BY MAY MCGOLDRICK

THE SCOTTISH RELIC TRILOGY

Much Ado About Highlanders
Taming the Highlander
Tempest in the Highlands
"A Midsummer Wedding" novella

THE PENNINGTON FAMILY SERIES

"Sweet Home Highlands Christmas" novella
Romancing the Scot
It Happened in the Highlands
Sleepless in Scotland

THE ROYAL HIGHLANDER SERIES

Highland Crown
Highland Jewel
Highland Sword

HIGHLAND
SWORD

MAY McGOLDRICK

St. Martin's Paperback

This is a work of fiction. All of the characters, organizations, and events portrayed in this novel are either products of the author's imagination or are used fictitiously.

First published in the United States by St. Martin's Paperbacks, an imprint of St. Martin's Publishing Group.

HIGHLAND SWORD

For information address St. Martin's Publishing Group, 120 Broadway, New York, NY 10271.

www.stmartins.com

ISBN: 978-1-250-31499-4

Our books may be purchased in bulk for promotional, educational, or business use. Please contact your local bookseller or the Macmillan Corporate and Premium Sales Department at 1-800-221-7945, extension 5442, or by email at MacmillanSpecialMarkets@macmillan.com.

Printed in the United States of America

St. Martin's Paperbacks edition / March 2020

10 9 8 7 6 5 4 3 2 1

To our loyal May McGoldrick readers
Resurrectionists all!

CHAPTER I
CINAED

Dalmigavie Castle, the Highlands
September 1820

The afternoon sun cast a golden glow over the high-walled garden beside the keep. The scents of autumn—rich and earthy—hung in the air, filling Cinaed's senses. His mother paused before a pair of rose bushes. The leaves were beginning to grow spotted and yellow, but a few red blooms lingered steadfastly in the protected space.

Caroline of Brunswick, Queen of England and Ireland, turned her gaze to him. Cinaed could see she was trying to keep up a cheerful façade, but her smile had been growing dimmer, her eyes mistier. She was leaving in the morning, and they both knew the likelihood of them ever meeting again was slight.

"If I could do it over, live my life over, I wouldn't make the mistake of letting you go. I would have been smarter. Fought harder."

Regrets almost always came too late, Cinaed mused. But he couldn't help his feelings. She'd made choices that didn't involve a four-year-old boy she'd sent off to be raised by strangers. All those years left their scars.

Growing up, he'd simply been Cinaed Mackintosh,

orphaned son of a sailor and Anne, the laird's sister. At the age of nine years, he'd been cast out by the only family he knew to become a ship's boy. No home. Unwanted. For years, he'd blamed Lachlan Mackintosh. No longer. The laird of Dalmigavie had a lad thrown at his feet. A boy who brought danger to his door.

Cinaed now knew why the Mackintosh clan protected him. He was the grandson of Teàrlach, the Bonnie Prince. He was the son of Scotland.

Caroline took his arm, and they walked in silence between the beds of flowers. The purples and yellows and reds were fading. Any night now, a killing frost would lay them all to waste.

"Family can inflict the deepest cuts and the sharpest pain. Disloyalty. Jealousy. Vindictiveness. The marks they leave rarely show to those on the outside. If you can survive, you become hardened to the world perhaps, but stronger."

He had become stronger, but she had no idea of what it cost him.

"I've survived," she continued. "As you have. I'm queen of a great land. You've made yourself into the man you are today. Master and commander of the seas. A hero to your people."

Cinaed thought about his lost ship, the *Highland Crown*. Of the men lost in that wreck. Not long ago, he thought he would be returning to the sea. Taking Isabella to Halifax. Building a life with her. All those plans, however, were now swept away by an ever-changing tide.

"For so many in the Highlands and throughout all of Scotland," she said, her voice growing stronger, "you are the future. You are the promise of a new rising. You embody the hope of a better world."

It was no secret a radical war of change was upon

them. Passions were running high. From the streets of Glasgow and Edinburgh to the docks and manufactories of Inverness. From the rolling farms of the Borders to the rocky coasts of the Northern Isles. Every week, protestors were assembling in the face of armed dragoons and being cut down by them.

"The time is now," she asserted. "You are the Highland prince emerging from the mists of the past with the royal blood of the Stuarts flowing in your veins. You are the warrior king who will set to rights the villainy of—"

He held up a hand and stopped her. "I have no desire to be king."

"Everything lies ready before you. We have important friends, both here and abroad. In coming here, I have affirmed who you are, who your father and grandfather were. Your time is now. Your people and your kingdom await. It is your destiny."

"*I* shall decide my own destiny. No one else."

"Not a fortnight ago, I watched powerful clan chieftains gather here at Dalmigavie to swear their allegiance to you. They're ready to go into battle for you against their English overlords."

"I'll not sacrifice Scottish blood in a futile campaign like the one that ended on Culloden Moor. I'll not blithely lead these Highlanders on a doomed, romantic quest that will crush us for another hundred years. War alone will not free Scotland from the oppressive yoke of England."

"Nations need leaders. Scotland needs a king to follow. They need *you*. A symbol to believe in. With you as their king, they will avenge the spilt blood of their ancestors, their fathers and mothers, their brothers and sisters."

Vengeance. This is what it came down to for Caroline. It was woven into the fabric of her soul. Vengeance for what her family did to her. Vengeance for the public venom of her husband. Vengeance for all those loveless years in exile.

"They have a king, despicable as he is. But no matter how desperate you are to see him gone, King George and his henchmen will never be ousted by a Highland revolt."

"Revolutions move earth and heaven. They pull down dynasties. But people can't rule themselves. They need a ruler."

"Not a ruler but a leader," Cinaed corrected. "What I want is justice for Scotland. I wish for a free and independent voice for its people. But to do this, we need a path that will unite the Highlanders of the north with the Lowlanders of the south. We need to become one Scotland."

Cinaed gazed at the silent figure standing before him. His earliest memory of her was of a young woman dancing with him in a garden like this one. The warm sunlight enveloped them as she sang a lilting French song and held him to her. She lived in a fairy tale.

She wanted reparation for what she'd lost. Caroline wanted her son to be king. She believed it was his by right. This was the world she had always lived in. It was all she'd ever known. Kings and courts. Power and conflict. Blood and passion. Thrust and parry. And revenge.

"I know who I am. And I know the path I must follow. I *am* the son of Scotland, and I'll do what I must, but I'll do it in the way that is best for the people."

CHAPTER 2
MORRIGAN

Inverness, the Scottish Highlands
October 1820

Morrigan Drummond stared at the half-dozen flyers posted to the wall of the abandoned malt house. Caricatures of Cinaed Mackintosh. Here in Inverness, within view of Maggot Green, where he heroically fought English dragoons trying to set the town on fire. She studied each unflattering depiction before peeling it off the bricks.

Unflattering was not the right term. Ruthless and false were closer to it.

One flyer showed Cinaed with a filthy boot pressed on the neck of a bairn. In front of him, ragged, starving people waited in a line to hand him their last ha'pennies from moth-eaten purses. Another showed what was supposed to be the son of Scotland's head on the body of a spider and a score of frightened poor folk caught in his web, about to be devoured. One more, depicting him, fat and drunken, with two Highland maidens on his lap as he leered lecherously at a third. Each sketch was worse than the last. All offensive. In every picture, he wore a tarnished and dented crown.

Morrigan had seen caricatures similar to these the last

two times she came to Inverness. While Searc Mackintosh and the fighters who escorted them from Dalmigavie Castle were off seeing to their business—she'd collected copies of the flyers. She found them pasted on walls throughout the town, and the same thought nagged at her. There was something more in this series of colored etchings than the obvious insults. Shadow figures lurked in the backgrounds of each one.

Back in Edinburgh, she was a fan of political carica-tures. For her, they were a kind of puzzle. They nearly all conveyed an obvious insult, but the better ones also con-tained subtle messages crying out to be discovered. The best artists used their platform to go beyond what he was ordered to draw.

This artist was talented, in many ways as good as those who worked for newspapers and publishers in Edinburgh and Glasgow. But Morrigan still needed to study his work more carefully.

A tall shadow blocked the late morning sun, and Mor-rigan stepped aside to make room for Blair Mackintosh. The leader of the fighters from Dalmigavie glowered at the flyers. "I'm looking forward to stuffing these down the throats of the bastards behind them."

With a scornful glance at the busy street, he ripped what was left of the caricatures off the wall.

"Not bastards. *One* bastard," Morrigan corrected, fold-ing the ones she'd peeled off and tucking them into her jacket. "This is the artwork of one person."

This much she'd deciphered. The use of curved lines to indicate motion, a similarity in certain faces, the some-what grotesque exaggeration of older figures all sup-ported her contention.

"Aye, but it takes more than one to print them." With the battered face of a brawler, Blair looked dangerous even when he wasn't angry. The fierce expression darkening his features now threatened violence. "And to pay for them."

The Highlander didn't care about details. He wasn't interested in subtle messages. On their last trip to Inverness, he'd called on every printing house in town. Whether the proprietors were being handsomely paid or were simply too afraid, no one was admitting anything. No one would confess they'd had anything to do with the scurrilous caricatures, though each of them was quick to point the finger at someone else.

Morrigan wasn't surprised when one shop owner suggested the flyers weren't even being printed in Inverness. Searc Mackintosh, the little bulldog of a man who had a piece of every illicit business transaction on the east coast of the Highlands, had his men questioning printers in other cities. The more Cinaed's name and popularity spread through the northern lands, the more virulent the campaign against him would become.

Morrigan was no politician. Still, she knew that while one person was drawing the caricatures, many stood to profit from planting the seeds of distrust regarding the son of Scotland. And not just the English military commands at Fort George and Fort William. The bloody aristocrats who were evicting thousands of families week after week, month after month, burning whole villages . . . they too had much to gain.

Perhaps not today, but someone would eventually pay the price. Of that, she was certain. It wasn't only the Mackintosh clan that were ready to defend their beloved native son. Many others in clans across the Highlands believed in Cinaed. In what he stood for.

"Searc wants to leave no later than noon. I need to help the men load up the carts. Stay close, lass."

Morrigan understood what the Highlander was telling

her. He wanted her within a stone's throw of Searc's house. Coming to Inverness with the Mackintosh fighters was a privilege that she'd earned, and she wasn't about to jeopardize it. She was smart, capable, and strong. And too restless to remain cooped up within the stout walls of Dalmigavie Castle.

She gestured down the crowded street toward the center of town. "I'll not go farther than the bookseller's shop."

Blair gave her a final nod and turned away.

As she watched him stride off toward Searc's house through the bustling throng of carters, vendors, and ragged, tired refugees, Morrigan thought of how much her life had changed in these recent months. She was fortunate to be standing here. The outwardly quiet life she'd been living in Edinburgh had been destroyed in a single afternoon's attack. A hussar's bullet had killed her father as he tried to protect his patients in his own surgery, and then they'd fled north.

Her stepmother Isabella was now married to Cinaed, and a bounty was being offered for the two of them. As a result, anyone connected to them was at risk of being taken by the British authorities.

Morrigan bent down and picked up one of the torn flyers. This one showed Cinaed, again as a fat king with his crown askew, seated in a throne that was being carried through a crowd of people by clan chiefs with the faces of wolves. Ahead of them, a passage toward a distant palace was being cleared by club-wielding brutes. On all sides, scores of people were looking on in fear and anguish. She felt her frustration rising as she looked from the sheet to the poor, harried Highland folk passing by this side street in the Maggot. They were trying to turn the people against Cinaed . . . those who needed him most.

"Sparrow?" the deep voice of a man called from a few paces off. "Robert Sparrow."

Morrigan didn't turn, but as she slid the flyer into her jacket, the reply came from someone closer to her.

"Aye, by my auld heart."

She stiffened.

"You two are a welcome sight to these sore eyes."

A trap door in her stomach opened, and her heart fell through it.

The name was strange to her, but she'd have known the voice if he'd whispered from the very gates of hell. She shot a quick glance over her shoulder. He was older, worn by the years, but she recognized him. Hell was where he belonged, with the rest of Satan's legions.

An old, painful sensation swept through her, a knife sliding between her ribs and into her chest. Cold lethargy slithered like an oily liquid through her body, seeping into spaces between her bones and her flesh. Numbness oozed into every joint, and pooled chill and dark in her belly. Then came fear. Her heart raced with the onset of memories. She forced herself to breathe.

"I was about to give up hope of you ever coming."

Anger sparked, quickly rising like a wildfire into her face, consuming her fear. Her breaths quickened, scorching her chest as they forced their way from her body.

Morrigan turned her head slowly in his direction. He stood with two other men by the brick wall. Gentlemen, by the way they were dressed. One was tall and broad-shouldered. The other stood half a head taller than his companion. They were speaking in low voices now.

The old myths told of swords and bows and spears that sang when the time came for vengeance. Hidden inside her boot, the keen-edged sgian dubh, forged by the smith at Dalmigavie Castle, pressed against her calf.

Morrigan heard its song. She heard the call to act. It was time.

CHAPTER 3
AIDAN

The Maggot, a tough and nasty-smelling neighborhood in Inverness, was little more than a rabbit warren of crumbling cottages, deserted warehouses, and ruined malt houses. On one side of the flat, muddy green used for drying wash, the blackened skeleton of a recently burned distillery stared with vacant eyes at the River Ness.

And everywhere, the poor milled about, crowded into shacks and decrepit houses and filthy alleyways. Mangy dogs and ragged children scavenged for anything of value on the riverbank. All of these Highland folk were victims of the clearances and of the lingering effects of the fateful Jacobite rebellion that had ended here, on a bloody field outside of Inverness, decades ago.

"You're my only chance, Mr. Grant. The only one I trust to keep me safe. You *must* keep me safe."

"I *must* do nothing," Aidan retorted sharply. "To be frank, I'd as soon feed you to a pack of hungry dogs, but I'm afraid they'd sicken and die from the effects of you."

Robert Sparrow, as he was calling himself at the moment, had good reason to fear for his life. So many people

wanted him dead that likenesses of him had been circulating among the societies of reformers in cities to the
south. But that hadn't stopped him from moving north and
continuing his work in the employment of the British authorities, assisting them in their spying and entrapment
operations.

Many Scots, including the throng of poor folk trudg-
ing by them now, would certainly relish the prospect of
killing this collaborator. Aidan didn't particularly blame
them.

"Beg pardon, sir. I misspoke. I . . . I'm pleading with
you. I'm desperate. I'm trying to make amends for my
mistakes."

Aidan thought of those who'd already been transported
or hanged in the cities south of here. It was too late for
them. But two more still waited to stand in the dock. It was
for their sake alone that he listened.

"You're the only one I know with a shred of honor.
You're the only one able to get me out of this trouble I'm
in." A wracking cough from deep in his chest shook the
man's body, leaving him gasping.

"What trouble?"

Sparrow was somewhat unsteady on his feet, and he
leaned heavily on an ivory-headed cane. Middle of height
and build, he was pale, almost ashen, and he was sweating profusely beneath his old-fashioned wig and tall bea-
ver hat. Under the sturdy travel cloak, Aidan caught sight
of a suit of forest green and a gold brocade waistcoat. A
thistle pin held a stock and cravat in place. He dressed well,
courtesy of the blood money received from the hands of
his British masters, but not so well as to attract unwanted
attention. He held a soiled handkerchief in one hand that
he used constantly, dabbing at the pinched corners of his
mouth.

"I've only just arrived in Inverness, and I can see all their eyes on me. They know who I am."

A group of young dockworkers coming up from the waterfront passed them, and the informer shrank away, using the tall figure of Aidan's brother Sebastian as a shield.

"They want me dead. Everyone wants me dead." Fear was written across Sparrow's face. "Please. Help me."

"You're afraid? Go to your masters."

"I can't. The English are after me too. I can't go to them."

"Why? What have you to fear from them?"

Sparrow glanced at two red-coated soldiers passing by. "I told them I'd done so much already. I couldn't help them anymore."

Aidan was certain the people working for Sir Rupert Burney, the director of Home Office activities in Scotland, had not taken the news too well. The decision to retire was not for an informer to make.

"Their response?"

"They told me to take the coach to Aberdeen. There'd be a packet sailing to Africa. To the new Cape colony. They were giving me land there. And money to make a go of it."

"Why didn't you go?"

"A friend sent word. Their plan was to punch a few holes in me and leave me under a dock." He clutched the cane tightly in his fist. "So I bolted. Wrote to you."

It was true that if the English thought there was a chance Sparrow would expose their underhanded actions, an assassin would cut out the double crosser's tongue and then put a dagger in his heart. The Home Office didn't look favorably on those who changed sides.

"Why did you write to *me*?"

"You're the best."

Aidan leaned forward, devouring the space between them. "Don't you dare flatter me."

Sparrow pressed against the wall and raised his hand in defense. "Sir, everyone knows who you are and what you stand for. For a decade now, you've argued for abolition, for better wages, for reform. You're the best lawyer Scotland has. You're the only one brave enough to stand up to Sir Rupert Burney."

What Henry Brougham, the queen's legal defender, was doing in Parliament, Aidan had been trying to do in Scotland. Both men wanted the same thing, a voice for their people.

"I also know the weavers' leadership committee and their people sent for you to come represent the Chattan brothers in their trial."

Edmund and George Chattan had been languishing in a cell, charged with planning an attack on the Lord Mayor's offices in Elgin at the time of the Military Governor's visit. The trial was not to take place in Elgin but in Inverness at the beginning of next month. Aidan had already met with the two this week. The brothers swore they'd been tricked by a fellow member of their reform committee . . . someone like Sparrow.

"You still haven't told me why I should help you."

"I told you in my letter. I have information. I can help you with names, places. I know the very one who was responsible for setting up the Chattans. He's gone, moved on already. But I'm here, and I can testify for you."

Robert Sparrow was a thief. An art forger. A villain who for years had committed his petty crimes with impunity by playing his part as an informer and an agent provocateur. His actions in entrapping leaders of the reform movement in Edinburgh had led to executions. He'd been moved north for a reason. Aidan had no doubt he had firsthand knowledge of government spying operations in the Highlands. His testimony could help Aidan.

It was impossible to ignore Sebastian's imposing figure beside him. Aidan's brother had been against coming here and listening to this viper.

"If I had one whit of assurance that you would help us, I would throw a rope around your neck and drag you to some safe house until the trial. But as my brother would no doubt remind me, you can't put a leash on a snake."

"I swear to you . . ." Another cough wracked Sparrow's body, cutting off his words. "I swear that I'll help you. No one knows what I know. No one has seen what I've seen. No one has done it as long as I have. I'll tell you exactly who gave all of us orders and what those orders were. The Chattan fools were only one case. There are others being lured into traps right now."

Aidan fixed his stare on the man with the same intensity he'd used on a hundred witnesses in scores of court cases.

"You still haven't said one word that would help me convince a jury that you matter, or that you're telling the truth, or that you were even working for the government as a provocateur."

"March twenty-first. I called together the committee in Glasgow. Everyone was arrested at that meeting. My partner was John King, a weaver working for the Home Office. April fourth. My plan incited three score men in Germiston to seize weapons from the Carron Ironworks in Falkirk. You had clients that were part of that committee. The dragoons were waiting for them. I was sent to Elgin right after."

Aidan exchanged another look with Sebastian. This was the kind of information that would influence a jury.

"We'll take you."

"I can't stay in Inverness. I won't be safe here."

"I said we'll take you," Aidan repeated more sharply.

"I need to fetch my bag. I'm staying at an inn by the river. I'd feel safer if you came with me."

Aidan heard knuckles cracking. He didn't need to look to know it was Sebastian, squeezing his hand into a tight fist.

"Go ahead of us. And do it before we change our minds."

The informer opened his mouth to argue but quickly snapped it shut, recognizing Aidan was done negotiating. He pulled up the collar of his coat and hurried along.

"He's playing you for a fool." Sebastian scowled as Sparrow edged past a group of street urchins.

"I need him."

"You think he'll stand before a magistrate and testify against the Home Office? He won't. This is a bloody mistake, and you know it."

"He's already given me more for this case than I had."

"Too trusting, as always. The cur is using you to slip out of the grip of his English paymasters. Either that, or he's setting *you* up."

His brother fell in step with Aidan as they started along the busy thoroughfare. The two of them were the only survivors of the father and four sons who'd gone off to fight against Napoleon, though Sebastian had lost an arm at Waterloo. After the war, Aidan quickly found that opposing the English government in politics and in the courts was a dangerous business, and his younger brother took it upon himself to become his protector. Aidan trusted Sebastian's judgment, but right now, the Chattan brothers' lives depended on Sparrow's testimony.

"We came. I spoke to him. And I have you beside me. There's nothing to be afraid of."

"You need to be smarter, or I'll be beside you on an English gallows."

A woman carrying a basket filled with wet clothes nearly careened into Aidan, but his brother pulled him out of the way.

"Come now. What did the bard say? Screw your courage to the sticking place—"

"How about if I screw my boot in your ear?" Sebastian scoffed. "I fear nothing."

"Watch him there," Aidan said as Sparrow turned down a side street. They quickened their steps.

By the time they reached the corner, the villain was some distance ahead of them. He was moving with a determined step, turning his head neither left nor right, like a wounded soldier lurching back toward his own lines. He was clearly laboring for breath, his shoulders rising and falling as he moved.

"He's moving as if the Grim Reaper is on his tail."

"He's thinking we're his only chance," Aidan replied. "He wants to get his things before we change our mind."

"If he turns into that alleyway halfway down, I still say it's a trap."

"Don't you think using this rogue to trap us in the middle of the day in an alley is a wee bit far-fetched?"

"You've forgotten High Street in Edinburgh. Midday."

He was right. In plain daylight. A ship's master who'd had his ship seized for transporting Africans to sugar plantations in the West Indies had attacked Aidan with a knife. Sebastian knocked him down with a single blow and disarmed him.

"And how about the Crown & Anchor? London."

That was in broad daylight as well. And within shouting distance of the Temple Bar. Aidan was on his way to meet his brother when two footpads attempted to waylay him. Sebastian had seen them from the doorway of the tavern and came to his aid. They turned out to be servants of Lord Horsley, another Tory foe whose nose Aidan had figuratively tweaked.

"The alley next to the Palace at Westminster. What time of the day was that?"

Blast. "And in every case, the two of us fought off the blackguards. Except at Westminster, where I was holding my own fairly well until you showed up."

Sebastian's answer was another grunt.

The truth was, Aidan could have been beaten to death that day. He couldn't prove it, but he was certain those assailants had been hired by the Home Office.

Aidan definitely had his enemies. And he knew he was more than just a burr under their gilded saddles. He was part of a reform movement that could unhorse the power of those in charge entirely. Many people in London, powerful men like Lord Sidmouth and his cronies, thought nothing of using a club or a dagger to eliminate foes like him.

"We're at home. We're in the heart of the Highlands. There are more sympathizers for the cause here than in the streets of . . ." He paused, motioning to a woman who was striding along in Sparrow's wake. "If she's unafraid of these back streets on her own, then I say the two of us have no reason to worry."

Now that he'd noticed her, Aidan paid closer attention. A grey dress was visible beneath her long coat. A single dark braid of hair hung like a rope from under an oversized knitted tam. She carried nothing in her hands, which he noted were fisted as they swung at her sides.

She moved with the smooth, lithe ease of a young

fencer, but she had a purposeful manner in her gait. Aidan glanced ahead at Sparrow and realized she was closing quickly on him.

The informer's words came to him, along with his own thoughts—there were many people who would readily take the sword of justice into their own hands.

At that moment, Sparrow turned into the alley without a glance back at them. The woman slowed for the briefest of seconds, bent down, and reached into her boot. He saw the flash of the knife's blade as she pressed it into the folds of her coat. In an instant she too had disappeared into the alley.

"You go after him," Aidan shouted, starting to run. "I'll stop her."

She whirled as they stormed into alley. Intent as she was on Sparrow, they'd caught her by surprise. The alley was short and dark, and the brick walls on either side glistened with moisture and slick green patches. Aidan went after the knife he'd seen in her hand, knocking it from her grip as she raised it. His momentum drove him into her, and he grasped her arms to keep them both from falling.

Sebastian raced past them, and she struggled fiercely to wrench her arms free. Her dark eyes flashed. Even in the dank dimness of the alley, her beauty was stunning.

"Let go of me."

"I'm afraid I—" he started to say but got no further.

Her knee came up sharply, knocking his bollocks halfway to Nairn. As he gasped for air, she nearly connected with another kick to the side of his knee, but he managed to deflect the blow, yanking her booted foot upwards and upending her.

Bloody hell. He was fighting with a woman. She was on the ground for only an instant. Springing to her feet, she glanced once at the end of the alleyway and then darted toward her knife, which lay on a tangle of discarded netting along the base of the wall.

Woman or she-devil, he thought, he wasn't about to let her use him for a pin cushion.

She reached out to snatch up the weapon, but Aidan caught hold of her coat, pulling her back. She spun away, yanking herself free of his grasp and falling on her face as she slid across the ground. Immediately, she was on her knees. She reached up to touch her rapidly swelling lip.

He staggered toward her, wincing at the pain between his legs. He leaned down to take her hand and help her up. Another mistake.

Without an inkling of warning, she reared back and butted him, planting her forehead squarely in his eye and knocking him onto his backside.

He sat for a few moments, dazed. When the cobwebs began to clear, she was gone. He looked around, but one of his eyes was not functioning. He touched it, but it was already swollen shut.

Aidan groaned and struggled to his feet. He scanned the alley with his one good eye, searching for any remnant of his manly self-respect. He spotted her knife and picked it up. Finding his hat where it had fallen, he sagged back against the wall.

A moment later, Sebastian came down the alley with Sparrow alongside of him. He paused by where Aidan sat in a heap, not even trying to hide his smirk.

"Perhaps next time, you should run after the sickly men, and I'll fight the women."

CHAPTER 4
MORRIGAN

At Searc's house between Maggot Green and the Citadel Quay docks, the Mackintosh men were tying down tarps on the loaded wagons. Morrigan nudged her horse a few yards down the lane toward the river. With her hat pulled low on her forehead and the collar of her coat turned up, she was doing her best to hide her face.

In the alleyway, she'd held her own and delivered more than the rogue had expected. Still, the cobblestone had left its mark. She couldn't tell the extent of her injuries, except it hurt to move her jaw. The bloody handkerchief tucked into her sleeve bore the evidence of the cut inside her lip. She ran her tongue along her teeth. She was lucky none of them had come loose.

She'd been careless, but even now she felt the heat rise in her face. A sudden rage had possessed her, and, hot for revenge, she'd been paying no attention to what was behind her. She was unaware of the two men following "Robert Sparrow." They had to be the same two who'd been speaking with him by the green.

Morrigan took a few deep breaths to calm herself, forcing her mind clear of his face, his voice. The blackguard was in Inverness, but for how long, she didn't know. Perhaps the next time she came into the city, she'd search him out and finish what she'd intended to do today.

One way or another, she *would* finish it. She'd killed once. The day they were fleeing their house on Infirmary Street in Edinburgh, she'd driven a knife into a man's heart to save the life of Maisie, Isabella's sister. She could kill again. Vengeance called for it. Justice demanded it. She'd do it if only to stop her nightmares. But would she be free when she left him lying in his own blood?

Her neck was already stiffening, and Morrigan rolled her head from side to side, stretching the muscles and thinking about the clash in the alley.

Morrigan was a skilled fighter. Since arriving at Dalmigavie, she'd been going to the training yard an hour before the men showed up four or five times a week. Some days Blair worked with her himself. Other days he put one of the Mackintosh fighters in charge of training her. Knife, pistol, even hand-to-hand, she could hold her own. She had the blessing of Isabella and Maisie. Both of them—and their husbands—agreed it was important that Morrigan be able to defend herself. Their enemies were numerous and too close to ignore. And being inside the walls of Dalmigavie didn't guarantee their safety either. Only two months ago, Maisie had been stabbed in a stairwell of the castle. She'd recovered fully, thank God, but all of them were far more cautious as a result.

A screech behind her startled Morrigan, and she reached down to find the empty sheath in her boot. Blast, she'd need to have the blacksmith make her another sgian dubh. Two urchins raced up the lane in a running battle, using sticks for swords.

Searc barreled out of his house with Blair on his heels.

He stomped around the wagons, pulling at tarps and ropes. With a grunt of approval, he climbed onto his horse and scowled back at Morrigan.

Black eyes peered from under his tall hat and bristling brows, and she fought the inclination to look away. Searc saw, heard, and knew everything and everyone. If he found out what she'd done—chasing a man into an alley and getting into a fight—he wouldn't be happy. Not that he was ever happy, but it would be detrimental to the trust she'd established with the Mackintosh clan leaders.

They were ready to depart for Dalmigavie. A dozen Mackintosh men—their weapons handily concealed inside coats and saddlebags—lined up behind the wagons.

"Ready, lass?" Blair called to her.

Her jaw ached, and she didn't trust her swollen lip to form any intelligible words. She nodded and nudged her horse, joining the line behind the carts.

A steady rain began to fall as they left Inverness and started the winding climb into the mountains toward Dalmigavie. The riders around her pulled their collars up and filed along, mostly in silence. The relative solitude of the ride suited Morrigan perfectly. If the men around her noticed the bruising on her face, they said nothing. She welcomed the drops of rain that cooled her heated skin.

Before they got back to Dalmigavie, however, Morrigan knew she'd need to come up with a believable story to explain her face. Telling the truth wasn't an option.

Night had fallen by the time they dismounted by the stables inside the curtained wall of the castle. Torches lit the courtyard, sizzling and hissing in the falling rain. A stable hand offered to take her horse. Morrigan handed the mare off reluctantly. She wasn't looking forward to facing Isabella and Maisie.

Six years ago, the three women had become a family, of

sorts, when Isabella married Morrigan's father and brought Maisie, her sister, with her. The relationship between them all had been a curious one. Sometimes strained, but for the most part defined by a cordial distance. Everything changed this past spring after they fled Edinburgh. Their bond now was one of true friendship and sisterhood. The three were closer than if they had shared the same birth mother.

Searc marched stiff-legged toward her, barking, "Be sure to tell Isabella you're back. The woman has been fretting since we left, I'd wager."

Searc was in charge while Cinaed and Lachlan, the Mackintosh laird, were traveling through the Highlands with Niall Campbell, Maisie's husband. But walking into the Great Hall with a battered face wasn't what she had in mind. Before word reached her sisters that the caravan had arrived, Morrigan needed to get up to her room and inspect the damage.

"Tell her I'll see her later, if you please. I need to change out of these wet clothes first."

Morrigan ran off before Searc could argue.

As she left the yard, others were emerging from the keep to help unload the carts.

Over the past month, this was the third trip they'd made to Inverness. By all accounts, Searc had his hand in dozens of businesses, but he'd also used the opportunity to bring back supplies. Morrigan knew the "supplies" consisted mostly of weapons, shot, and powder. It was no secret Dalmigavie was in danger of attack by troops stationed at Fort George and Fort Williams.

Before those regiments were prepared to attack the Mackintosh stronghold, however, there needed to be a build-up of troop numbers in the forts. And so far, Searc's spies confirmed no additional reinforcements had been sent north.

The noises from the Great Hall became muffled in the stairwell as Morrigan hurried up to her bedchamber. Safely inside, she dropped the latch in place and lit a candle. She peeled off her coat, tossed her hat on a chair, and moved to the mirror.

"Blast," she murmured, cringing at the sight of her reflection in the glass. Her bottom lip was the size of a fat mouse. Dried blood clung to the corner of her mouth. Her forehead and chin were marked, red and rough, and a shadow stained her puffy cheek and jaw. She prayed some of it was dirt that would wash away, but she wasn't particularly hopeful.

"Morrigan?" Maisie called, knocking sharply. "Unlatch the door and let me in."

Too soon. Too soon. She looked around her in panic. The dried blood made everything look worse than it was. If she could only wash her face.

The rapping on the door grew louder and more persistent. Over the years, Maisie's sweet demeanor and beautiful face had fooled many into thinking she was quiet and docile. But they were so wrong. Kicking this door open was not beyond her. Morrigan needed to act quickly.

"You didn't have to come after me. I'm changing into a dry dress." She moved the candle to a side table where it would shed less light in the room.

"Open. Please. Now."

"Just a moment." Morrigan pulled open the wardrobe and grabbed a clean shift and the first dress her fingers brushed against. She tossed it over her shoulder, hoping her face was partially covered and unlatched the door. She turned away as Maisie stormed in.

"What happened today?"

"Nothing. I just returned."

"Morrigan?"

"I went to Inverness. It rained." She hurried to a screen

standing in the corner of the room. "I need to change out of these wet things."

"I knew it. Searc was right. Something did happen."

Morrigan hid behind the partition. "Searc? I spoke to him a moment ago. I told him I had to change."

"Searc *sent* me up here."

Undoing the fasteners on her dress, she winced as she bumped her jaw. Maisie was moving around the bedchamber, and Morrigan heard her lighting the fire in the hearth.

"What's wrong with him? I didn't give him a single reason to complain about me today."

"Exactly. You gave him no reason to complain, and that alarmed him. On the way back, not once did you ride ahead or wander off on your own."

Maisie fell silent beyond the screen. Morrigan peeked over the top and found the younger woman inspecting her coat and hat.

"He's certain something must have happened in Inverness that he doesn't know about."

Damn that Searc. Such a meddling busybody. Morrigan shoved the wet dress down over her hips and was startled when Maisie appeared beside her, holding the candle up.

She gasped. "Who did this to you?"

There was nowhere she could go. It was useless to turn around. Morrigan was trapped. "No one."

"Were you attacked?"

"Not attacked. It was an accident. I stumbled. Fell on my face. It's nothing. Really."

Maisie tried to reach up and touch her face, but Morrigan pushed her hand away.

"Where did you fall?"

"In Inverness. Where else?"

"I don't believe it for one instant. I've never seen you trip and fall. Not once."

"Well, you have proof of it now." She exchanged the dry shift she'd draped over the top of the partition with her wet dress. "Let me change. I'm getting chilled."

"You're lying." Maisie wasn't budging. She lifted the candle closer to Morrigan's face, inspecting every bump and scratch.

"Why should I lie?"

"So you don't lose your freedom. So you can continue to come and go as you please."

"You're reading far too much into this."

"Am I?" Maisie scoffed. "We've been here before. You and I had this same conversation in Edinburgh. Except it was you questioning me. And we promised each other there'd be no more lies. Remember?"

Maisie was right. Morrigan had confronted her in the stairwell of the house on Infirmary Street after one of the reform protests this past winter. They'd had a very similar conversation because she was concerned about the bloodied condition of the other's clothing. She'd been ready to tear apart whoever was responsible for hurting her. Maisie looked ready to do the same for her now.

"We vowed to be sisters and be honest with each other. Have you forgotten?"

It was more than her face that was bruised right now. Morrigan *wanted* to tell her the truth. But she couldn't. Her past was complicated. The years—and her father—had taught her that silence was the best path. In order to heal, she had to forget. But Maisie wasn't going anywhere unless Morrigan could concoct a better story.

"Very well. I didn't just fall. I was chasing after someone when I fell. But Searc can't know. You have to promise me."

"You chased after someone?" Isabella's dismayed cry came from the far side of the room. "Where was Blair? You were to stay with the Mackintosh men the entire time."

Morrigan closed her eyes and shook her head. She hadn't heard the bedroom door open again. Of course, both women would come up here. Here was a lesson learned. From now on, regardless of what kind of day she had, she'd be certain to torment Searc.

Isabella poked her head around the edge of the screen, holding another candle.

"For the love of God!" Morrigan exploded. "Why don't we invite everyone up from the Great Hall?"

She pushed Maisie toward her older sister.

"The two of you will have to wait until I change."

They followed her order, but that wasn't the end of the inquisition.

"Is she hurt?" Isabella asked Maisie.

"I'd say!"

"No, I'm *not*!" Morrigan denied loudly. She draped the wet shift over the screen. Quickly, she began pulling on the dry one.

"You'll see, as soon as she comes out of hiding," Maisie retorted. "Her mouth is bruised, and her lip is badly swollen."

"You're exaggerating." Morrigan tried to make less of it.

"I'm not," Maisie contradicted. "I think her nose is broken. It looks quite crooked to me."

"My nose has never been straight, thank you."

"There was nothing wrong with your nose before," Isabella replied, her tone rising with concern.

"I think she may have lost teeth, but the swollen lip makes it difficult to tell."

The wet dress disappeared over the top of the screen.

"This is ridiculous. I didn't lose any teeth."

"Whom were you chasing?" Isabella demanded.

Morrigan shoved her arms into the sleeves of the clean dress. She knew she had only one chance at an explanation.

It had to be believable. Would she chase after a child trying to pick her pocket? That wouldn't do. There were too many hungry children on the streets who would do anything to survive. Was she accosted by a sailor or a tradesman? No, that would simply get Blair and Searc in trouble.

"Look at all the blood!" Maisie exclaimed.

She must have found the handkerchief in the pocket. Morrigan had to face these two. There was no avoiding it. She stepped around the divider as she buttoned her dress.

Isabella stood staring for a few moments, speechless. Her anger was evident in the scarlet rash spreading from her throat into her cheeks. Unlike Morrigan, the young doctor used to be adept at controlling her temper, but she was a different woman from the one she once was.

"Who did this to you? By heaven, I'm going to make them suffer. They were supposed to take care of you. Protect you. Watch you every minute."

Morrigan imagined Isabella rushing down to the Great Hall in search of Blair and Searc and the other men with every intention of thrashing them soundly.

"It looks far worse than it is," Morrigan said calmly. "Let me wash my face first and you'll see."

It took a few moments for the young doctor to quiet her temper, but after inhaling a few deep breaths, the protective tigress in Isabella subsided slightly, allowing the physician in her to surface. She sat Morrigan in a chair by the hearth and held the candle closer. "Tell me what hurts."

"Nothing hurts." She forced herself not to flinch when Isabella touched the side of her chin.

"I know of no woman who is physically tougher than you, my love. But right now, I need to see how much damage was done."

Morrigan gave herself over to Isabella's ministrations.

Her head was moved from side to side. Her mouth was opened gingerly, her teeth checked. The bruise on her forehead touched. Maisie placed a towel and bowl of water at her sister's elbow. The care continued. The cut on her lip was cleaned. She had a scratch on the side of her face that she hadn't even been aware of, and there were other cuts and bruises on her wrist and hand, all from trying to control the fall.

"You're going to need to keep cold compresses on your face to reduce the swelling."

Looking up into Isabella's focused and caring expression, emotions rose and filled Morrigan's chest. There was so much she wanted to talk about and confide in these two women. But she couldn't. Before they came into her life, she had only her father. He was a busy man, a dedicated radical and an activist who fought for the rights of common folk who were suffering from economic hardship. He pushed for reform and a voice for the people in government through assemblies, marches, and protests.

When it came to issues of their own lives, however, he didn't want any discussions. He wanted their problems buried, and Morrigan had followed his lead. She'd kept her own counsel and refused to wallow in past things she couldn't change. But he was gone now, and she'd been left to deal with the squalid aspects of life. It had never been easy. But it was worse now, especially today, seeing that foul man standing a dozen steps away. *Robert Sparrow.* Knowing he still lived and breathed brought back the same anger and hurt she'd felt at Maggot Green.

"You are hurting. And I'm not only talking of your bruises. Why don't you tell me what's wrong?"

Isabella's soft voice pierced Morrigan's heart. She wanted desperately to talk about the past, but the tightness in her throat wouldn't allow the words to form.

Maisie's voice cut into the momentary silence. "Are these the reason you were chasing after someone today?"

The flyers she'd stuffed into her coat. Maisie was unfolding them. One trouble was replaced by another. Morrigan shook her head once at the younger woman, but it was too late. Isabella saw the pages.

Ever since the first of these showed up in Inverness, Searc had ordered her and Blair and the men not to mention them to anyone at Dalmigavie Castle. Especially to Isabella. With Cinaed traveling right now, he didn't want her to worry about this nonsense. Morrigan had seen the wisdom in his direction. It was too late now, however.

Isabella glided across the room to her sister, and the two stared for a long time at each sheet of paper. Inwardly, Morrigan cringed, recalling the images. She thought how difficult it must be for Isabella to see these horrible depictions of the man she loved.

"Where were these posted?"

"By Maggot Green," Morrigan replied. "Not far from Searc's house."

"Does he know?"

She nodded. "Searc saw them. He said he and Blair will find out who's behind it all."

Isabella handed the flyers to Maisie and came back to the fire. Morrigan noted the rigid set of her shoulders, the fisted hands.

"They'll put an end to it. Trust them."

Isabella wrung the cold water from the towel. Her eyes were clear and her chin high when she went back to tending to the bruises. "The three of us know who is behind this. Sir Rupert Burney and his vile cronies. But I'd like to believe the folk these were intended to influence have seen enough English oppression to know it too."

Morrigan shot a quick glance up at her. Isabella had

always kept herself so focused on medicine and her patients. She didn't know how persuasive these satirical images could be. When people all over Britain thought of Napoleon, they saw Fores's little "Corsican monkey" in a uniform, or Gillray's jester-like figure in an oversize military bicorne hat.

The public's view was formed by these caricatures, and their opinion was shaped in the same way. Even in the days before Morrigan, Isabella, and Maisie left Edinburgh, Whig printers were carrying on a campaign against Queen Caroline, depicting her as a voluptuous, painted harlot chasing wildly after Italian men. Luckily, the king was being portrayed in "Queenist" caricatures as a haughty and lustful fop bursting out of waistcoats and breeches with his current mistress fawning at his feet.

These images had shifted the favor of the people in the past, and they could do it now. But this was no time to worry Isabella about such things.

"I saw no mobs marching in the streets, cursing the son of Scotland," she said. "And yet, tens of thousands, in every city, are raising their fists against Crown rule."

Isabella nodded in agreement and caressed Morrigan's face. "I don't want you ever to do anything as foolhardy as this again. No chasing down rogues and villains. We don't need another martyr in this family. Do you hear me?"

Morrigan would gladly fight anyone who spoke against Cinaed and what he was trying to do for the Scottish people. Today wasn't the day for that, however. Isabella and Maisie misunderstood what happened in Inverness, but she wasn't about to enlighten them.

"I shan't," she replied. "Unless I have you two beside me to chase down the blackguards."

CHAPTER 5
MORRIGAN

For two days, Morrigan had confined herself in her chamber to allow the bruises to heal. The swelling of her lip was much improved, but in its place, hideous patches of purple and green discolored the skin on her forehead, cheek, and jaw.

If it were left up to her, she'd have stayed in her room for a week, but Isabella had other plans.

The physician stood in her doorway, wearing her coat and hat and holding her medical bag. "I am going into the village to see a new patient. I need you to come with me."

"Can't you ask Maisie?"

"She already has plans for an outing this morning with her sister-in-law Fiona and the girls. Put on your coat. It'll do you good to stretch your legs."

As a university-trained physician, Isabella was an anomaly everywhere, and not only in the Highlands. She was devoted to the art of healing. Since arriving at Dalmigavie, despite being Cinaed's wife, she'd continued to treat the sick and the injured. Her reputation was quickly spreading, for she was quite good at what she did. Still, she was an outlaw in the eyes of the Crown, so the infirm traveled to her when they could. Some she saw inside the castle walls. Others she treated in the village.

As a female doctor, she followed the same routine that she had in Edinburgh. Someone accompanied her when she tended to the sick. At Dalmigavie, her only options were Morrigan or Maisie.

"Who is sick?"

"I'll tell you along the way."

"A villager?"

"An outsider."

Isabella motioned for her to hurry. Between the large, woolen tam and the high collar of her coat, Morrigan could keep at least some of the bruising hidden. After changing from her slippers into sturdy boots, Morrigan followed the other woman out into the corridor and down the dark stairwell.

"Has anyone asked about me?"

"Everyone. Auld Jean. Searc. Blair." Isabella glanced back at her. "Fiona's daughters get up early every morning just to sit at the window to watch you exercise in the training yard. This morning alone, a dozen people must have asked me what's ailing you."

To know so many cared warmed her heart. She was accepted here, welcomed, liked. These people were her chosen family. "What did you tell them?"

"The truth, of course." Isabella sent her a sidelong look. "I should tell you, however, Blair and his men were highly entertained at the image of you stumbling over your own feet and giving yourself a fat lip."

"I don't care if they laugh, so long as Searc doesn't stop me from going in to Inverness with them."

"Well, about that . . . we need to discuss the topic a

wee bit more before you step foot away from Dalmigavie again."

A maternal warning or a sister's friendly word of caution? Isabella had the ability to shift her role easily, depending on what the situation warranted. But regardless of the part she played, she was always the lioness, ready to protect Maisie and Morrigan.

Blair was waiting by the courtyard door to escort them into the village. The tall Highlander cocked his head to the side, assessing Morrigan's face as she stepped out into the sun.

"I never thought of ye as the clumsy sort, lass. Why didn't ye tell us on our way back from Inverness that ye were hurt?"

"What for?"

"I'd have gone back and given the cobblestones of that street a pounding for tripping ye up."

"I couldn't say anything. I was worried that you or Searc might faint dead away at the sight of a few drops of blood."

Blair grinned. "Well, I can see yer mouth is still working."

They hurried to catch up with Isabella, who was striding off at a quick pace. It was good to be outside. Two days of self-imposed isolation in her room might have been important for her physical healing, but they'd been brutal on her mind. Far too much time to think, to remember the things she was supposed to keep buried.

Morrigan took a deep breath of fall air and turned her attention to Isabella. "So, who is this we're seeing? What's wrong with him . . . or is it her?"

"Him."

For many years Morrigan had shadowed her father at the medical clinic he and Isabella ran on Infirmary Street in Edinburgh. As a result, she had a solid grasp of diseases, as well as what to do to be useful at a sick person's bedside.

"What's wrong with him?"

"He has some kind of lung disease, struggling to breathe."

"Consumption?"

"I haven't seen him. We'll soon find out."

So many were dying of the disease all over Europe. She recalled discussions of the growing epidemic in Edinburgh. "Where are they keeping him?"

"In the empty cottage on the far side of the fields, the one by the edge of the forest. Before coming here to Dalmigavie, they stayed at the hunting lodge," Isabella told her. "Apparently, he needs a doctor badly, but Searc didn't want me going so far to see him. This morning, they brought him up to the village."

Morrigan glanced at a group of children running with a pair of dogs between the cottages. "Is it safe to bring someone so sick to the village?"

"They're keeping him inside. I don't want you to come past the threshold."

"How about you?"

"If it is consumption, I've treated patients with it before. But he could have something else entirely." Isabella squeezed Morrigan's hand. "I'll be fine."

There was no sense in arguing when the physician side of Isabella took over. She didn't see danger. She didn't care about her own safety. There were no faces, only patients. She became totally focused on what she had to do. Friends and enemies were treated the same.

"Who brought him here? His kin?"

"Not his kin. I don't know their connection, but he's traveling with the Grant brothers."

"Don't know them."

"Aidan and Sebastian Grant. Aidan is an Edinburgh barrister. From what I hear, he is a young man of great character and promise. Queen Caroline and Mr. Brougham, her attorney, wanted Cinaed to meet him. Sebastian, the younger brother, is a solicitor. A war hero too, they tell me."

No one had any prior knowledge of Cinaed's mother's visit to Dalmigavie last month, except Maisie's husband, Niall Campbell. And much of Queen Caroline's time here was spent behind closed doors, visiting with her son and Highland clan leaders.

"Aidan Grant could be a strong contender to represent Inverness-shire in Parliament. That is, if my husband can get him interested in running in the next election and then gather enough support for him."

In spite of the defamatory flyers, Cinaed definitely had the Highland's attention and support. As far as a military expertise, he had Niall Campbell, a former lieutenant in the 42nd Royal Highlanders. Morrigan could see that political allies working inside the system, especially in Parliament, would be a necessity, as well.

She recalled the men who'd traveled to Dalmigavie with Queen Caroline last month. Fashionable, courtly attire. Refined manners. Most of them totally ill at ease in the rugged fortress and at close quarters with the tough, plain-speaking Highland folk. She glanced around, taking in the sights and smells of the rustic village. Farm animals wandered freely in the muddy lanes and between the cottages, where smoke from cooking fires hung thick and pungent over thatched roofs. This place was far different from London or the cities of the continent the outsiders were accustomed to.

Heads turned in the village center as they passed the

kirk and the market cross. Isabella received the courtesy of doffed caps and curtsies, and she paused several times to speak with villagers before they continued on.

"I assume the brothers aren't sharing the cottage with the sick man."

Isabella shook her head. "They have a clerk traveling with them as well. He's staying with the patient. Searc wants them at the castle until Cinaed returns."

Morrigan considered this news. Everyone was expecting the son of Scotland, the laird, and Niall to return by the end of the month.

Everyday life at Dalmigavie was a communal affair. In the same way as it had been done for as long as anyone knew, most meals were shared in the Great Hall. Guests dined in a rustic style along with Mackintosh retainers. The fact that the Grants were staying at the castle meant Morrigan would be seeing quite a bit of them.

"Tell me more about them."

"The Grants are a large and important family, I'm told. The chief is building a town on the Spey River with the idea of employing Highland folk who have been evicted from their homes. These two grew up on a family estate called Carrie House, which is two days' ride to the west of us. Apparently, they refuse to clear their tenants, as many of the large landowners are doing. A cousin manages the properties while the brothers practice law in Edinburgh. For the next month or so, they have business in Inverness."

"Why Inverness?"

"Aidan is representing the Chattan brothers in court."

Many conversations as of late in the Great Hall had touched on Edmund and George Chattan. They were due to be tried for planning to murder the Lord Mayor of Elgin and the Military Governor of the Highlands, but the trial was being moved to Inverness for fear of riots in Elgin.

"Have you met them?"

"Not as yet. They only arrived this morning."

"You know a lot about them."

"From Searc. You know the way he is." They exchanged a look. "He's known the family for years. He did some business with their late father, though he was characteristically vague about the specifics. While the trial is going on, the brothers will be staying at his house in Inverness."

Morrigan thought about the rambling house in the Maggot with its many wings and mazelike corridors. On any given day, friends and enemies and business partners paid calls on Searc when he was in town. That house was a hub of both legal and illegal activity in the region.

As they crossed through the stubbled remains of harvested barley, a flock of wild geese took flight on the far side of the field. Morrigan eyed the cottage in the distance. She'd been here before. Isabella had more than once seen patients from neighboring villages in this same building.

A tall man stood by a wall that enclosed the cottage yard, talking in a vigorous manner with one of Blair's fighters. He wore no hat and his face, though young, bore evidence of hastily stitched battle wounds. Morrigan's eye was drawn to the empty sleeve tacked at the side of his coat. She stared, knowing she shouldn't. The gnawing sadness she felt was the same that filled her every time she came face-to-face with someone who'd lost an arm, a leg, a part of themselves to war. Innocent men who'd been duped into fighting for an empire that cared nothing for them.

The stranger came closer as the women approached, and Blair made the introductions. Sebastian Grant, the younger brother. She felt as if she already knew so much about who he was, just from the information Isabella had given her, but there was more to it. His face, his build . . . there was a familiarity about him that made her think she'd seen him someplace. But where?

"Have we met before?" she asked, interrupting whatever was being said.

"I don't believe we have, Miss Drummond." Black eyes, dark as coal, sparkled with amusement as they lingered on her bruised cheek. "Your face is one that I could never forget."

She stared back. His flattery—or his teasing—was wasted on her. Still convinced that she'd seen him before, Morrigan thought of the busy streets of Edinburgh. Isabella said the Grants practiced law there. The house on Infirmary Street was not far from the courts in the old Parliament Hall. There was a strong possibility she could have encountered him on any number of occasions. He would have stood out in a crowd. Or maybe at one time or another, he'd been a patient of her father's. Many retired military men, including amputees, came to the clinic.

A sound from the cottage made Morrigan shift her gaze to a shadow moving in the doorway. It materialized as a large man. Wide shoulders blocked the entrance. No hat, no coat. His sleeves were rolled up, exposing powerful arms. From the fashionable cut of his waistcoat, she guessed this had to be the other brother. The barrister.

Morrigan looked at his face, and she cursed under her breath.

A nightmare. Disaster had come to her door. Panic washed hot and cold down her back. She fought the urge to run; all she wanted was to be miles from here.

"Aidan Grant . . ."

He stepped out. She took an involuntary step back. Morrigan didn't hear anything beyond the name. She paid

no attention to the introductions. He'd be a guest here for
the devil knows how long. A guest of Cinaed. A future
ally. A blasted politician. She was finished. They'd lock her
in and bolt the gate.

She had no doubt he recognized her. One look at her
and his face hardened. His stance became combative. Morrigan recalled their scuffle. Her forehead ached as she
stared at his blackened eye, still swollen partly shut.

More introductions. More talk. A buzzing in Morrigan's
ears muffled the words being spoken. Devil take him.
Aidan Grant bowed to Isabella, but his glare never wa-
vered from Morrigan's face. She'd hedged the truth with
Isabella and Maisie, and he would expose her.

His step brought him closer to her. This time, she refused to budge.

He was armed with the truth, and she should surrender
ground. But she wouldn't be routed. She had to hold out,
take his assault and then parry.

"Miss Drummond." He drawled her name. He was
taunting her.

"Mr. Grant."

"You look quite familiar to me."

"I can't say the same thing."

"We *have* met."

"Wrong, sir. You brother says we haven't."

"Sebastian and I have been known to travel in separate
society. We're not conjoined twins."

"That's quite obvious. He's much taller."

"And much younger."

"And less argumentative, apparently."

"He's a solicitor. I, a barrister. Hazards of the profession."

A silence fell over the group, and she realized she was
tempting fate. One word from him would expose her.

Morrigan's heart raced as their gazes remained locked. He had one grey eye. The other—he should have worn a patch to cover it—looked hideous. She'd done an exceedingly gratifying job on it.

He finally broke the silence. "If you're certain our paths have not crossed—"

"I'm certain." She turned to Isabella, who was looking on with a curious frown.

Morrigan's thoughts uncontrollably turned to their meeting in Inverness. The brothers had been speaking to Sparrow. But Isabella said these two were representing the Chattans. She guessed there were many people they had to interview for the court case.

All eyes were on her. She squirmed under the pressure. This wasn't the end of it. All who stood watching their exchange had to see the tension sparking between them. There would be more questions. More answers to invent. But for right now, all she could think was that she needed to get away from Aidan Grant.

Morrigan nodded to Isabella and motioned to the cottage. "I know this is not your only patient today. We should go in."

CHAPTER 6
AIDAN

Beneath the tam and the dark brown hair, the hellion's eyes flashed with challenge. He had a strong feeling that if he didn't move out of her way, they'd be brawling again. The mysterious woman Aidan encountered in the alleyway in Inverness was the daughter of Archibald Drummond.

It was a very small world.

Before traveling to Dalmigavie, he'd learned a great deal about Cinaed Mackintosh's wife. Henry Brougham's message had informed him that Isabella had arrived in the Highlands with her sister, Maisie, who was now married to Niall Campbell, a man he and Sebastian had served with during the war. And the young physician's stepdaughter, Morrigan, was traveling with them.

This past April, on a day of violent protests in Edinburgh, Archibald Drummond was shot dead by British soldiers swarming into his clinic, supposedly in pursuit of wounded protest leaders. Aidan's own clients told him they were certain the Infirmary Street house was on the government's watch list, thanks to one informer or another.

Henry Brougham believed Dr. Drummond himself had been targeted for elimination. Whether that was true or not, Morrigan going after Sparrow made sense now. Clearly, she held him responsible for her father's death.

The blackguard probably wasn't the informer, but that didn't change things.

Morrigan approached him, expecting Aidan to step aside, but he refused to move.

He'd never met a woman so effectively prepared for wreaking vengeance. Two days ago, in the quiet of an alleyway, Morrigan's smooth, controlled movements were deliberate, not impulsive. She was not a novice, but rather a trained fighter. Aidan's left eye, still swollen from the well-placed blow from her head, twitched as he recalled how expertly she'd incapacitated him before walking away. The city-bred daughter of a physician, indeed.

"I need you to stay out here." The physician directed her words at Morrigan as she moved past them and disappeared into the cottage.

Morrigan glared up at him. He glared back. She refused to back away.

"If you'd kindly move, sir, I should be assisting in there."

She took a step to the side, and Aidan followed suit, blocking her.

"If you don't mind," she said, an unmistakable note of threat in her tone.

"I *do* mind, Miss Drummond. I just heard the doctor say you were to remain out here."

Blair Mackintosh went around them and looked in through the doorway before joining his man and Sebastian by the low wall surrounding the cottage, leaving the two of them alone.

"So, you maintain that we've not met before?"

"Absolutely certain of it." She turned and stalked off a few paces before marching right back to him. "Isabella doesn't like to be alone with patients."

"She's not alone. My law clerk, Mr. Branson, is in there."

"He'll be no help to her."

He cocked an eyebrow. "And you would be?"

"Of course. I assist her regularly. While we lived in Edinburgh, I always helped my father with his clients."

"You . . ." he scoffed. "Helping to *preserve* lives?"

"You don't believe me?"

If one ignored the bruises, Morrigan Drummond was certainly a striking beauty. Large eyes of the deepest brown perfectly set in an oval-shaped face. If he hadn't witnessed her lightning-quick reflexes and unexpected talent for inflicting pain, it would be easy to imagine this lovely young woman as an angel of mercy.

He lowered his voice. "I believe you had every intention of taking a life the other day."

She stared at him, saying nothing.

"Tell me, was it revenge you were seeking?"

She tried to appear calm, but the color rising into her face betrayed her. "I don't know what you're talking about."

"I'm talking about revenge for your father's death. Is that why you were trying to kill him?"

She cast a quick glance over her shoulder. The three other men were occupied in their own conversation.

Her eyes narrowed to thin slits. "I tell you we've never met."

"You can save that tale for others. You and I know the truth." He held her gaze. "But if you refuse to be forthright, then perhaps you'll not mind me telling the doctor or Searc Mackintosh the manner in which we ended up with our bruises."

"You're supposedly a gentleman. You wouldn't betray me."

"I would, indeed, for you've not provided an explanation for your actions. I owe you nothing. Neither have I made any offer to keep your secret."

"I'll simply deny it."

"In the face of the proof I have?" He reached for a satchel behind him by the door. "The handle on your sgian dubh is quite distinctive. Shall I take out your knife for everyone to see?"

"No," she said through gritted teeth.

At any other time or place, Aidan was sure she'd be at his throat.

"So, what will it be, Miss Drummond? Shall we tell them together? Or would you care to explain yourself to me?"

She didn't need any weapons. The flash in her eyes were sharp enough to cut him down.

"There's still a chance that I'll remain silent."

She looked over her shoulder at Blair and the others again. When she turned her attention back to him, the scarlet hue in her cheeks was a few shades darker.

"I'm told you'll be staying here until Cinaed returns."

"That's correct."

"Then we have time to discuss this. And I shall explain. For now, however, I'm asking you to keep our secret."

Morrigan assuredly held the same political sentiments as her father. She wouldn't be here at Dalmigavie Castle otherwise. This put the two of them on the same side. Aidan knew it was certainly in his own best interest to say nothing more about their scuffle in Inverness. But it occurred to him that she probably had no idea who was lying inside that cottage right now.

"Before I make any promises, I need to know that you can be trusted, something which is doubtful at the moment."

"I've told you that I'll explain."

He waved her off. "Tell me, who is your role model when it comes to offering medical care, Miss Drummond?"

Her furrowed brow showed her confusion at his question. "My late father . . . and of course, Isabella."

"Then it's safe to say you've never entered their surgery and cut the throat of a patient who was under their care?" He paused, his gaze moving to the pouch containing her dagger and back to her face.

Her mouth dropped open in shock, but she quickly closed it and took a deep breath. "Of course not. I could never do such a thing."

"Are you certain? I would assume that any number of British officers must have sought out your family's medical assistance in the past. People you possibly saw as the enemy. Have you never been tempted to injure them in their weakened state? Make them suffer?"

Aidan sensed she was angry enough to slap him, or perhaps stab him. He wasn't sure which.

"What kind of a monster do you think I am?" Morrigan seethed, struggling to keep her voice down. "Whatever impression you have of me, sir, it is completely unfounded."

Aidan certainly hoped so. He needed to keep his informant alive. Over the past two days, he'd heard accounts from Sparrow of additional government plots to ensnare reform activists. He was even more convinced than before that the sick man's testimony could not only save the lives

of his clients but publicly shame the Home Office enough to stop future entrapment schemes.

The last thing he wanted to do was deliver Sparrow up to the sharp-edged vengeance of Morrigan Drummond.

"Then I have your word that you'll . . ." Aidan paused as Mrs. Mackintosh stepped out of the cottage.

Isabella had left her coat and medical bag inside. Before she even spoke, the stern expression in her eyes and the grave frown told him the news was not good. "Your companion is not suffering from consumption."

"*Not*, you say?" He was no physician, but from the little he'd witnessed of the man's condition, Aidan thought consumption was the worst thing Sparrow could be suffering from right now. "What is it, then?"

"Based on what he's told me, and what I have seen, I believe his condition is quite different. Apparently, his cough has been present for months and is gradually getting worse. But no fever. No chills. No sweating at nights. Always tired." Her voice was lower, the words intended only for them. "In addition, there is blood in the phlegm. The shortness of breath and hoarseness of his voice support my diagnosis."

Aidan waited to hear more. Sparrow had wronged a great many people. No doubt the man's death would be celebrated by many, including the young woman now standing at his elbow. But Aidan needed time. And more information. A day in court, preferably. Testimony.

"I suspect his lungs are riddled with cancer," the doctor continued. "Unfortunately, there is nothing I can do for him. Nothing anyone can do but give him some relief from the pain and allow him to die in peace."

This explained the change of heart. The sudden effort to make amends. Sparrow's willingness to help him was

now clear. *There's special providence in the fall of a sparrow.* The man knew he was dying.

"How much time does he have? I need about two months."

His abrupt questions and comment drew Isabella's sharp gaze. She no doubt thought him heartless. Her impression of him didn't matter. Other lives were at stake. Innocent lives. And she didn't know who lay in that cottage.

Isabella shook her head and glanced back at the doorway. "Seeing him once, I can't tell how long he has. Perhaps after I observe him over a period of time, I'll be able to give you a better idea of the speed of his decline. But even that would be conjecture."

Sparrow was dying. That was not good news for anyone. He imagined it would be easy to convince Morrigan to let him be and die a slow and painful death. He would keep her secret from the Mackintoshes, for now.

The physician gestured to Morrigan. "Come inside with me."

The young woman's eyes immediately found Aidan's. A question lingered in the dark depths along with a fleeting look of vulnerability.

Aidan stepped aside and followed them in. The cottage was dark. The air inside damp and chill. His law clerk, Kane Branson, bowed to Morrigan as Isabella made a quick introduction.

Aidan stood inside the door and watched her. He doubted Morrigan would hurt Sparrow now. Not after what the doctor had shared about the man's poor state of health. Not after their conversation. But he also wanted her to know about the informer's value to the cause.

The moment Sparrow turned his face toward them, Morrigan's shoulders stiffened, and she rocked back as if

she'd been stabbed. The sick man's reaction, however, was far different.

"I can't believe heaven would smile so on a poor sinner like myself," he rasped haltingly between labored breaths. "I must have done something right in my life for such a blessing. To find my own kin beside me at the end of my miserable life."

A spasm of coughing shook him, and he struggled to breathe.

Kin? Aidan looked from Sparrow to Morrigan. She'd turned to stone. No visible movement. Silent as death.

Looking perplexed, Isabella touched her hand. "You know him? Is this true? This man is a relation?"

Aidan thought back to Inverness. She'd drawn a weapon. He had no doubt she'd intended to kill Sparrow.

"I know it's been a long time, lass." He raised a shaking hand to her. She made no move to take it. "The years have been hard and cruel on me. But don't tell me you don't remember your own uncle."

The cottage became a sealed crypt, the air thick and heavy. Every sound died, inside and out. Aidan couldn't tear his gaze from Morrigan. Her hands, hanging flat against her sides, ever so slowly curled into fists.

"My sweet child . . ." Sparrow managed to gasp.

Without uttering a word, Morrigan turned sharply on her heel and strode to the door. The dark eyes in her ashen face looked straight ahead. Her shoulder bumped against his as she passed, but Aidan didn't think she noticed.

Wherever she was going, she never paused or gave any sign that she even heard Isabella calling after her.

CHAPTER 7
MORRIGAN

Morrigan couldn't breathe. She felt trapped, weighted down, buried alive. She needed to go somewhere, hit something, break free of this horrible feeling. Thankfully, the training yard was empty when she reached it.

Tearing off her tam and coat, she tossed them aside. She drew a backsword from the rack and swung the single-edged blade as she strode onto the yard.

The straw-covered pell summoned her. A dozen steps and she was thrusting, cutting, slicing, hitting the target with vicious strokes, again and again. Her heart raced. A fever raged through her, threatening to reduce her to fiery ash. But she continued with the assault on the training pillar.

She'd been only twelve years old when her father left her in the care of family in Perth. A motherless child. They were supposed to protect her, watch over her, keep her safe. *Safe*. Pain shot through Morrigan's arms, jarring her from the force of the sword connecting with the wood through the sacking and the straw.

Kin! How dare you call yourself that? Blackguard!

The weapon whirled in an arc over her head and smashed down on the pell. She drew the sword back, striking again.

Her throat burned, but she refused to shed a tear. When had she become so stupid? She should have guessed he was in that cottage. The Grants had been speaking to him in Inverness. But she'd justified in her mind that they'd been speaking to many witnesses. *Fool!*

Over and over, Morrigan delivered more blows, feeling the impact of each one across her shoulders and down her back.

Seeing him here at Dalmigavie or a half-day's ride away in Inverness, the effect was the same. The monster was alive. Every painful memory was back. Ever since hearing his disgusting voice and seeing his horrid face, she'd had no control over her thoughts. Her insides burned with sadness, with rage.

All these years, her father had been right. *Forget. Pretend. Forget.*

Her arms were burning, but she continued to swing the sword, punishing the sacking, straw, and wood.

Her father had taken her away. They went to the continent. To Wurzburg. The past was buried, never to be talked about. Their family was dead to them. It was easier to forget, not to remember, to pretend nothing had happened. Morrigan wished she could do the same thing now. She wanted this anguish to be gone.

She raised the sword high and brought it down with all her strength near the very top of the pell. The blade's edge buried itself deep in the wood. Her head and shoulders rang with pain from the force of the blow. She tried to wrench it out, but the sword wouldn't pull free. She let go of the handle of the weapon and kicked at the post, again and again, until her toes went numb.

"Should I fetch you another sword from the rack?"

Yanked out of the blur of self-inflicted pain, Morrigan whirled and faced her audience.

Aidan Grant stood at the entrance of the weapons shed, leaning one shoulder against the jamb. She didn't know how long he'd been there, how much of her fury he'd witnessed. A handful of lads, helpers in the yard and the stables, were watching too.

She stepped back from the pell, her breathing uneven, drops of sweat running down her face. The roaring in her head had started to quiet. In spite of the fiery pain in her arms and shoulders, she was feeling better, more in control of her emotions, more clearheaded about what she needed to do.

"Thank you, but no. I'm finished."

"Excellent." He straightened up in the doorway. "Then, since you're unarmed at the moment, perhaps this is a good time to speak?"

Her nod was curt. He had brought her enemy to Dalmigavie. But she couldn't blame him. He didn't know. In the same way, Isabella was clueless as to why she'd charged out of that cottage. There were lies she'd need to tell to protect herself, starting with this man right now.

The truth about what happened to her was painful. But the tragedy didn't end in Perth. An admission would bring shame to her, to Isabella and Maisie and all the people she now considered her family. She'd be at the very center of a storm. But it wasn't only her own reputation that she was worried about. She saw how her father had been affected. She wouldn't put that burden on the women she loved like sisters.

Before she reached the place where she'd tossed her tam and coat, he was offering them to her. Morrigan didn't want to notice his attempt at either humor or courtesy.

"When we met earlier, you hinted that you wanted to keep our discussions private. Where would you like to talk?"

She donned her coat and pulled on her hat. "The walled garden beside the courtyard."

Morrigan led the way. It wasn't the best place. Many members of the Mackintosh household would see them in there. Their conversation might be overheard. The bruises each of them was sporting and the way they'd interacted from the first moment they were introduced would cast her earlier explanation in a bad light. The time had come when she'd need to admit a partial truth about Inverness.

He caught up with her and spoke first once they passed through the stone archway into the garden.

"Your sentiments toward Sparrow are very clear to me. I want you to know that the man is no friend of mine. I personally think him a rogue and a cur, and I say that even knowing now that he's a relation of yours. But it's my responsibility to keep him alive."

Perhaps there was a glimmer of hope for Aidan Grant. "Why?"

"Because I have clients who are about to face a jury in Inverness. This man's testimony could mean the difference between life or death."

Morrigan refused to sit when he motioned to a bench. She had a hard time believing there was a shred of humanity in "Sparrow."

"What is it that he could say in court? Why would anyone believe him?"

"First, is he really your uncle?"

They were again at an impasse. She looked up into his face. Since their meeting outside the cottage, he'd pulled on his coat but still wore no hat. The wind tossed a few strands of dark hair over his eyes. She imagined that women might find the barrister quite handsome when his face was unmarked by bruises and he could see out of both eyes.

"Does it make a difference if he's related to me?"

"Yes."

"Why?"

"To start, because I'd like to know his real name."

She shook her head in disbelief. "You're prepared to present this villain in court as a witness, and you don't even know his real name? How long have you known him?"

"Two days, not counting written correspondence. We met in person just a few moments before you and I—"

"Had our little disagreement," she interrupted, finishing his sentence as two kitchen workers walked past them, carrying baskets of cut herbs.

"I've known him by reputation far longer. I've heard many tales about the damage he's done."

"What kind of damage?"

"*Is* he your uncle?" he persisted.

Morrigan noticed that information was being exchanged in a kind of negotiation. One offers something; the other offers something in return. What else should she expect from a barrister? "He's my late mother's younger brother. We've been estranged from that side of the family for a very long time."

"His name?"

"Robert Wemys." Even the sound of it on her lips made her ill.

"I wonder how many others he's used," Aidan mused, his attention wandering to the garden entrance.

"Your turn," Morrigan prodded. "How can he help your clients? What can he say that will make a difference?"

His gaze moved over her face. Lingering. Studying her. This time, she sensed what appeared to be a hint of regret as he stared at her bruised mouth. His intensity was somewhat unsettling. For years, Morrigan had been an expert at warding off men's attentions. Her usual abruptness with would-be suitors intentionally bordered on rudeness, pushing them away at the very moment introductions were being made. She knew she was reasonably pleasant-looking, and many found her odd sense of humor charming. But no flattering compliment ever affected her. She had no interest in any relationship that could lead to romance or marriage. No interest at all. Her past scandal guaranteed it.

The trouble was, she realized, the two of them had skipped that initial introduction.

He motioned to the bench again, and for a second time, she declined.

"Would you be kind enough to speak plainly, sir? We had a bargain, of sorts."

"Did we?"

"I have no reason to be open with you if you'll not be open with me."

"And if I hesitate, do you plan to use me in the same manner that you used the post in the training yard?"

"Are you trying to rile me?"

He smiled, a gesture that made a marked improvement in his looks.

"Your uncle—"

"*Never* refer to him that way again," she interrupted sharply. "You have a name for him now. Pray, use it."

"Very well," he continued, clearly undeterred by her curt tone. "Wemys was one of dozens of men and women the Home Office and local authorities have been paying to subvert the reform movement by infiltrating committees and entrapping the leaders."

A rat, Morrigan thought. A spy. How appropriate. She

now knew her father's immediate circle of friends had harbored such men too.

"Regarding my clients, I plan to have him testify in their trial," he continued.

"So you said. The Chattan brothers, I hear."

"You know about them?"

"They're famous here. The Mackintoshes, the Drummonds, and the Murrays—being radicals—have a stake in the outcome."

He tugged at his ear thoughtfully and looked pleased with her response. "Then perhaps you already know the two men were drawn into a snare."

"So everyone says." Morrigan frowned. "Was it Wemys who did it?"

"No. Someone else. Someone who worked for the same people."

She waited. She already knew how the entrapment schemes worked. The English government used many underhanded methods to coerce or dupe people into doing their bidding. Maisie's husband, Niall Campbell, was one they targeted this past year. They held Fiona, his sister, as a prisoner without ever charging her with a crime.

Aidan continued. "Wemys has, or had, a talent for insinuating himself into the circle of trust in the society of reformers. He would put forward plans for acts of violence, plans developed by Sir Rupert Burney and other scoundrels working for Lord Sidmouth, the Home Secretary."

"And I know the outcome," Morrigan responded. "The plot gets 'miraculously' discovered, the leaders arrested, and the orchestrated disaster thwarted. The event—as well as the subsequent public outcry—is then used to justify tougher laws and more restrictions on people's right to gather and protest."

He cocked an eyebrow at her. "You're well-informed about their tactics."

"I lost my father to these villains."

Silence hung between them for a heartbeat. Morrigan didn't want his pity, however. She motioned to him to continue. "And you think this . . . relation of mine can help?"

"In past cases, by the time the accused radicals have arrived in court, Wemys and others like him were long gone, squirreled away in a new place, with a new name, and with a new plan to ruin some other group of trusting idealists."

"And you say he is now willing to testify on your client's behalf?"

"I believe he is." Aidan plucked a remaining petal from a nearby rose. "He promises to tell the truth."

"But you said he didn't set up the Chattans himself."

"He didn't. But he knows who did. He can provide names and dates and where the agent provocateur was sent after the arrests. Wemys's testimony will be crucial."

Morrigan had no doubt Aidan Grant was a capable barrister.

"When I met your . . . met Wemys, he said he didn't care to be sent to the Cape colony in Africa," Aidan continued. "He asked me to protect him in return for his testimony. Now, however, I know it was because he's dying. I think he's known it for some time."

Morrigan recalled the momentary shudder that ran through her when Isabella mentioned cancer. She knew it was not a good way to die. But that was before she knew the devil himself lay in that bed.

Aidan's grey eyes focused on her face. "I'm asking you to let him be. Let him live until his sickness takes him."

"I'm not an assassin, Mr. Grant."

"I saw the way you attacked that pell in the training yard."

Morrigan wasn't sure if his words were spoken in seriousness or in jest. "Assassins kill without passion. And as you now know, I do have a temper."

"Tell me why you were following him in Inverness."

Morrigan considered but then dismissed the possibility of an evasion. She doubted the barrister would let her be until he had a satisfactory answer. She shrugged. "I thought I recognized him. I wanted to be sure."

"Do you hold him responsible for your father's death?"

"No," she replied truthfully.

"Then why the dagger? Why try to kill him?"

"That's what you thought?" Feint, sidestep. "I was walking in a deserted alleyway in a dangerous seaport town with no escort. Don't you think it reasonable to be ready for any possible threat?"

"You could have explained this to me when—"

"Explained to you? To a stranger?" Parry, lunge. "You attacked me, sir."

"I knocked the knife out of your hand."

"In my eyes, you were a brute, showing up suddenly from behind, physically assaulting me."

"You nearly unmanned me."

"And you caused this." She pointed to her mouth and chin.

He jerked a thumb toward his swollen eye. "I didn't come by this banging my head against the wall."

Morrigan and Aidan glared at each other.

"How convenient. Just the two I hoped to find."

They turned in unison, surprised by the sound of another voice. Isabella stood, medical bag over her shoulder, near enough to have heard their discussion.

"Is this true, Mr. Grant? You are responsible for the bruise on Morrigan's face?"

Isabella's tone was sharp enough that Morrigan feared she might order Blair to throw Aidan into the dungeons.

"I confess that I am responsible."

"He's not." Morrigan turned to him. "You're not at fault for this at all."

"But I am. Clearly and regrettably."

She ignored him and turned to Isabella instead. "There's an explanation. Mr. Grant misunderstood my intentions. He thought I planned to do harm to someone."

"I know now that Miss Drummond was seeing to business of her own. I'm entirely at fault."

"You, sir, have obviously not visited Dalmigavie's cells," she hissed under her breath at him. She turned back to Isabella. "He didn't hurt me. I tripped and fell. But it's true, we fought."

"We didn't need to. It was wrong of me to interfere."

Morrigan couldn't understand why he was being so deucedly agreeable. "It's completely justifiable to interfere when one sees a person draw a knife on a deserted street. I'd say that's a reasonable cause for alarm."

"Not if that person is a woman. You were rightfully concerned when you heard the sound of footsteps behind you. I'll not have you take the blame for this. You were in the right. I was wrong."

"But you simply knocked the knife out of my hand. I kicked you in the . . . the . . ." She wanted to motion toward his groin area but thought better of it.

Isabella cleared her voice, drawing their attention back to her. She stared at Morrigan, then at Aidan, and then back at her again.

"I suggest you two agree on a story. A good story. A plausible story. Then tell it to anyone who asks." She shook her head in disbelief and walked away.

Neither said anything until Isabella went into the castle through a door leading to the kitchens.

"I have it," Aidan said, breaking the silence. "A company of British dragoons. Dozens of them. All drunk. They cornered us. You used your knife. I used my fists."

With a story like that, Morrigan knew she'd never be able to leave her room, never mind the castle grounds.

"It would be best if you allowed me to handle this. You, sir, cannot be trusted."

CHAPTER 8
AIDAN

While staying at Dalmigavie, Aidan needed a place to work. He had correspondence to keep up and legal briefs to prepare. Searc suggested the small library upstairs from the Great Hall. It had once been the domain of the laird's sister, who'd been companion to Queen Caroline. Though it was situated next to a drawing room often used by others, the room was quiet, hardly used, and it had a small fireplace to take the autumn chill out of the air.

After dinner, he took his satchel and went up.

His destination was easy enough to find. Passing by the empty drawing room, he was surprised to find the door to the library open and light spilling out into the corridor. He stopped in the doorway.

Bookcases lined one entire wall, and a writing desk stood by one of two heavily curtained windows. Two up-holstered chairs flanked a small fireplace that hadn't been lit, and a table was stacked up with four or five books and a lamp. None of that interested him as much as the figure of the woman standing on a short library ladder against the bookshelves. She had her back to him as she reached for a volume, but he recognized her immediately.

"Miss Drummond." He hadn't seen her since yesterday.

She almost fell off the ladder but caught herself. Her dark eyes flashed in the lamplight as she turned.

"I'm very sorry." He dropped his satchel by the door and crossed the room to her. "I didn't mean to give you a start."

"Then perhaps you shouldn't make a habit of sneaking up on people." She reached up and took down the volume she was after.

"Searc said I'd be safe working up here."

"If Searc only knew our history."

The dark blue dress hugged her curves perfectly. Her pretty face still sported bruises from their skirmish. This explained why she wasn't taking meals with everyone else at the Great Hall. Aidan held up a hand to help her down. Morrigan shot him a look that told him she needed no assistance. He remained rooted on the spot.

"The ladder is unsteady. I'd hate to have you fall on whatever deadly weapon you're concealing tonight."

"Good point . . . and I don't use that word lightly." With a quirk of her lips, she accepted his offer and descended. Her hand was warm and strong and had none of the softness of most city lasses. The skin had clearly been toughened by hours of work in the training yard. And he knew from personal experience, the time had not been ill-spent.

He watched her. She ignored him. Studying the volume, she headed toward the table.

"I didn't mean to intrude. I'll be happy to come back later."

"Not at all. My work is done here. I have what I need. I'll take the books back to my room."

Aidan eyed the stack. Each of the volumes was heavy. Altogether, it would require more than one trip. "Allow me to carry them for you, then. That's quite a collection."

She separated two of the books from the others and added the one she'd just retrieved. "I don't need any help. These three should suffice."

"I'm a highly skilled beast of burden."

"I'm perfectly capable of carrying them, thank you. But since you insist on being useful, you can help me put the others back on the shelves."

"As you wish." He studied the bookcases. Spaces between volumes made it obvious where the books had been pulled from. "You tell me where they go and—"

"If you'd like to help, then please hand them up to me."

She was a woman who knew her mind. He was wise and would never remind her that he was taller and had a greater reach. But he also had no desire to curtail this unexpected encounter.

Morrigan climbed the ladder and stretched a hand down to him.

For a moment Aidan stared, admiring the loveliness of the woman before him. Her hair spread like a blanket of soft curls around her shoulders. Her eyes were magical. Her face, when healed, would be the kind poets wrote about.

"Do you intend to help or just strike a pose, Mr. Grant? I'm not planning to paint your portrait."

Her wit was as attractive as the rest of her, but he'd be a fool to give her a compliment on it. She'd cut him to ribbons.

Aidan picked up the first book off the desk and read the title aloud. "*Hungarian and Highland Broad Sword.* I see you have a devoted interest in the martial arts."

She took the volume out of his hand and slid it on a shelf.

"*The Military Adventures of Johnny Newcome.*" He read the second title. "What British fort do you plan to storm?"

"Any suggestions?"

"Fort George? It's handy, a wee bit more than half-a-day's ride."

She found the spot for this book, as well.

"Or are you going right for the heart of the empire. Parliament itself."

"I was thinking St. James Palace. I believe we should roust that fat little Hanoverian king."

"Very ambitious," he said as he picked up two volumes. "*Reft Rob; Or, the Witch of Scot-Muir, Commonly Called Madge the Snoover.*"

She reached for it, but he held back for a moment. "A classic of modern literature, to be sure, but it won't help you with your military ambitions."

"You don't know how useful snoovering is in a campaign." She crooked a finger at him.

Aidan grinned and handed it up to her. "What does snoovering mean?"

"I have no idea."

"But you pulled it off the shelf."

"I didn't. Or at least I don't remember doing it. I really don't know how that got mixed in with my books."

"Perhaps this one is also not one of yours. *A Modern Anecdote of the Ancient Family of the Kinkvervankotsdarsprakengotchderns.*"

"Now you're just making things up."

"Me? Telling stories? Yesterday, you told me that I'm horrible at it."

"I said no such thing. I said that you are not to be trusted."

"Well, what do you say to this?" Aidan opened the book and showed her the title page.

She had to lean toward him to see. The ladder shook and Morrigan had to put a hand on his shoulder to steady herself. Her hair brushed against his face. The incredible softness, the fresh scent made him want to touch the silky ringlets.

The moment was fleeing. She took the book out of his hand and turned away.

"I'm just so curious about the range of your interests."

"There are lots of things that would surprise you about me. But that volume must have been sitting on the desk before I arrived here, as I don't—"

"These two must be yours. *Love And Madness. A Story Too True.*" Aidan tried to cock one eye at her, but it was too painful. "And *Studies in the Nude.*"

"They are not."

"Then perhaps I'll hold on to the second volume."

"Suit yourself."

"On second thought, perhaps when I have more time for leisure reading."

Morrigan snatched the book from him. "That's not the title at all. It's Rowlandson's *Miseries of Human Life.*"

"So it is. The light is not very good over here. I must have misread it."

Morrigan shook her head at him. She turned to slide the volume into the bookcase, but he saw the smile.

Aidan considered pulling a few more books off the shelf so they could continue to play this game. But Morrigan was too quick for him. She was down the ladder and had the selected books in her arms in an instant.

"Thank you for the entertainment, Mr. Grant. Good night to you."

He bowed, regretting it as she started toward the door.

"Have you decided what story we shall use to explain our bruises to the people of Dalmigavie?"

"After tonight, sir, you've gained my confidence. Go ahead. Tell them whatever you wish."

And without another word, she went out.

CHAPTER 9
MORRIGAN

The shutters and curtains were drawn back. The mid-afternoon sun illuminated the three rows of etchings arranged neatly on the desk near the window. Morrigan had lined them up in the order she'd gathered them in Inverness.

Now, she and Maisie scrutinized each one.

"I barely had a chance to look at them the other night with Isabella here," Maisie said, picking up a flyer and studying it thoughtfully.

Trying to learn where these caricatures came from was a diversion. Morrigan needed a way to distract herself. There was little else she could do about the fact that Wemys was so near. Isabella continued to visit him. Thankfully, Maisie accompanied her sister to the cottage.

The villain was dying, Morrigan kept reminding herself. Dying a slow and painful death. She couldn't think of anything more fitting, even if she herself wasn't inflicting it.

Maisie put the flyer back down in its ordered place. "I know it's foolishness, but whenever I think of satirists—and artists in general—I assume they're progressive and radical. That they have a natural interest in alleviating the suffering of people and use their talents to help their fellow man in some way."

Morrigan bumped her sister's shoulder affectionately. "That's because you have a good heart. A clear conscience. You always see the best in people. And you try to improve the world."

A year ago, Maisie and Fiona, Niall's sister, had founded Edinburgh Female Reform Society. True idealists and revolutionaries, their efforts stopped dead and Fiona was arrested when the government used its iron fist to crush all opposition and protest. Since then, here in the Highlands, Maisie had continued her reform work, using the sharp point of her pen. And now, with Fiona again by her side, she was planning to start another chapter of the Female Reform Society in Inverness.

"Artists generally put a signature of some kind on their work."

"This one is too much of a coward to put his name to them."

"If we look close enough, however, he might still reveal something about himself." Her sister ran her fingers around the outside edges of one. "I've never known an artist who didn't ache for some kind of recognition."

"When Searc or Blair get their hands on him, he'll learn the real meaning of *ache*."

"I suspect he does this work for the money," Maisie said. "For a Highlander to do this, I have to assume he's starving. Maybe he has a family he needs to feed. You and I both know who'd be paying for such underhanded disparagement."

Morrigan knew. They all knew. Sir Rupert Burney had been moved from London to Edinburgh to Glasgow to Inverness this year to crush the reform movement and the threat Cinaed posed in Scotland.

"The artist is also a storyteller, and there's more than one story being conveyed here." Maisie traced a circle on one, then the next and next. "Look at this area of each etching. Do you see the similarities? They're all women."

"You're right." Morrigan looked closely. "Are those crosses on their coats?"

"I believe they are."

"They're nuns." Whether the etchings depicted a mob or not, the figures were repeated, artfully worked in. "Are there any nuns living in the Highlands?"

Maisie shook her head. "I don't know."

"Is he saying that Catholics are behind the movement?" Cinaed and the reformers were on the same side, but these etchings cast them as opposites, with the son of Scotland depicted as corrupt, power hungry, and a potential tyrant.

"Perhaps." Maisie leaned closer. "But look at the smaller faces, mixed in with the nuns. Children are standing with them."

"School children," Morrigan suggested. "A Catholic school?"

They both knew that practicing Catholicism had been illegal in Scotland and England for centuries, but the faith had survived in the Highlands by going underground, particularly in the north and in the Western Isles. It had to. The religion had too many ties with the old Jacobite loyalty to the Stuarts.

"Could there be such a school in Inverness?" Maisie asked.

"Blair might know."

"Searc definitely would."

A knock on the door had both women hurriedly stacking books on top of the flyers. Despite the fact that Isabella had already seen them, she didn't need constant visual reminders that the man she loved was at the center of a growing storm.

She was relieved to find Fiona at the door. Sister-in-law to Maisie, the young widow had spent some time in a British prison before being freed. As of last month, she and her two daughters also had found a refuge behind the walls of Dalmigavie Castle.

"Where are the girls?" Maisie asked.

"Terrorizing their grandmother."

"How is John doing today?"

John Gordon had helped Isabella, Morrigan, and Maisie flee Edinburgh, traveling with them to Inverness. Because of his assistance, the young Edinburgh lawyer was arrested by the dragoons pursuing them and tortured until Cinaed and Blair managed to free him.

"Better than I've seen him since I arrived. He joined me and Catriona and Briana on a walk to the village and back."

"He clearly enjoys your company," Maisie said.

"We have a great deal in common."

A shadow crossed Fiona's face, and Morrigan knew she was still haunted by her months in captivity. Since arriving at Dalmigavie, she wouldn't talk of it. She never shared how she was treated or what was done to her. Morrigan understood. She knew that dwelling on some evils only made them loom larger in your mind. It only made matters that much worse.

And then the doubts took root and sprouted. What if people looked at you differently? What if speaking about the past brought the nightmare back? What if one lost the ability to forget?

Morrigan realized she was thinking of her own demons and not Fiona's.

"I heard you and John Gordon are getting married," Morrigan teased, deciding to lighten the mood.

Fiona planted her hands on her hips and flushed an unexpected shade of red. "Aye, right after you and that Aidan Grant fellow are wed. The word going about is that you two are long lost lovers."

"Lies," Morrigan gasped. She thought of the few moments they'd spent in each other's company in the library a couple of nights ago. "Who's been saying such things?"

"If you came down and took a meal or two in the Great Hall, then you'd know."

She wasn't ready to circulate amongst the castle folk. Not yet. A few more days, perhaps, when the bruises were gone.

"All I can say is," Fiona continued, flashing a quick grin at Maisie, "a handsome young man has been mooning about."

He *was* handsome . . . and mildly amusing. Not that she'd admit any such feelings to anyone. She did give him permission to make up a story. But would he go so far?

"I'll blacken his other eye if he's been lying about us." Morrigan turned to Maisie. "Has he?"

"Now, that's not very ladylike, is it?"

"I'll cut his tongue out."

"Much better," Maisie replied. "The truth is, he hasn't said a word. In fact, he's been very much the gentleman. He says nothing at all in response to the tales Sebastian Grant is weaving at supper every night."

"What tales?"

"That his brother made the mistake of getting too close to you in an alleyway in Inverness. That you thrashed him like a Latin master on examination day."

"I'll never be allowed to go back to town," Morrigan huffed, walking back to the table. She removed the books from the flyers. Even from the few words she'd shared with Sebastian, though, she could see the man had a sense of humor.

She'd learned a little more about the Grants since that first day. The brothers had come north to take up the case of the Chattan brothers at the request of Searc. Aidan was quite famous, apparently, in Edinburgh and Glasgow. But this case would help his standing in the Highlands, and it would help him move a few steps closer to a seat in Parliament.

Morrigan's thoughts again meandered to their moments in the library. She wished she'd been brave enough to stay longer and continue their sparring. Or go back to that room the next night, knowing that was where he'd be working. The quickening of her pulse was as unwelcome as it was troublesome.

"Why are you staring at this twaddle again?"

Fiona's question shook Morrigan free of her musing about Aidan. The young woman was standing at her shoulder and gazing down at the flyers spread out on the table. She'd seen the sketches the last time she wandered in here. Maisie explained what they'd discovered earlier.

"It's a curious thing that he should repeat these suggestions of Catholicism in every one of the etchings we have," Morrigan added.

"And you believe this is part of his signature?" Fiona asked, reflecting on it.

"Other than the nuns," Morrigan asked, "do either of you see anything else?"

From the first time Morrigan laid her eyes on these flyers, she'd sensed there was something hidden in them.

"I wonder if this *he* might actually be a *she*," Fiona suggested suddenly, motioning to the caricatures. "In several of them, you can see a ring of women looking at the central images. We also have the nuns. The children, which appear to be girls. It's the same thing in several of the others. It's mostly women."

Morrigan leaned over the table again. "It's a possibility."

Maisie nodded. "Particularly if she is somehow connected with nuns or a school for Catholic girls."

There was a great deal more to these than immediately struck the viewer. Morrigan tried to justify in her mind why a woman, a talented artist living in the Highlands, would draw these for the enemy. She recalled what Maisie said only a few minutes ago. People were hungry. Jobs were scarce. Perhaps she had children with no roof over their heads and no food to sustain them. Desperation made people do terrible things. And there were thousands upon thousands of struggling war widows throughout Scotland.

If this was indeed the work of a woman, perhaps she was being forced to do it against her will.

The three turned as one at the sound of another knock at the door. Morrigan opened it to Auld Jean, John Gordon's aunt. Though the old woman was afflicted with shaking palsy, nothing slowed her down. She'd taken it on herself to bring up Morrigan's clean, mended dress from the seamstress. The outfit was the one she'd worn to Inverness.

Morrigan took the dress and invited her to sit. Jean shuffled across the floor, limping slightly. She hadn't seen the caricatures on the flyers, and it didn't make any sense to show them to her now. She was devoted to both Cinaed and Isabella, and there was no point upsetting her.

Once settled into her chair, she looked suspiciously at the three of them. "What goes on here? Ye look to be a gaggle of witches getting up a brew for Samhain." She lowered her voice conspiratorially. "Well, ye'll not be leaving me out. I been doing it since I were a wee lass."

Auld Jean was from a village huddled beneath a rugged headland east of Inverness. If not for her involvement with Isabella and Cinaed, she'd still be there. But her old life was gone too, and she now lived at Dalmigavie, where she watched over everyone while her nephew mended.

"No witch's brew here," Maisie assured her.

"Actually," Morrigan said, "we could use your knowledge of the area."

"What knowledge?" Her old eyes flashed. "I'm no mountain ewe, lassie. Born and bred in the shadow of Duff Head, I was, and I've got naught but seawater running in these auld veins. So, if yer thinking of running off through these hills—"

"No, that's not it," Morrigan said, fighting back a laugh. "Inverness. I heard you say your husband sold his fish in town."

"Aye, that he did. From the time he was a wee chack, bless his tough hide."

"You helped him, didn't you?"

"Aye." Jean nodded cautiously.

"So you know the area."

"Very well. Out with it," the old woman snapped. "I cannot be sitting about all day with a bunch of cackling hens. What d'ye want?"

"Do you know of a convent of Catholic nuns who live around Inverness? Or a school that might be run by them?"

Jean's gaze moved from one woman to the next and finally came back to Morrigan.

"Are ye all daft?" she barked. "Does Mistress Isabella know?"

"What do you mean?" Maisie asked quietly.

"Are ye thinking of taking up with the papists now? Joining a nunnery?"

"No," Morrigan shot back.

"Damn me if I'll be responsible for ye leaving off kicking the arse of handsome barrister, and running off to be some nun."

Morrigan caught herself gaping. Whether the old woman was teasing or not, she couldn't believe that Aidan could be happy with this kind of talk. "I'm not interested in running off anywhere!"

"Who then? This one's got herself a dashing Highland lad now." She motioned to Maisie and then to Fiona. "And this one and her sweet lasses are putting a smile back on my John's face. So don't come looking to me for help."

"We're trying to find someone," Morrigan said. "I promise. None of us have any intention of running off."

It took a few moments to assure the old woman they weren't all planning on leaving or becoming nuns. She finally calmed down. "A convent, you say?"

"Or a school?" Maisie asked. "A place where one might find nuns and girls boarding there."

"Aye, I do know a place." She thought some more. "Barn Hill, away from the river, up past Castle Hill."

"Can you tell us anything more about the place?" Morrigan pressed.

"Aye, it's all coming back to me. With the exception of a lad or two to help with the farming, they're all women. Been there a long time, I'm thinking. I went up there more than a few times with my old man. Chatted with a few of 'em. Going back a ways, but the womenfolk living there were mostly widows and spinsters."

"And nuns?"

"Aye. French and Irish amongst them too, blast 'em. Brought in to teach the young ones, though some lasses were old enough to wed. Waiting, I suppose. Not enough men about, maybe, what with the wars."

"Whose children went there?" Morrigan asked.

She shrugged. "Folk holding on to the auld ways. Unwanted lasses too, I reckon. Been some time since I visited there. Might all be dead or run off by now, for all I know."

"That was a great help to us," Morrigan said, taking her hand.

If she could convince Searc to let her join him the next time he went to Inverness, perhaps she could find this Barn Hill. If their guess was correct—and if the women were still living there—they might be able to tell her who could have drawn these caricatures. Talent of this kind was rare.

"Well, ye lasses can sit about all day, jawing and the like, but I'll be—" Before the old woman could finish her sentence or push to her feet, another knock on the door interrupted her. "Damn me, but it's busier in here than a harbor in a harrycain."

As Morrigan opened the door to find Isabella, she was conscious of the shuffling of paper and books across the room.

"Why are you all here?" Isabella asked as she came in and eyed the four women.

"Plotting against yer husband, mistress." Jean waved a wrinkled claw of a hand. "I tried, but there's no stopping these ungrateful hussies."

"I see. Well, you're the person I've been looking for." Isabella went to Jean and crouched before her. "Your shoulder is bothering you. Your knees are swollen. You have a sore on your heel. I told you this morning not to climb the stairs until I came back from the village."

She tried to reach for her foot, but Jean tucked it under the chair.

"When's the ship captain coming back?"

"Before the end of the month, God willing."

"Not soon enough, to my thinking, what with yer sulking and bullyragging."

"Bullyragging, is it?" She grabbed the foot and removed Jean's shoe.

Morrigan didn't need to be prompted. She poured water in a basin and carried it over.

"They've moved the dying man into the keep," Isabella told her in a low voice. "Searc insisted on it. He didn't think it prudent for me to be going to the cottage twice a day to look in on him."

Though the old woman was watching them both, the information was intended only for Morrigan. Their gazes held. After that first day when she'd charged out of the cottage, Isabella had asked no questions. And when it came to have someone accompany her to the village, she took Maisie with her each time. Morrigan was not being pressed to explain.

"Where have they put him?" she asked, forcing the words past the tightness in her throat.

"In one of the rooms in the old tower."

She passed those rooms frequently when she climbed the stairs to the top of the tower, where the parapets overlooked the gardens and the hills.

"Searc says, regardless of the man's past, he poses no danger to anyone here."

Wemys was getting closer and closer. Morrigan's heart began to race. She felt the pressure building in her temples. Anger clawed at her insides. She didn't want Isabella to see how this news affected her.

"You need your ointments, don't you?"

The doctor turned her attention to Jean.

"I do."

"I'll fetch them."

Morrigan ran out, fighting the bile rising into her throat.

CHAPTER 10
AIDAN

Dalmigavie Castle was untouched by time.

The fire in the huge open hearth, the tapestries and weapons adorning the walls, the smells of bread wafting in from the kitchens.

As Aidan descended to the gallery and looked down over the railing into the Great Hall, the thought occurred to him that if he'd come down here three centuries ago, the sensation would be the same. The change sweeping through the Highlands was called progress, but thankfully, not here.

As other landowners evicted tenants in order to raise sheep, Lachlan Mackintosh kept his people farming the land. Preserving the best of the past was important here. Lady Sutherland and others like her blithely turned families out, ordered their homes burned, gutting traditional clan relationships—all from their mansions in London—but the Mackintosh clan was determined to keep alive the old way of life. Scores of people elsewhere were being driven off to the cities to work in the factories or to the colonies or to unsustainable crofting communities along the coast, but life here was unaffected.

Aidan had been here nine days, but he was already quite familiar with their ways.

The day started at sunrise and ended with a late supper in the Great Hall. In between, the domestic staff went about the business of cooking, serving, cleaning, and everything else required to sustain a large community of people, both inside the walls and extending into the village beyond. Clan folk worked the farms and pastures that spread out across brae and glen, adding to the clan coffers.

The Mackintosh laird also maintained a company of fighters that trained daily and were well prepared to protect the people of Dalmigavie. And then there was the occasional horse and cattle raiding from the English military to keep them active and maintain the herds.

Decades ago, the fortress had been spared from the carnage following the Battle of Culloden. Its peculiar geographical positioning and the ferocity of its people had made negotiation preferable, albeit unusual, to assault. But the English army was now more confident and entrenched, and their artillery modern and powerful.

No reasonably intelligent Highlander wanted another war that would ravage their lands and kill their people. And times were changing. Loyalties were now divided, families torn apart. So many Highlanders had been recruited into military regiments over the past few decades. They'd fought side by side with the English soldiers on the Peninsula, in France, and on the fields of Belgium. In spite of it all, however, people were rightfully unhappy.

Aidan had not yet met the son of Scotland, but from what he was told, the man was selfless and smart. He longed for no personal glory and no crown. According to

Henry Brougham, Cinaed Mackintosh only wanted what was best for the people.

This was why Aidan had come to Dalmigavie. To meet him. And now that he was here, he realized why he and Sebastian felt so at home in the Mackintosh keep. The traditions of this clan brought back memories of their own upbringing.

They lost their father and brothers in battle the day before Waterloo swept away the threat of Napoleon Bonaparte forever. After that, Carrie House became his responsibility. Their mother had passed away when they were still children, but luckily, their first cousin was attached to the place. He ran the estate well, caring for the tenants as they'd always been cared for. The two brothers were grateful to have him, for they were never intended to inherit Carrie House. And now their law careers—and the affairs of politics—kept them far away. But in truth, Aidan knew that neither he nor Sebastian wanted the daily reminders of the family they'd lost.

This morning, Aidan was going to join Sebastian in the training yard, but he stopped in to see Wemys first. Since they moved the ill informant up from the village to this old tower room, he made a point of checking on him frequently.

"Rough night," his clerk told him. "Better after Mrs. Mackintosh came to see him, though." Kane Branson was worth his weight in gold. He'd arranged to have someone sit with the miserable cur continually, day and night.

Aidan looked at the sleeping figure across the room. His breathing was ragged and labored. "Did he say anything overnight? Mention any names?"

Branson shook his head. Wemys had made many promises to save his hide, but since then, he'd not revealed even an ounce of useful information.

Aidan went down the tower steps to the courtyard and found Sebastian waiting for him.

"Not much time left before we go to the trial, but I have no confidence that Wemys will still be alive," Aidan said as they made their way toward the training yard.

"What does the doctor say? Does she have any hope?"

"She's giving him some concoction to ease the cough. He spends much of the time sleeping. She doesn't pretend to be a fortune teller. She can't say how long he'll last."

"Too bad the trial isn't sooner."

Aidan agreed. But the government wasn't going to proceed until Lord Ruthven arrived from Edinburgh. The man was firmly in line with what the Crown wanted, and the entire proceeding was designed to cut gaping holes in the sails of reform.

Sir Rupert Burney was behind it all, directing everything. He'd had them change the trial location, proclaiming that too many people knew the Chattan brothers in Elgin. That illegal protests and violence would occur if the trial went forward there. The truth was that the Home Office preferred Inverness where the outcome was a forgone conclusion.

"I know they're intent on waiting to have their own man convene the court," Sebastian said. "But do you think the authorities have gotten wind that we have Wemys?"

His brother knew everything that Aidan had learned from Morrigan about the informant.

"I don't know. But it would be far better to keep that information hidden until the trial begins." If the man lived that long.

"Not much chance of keeping him a secret if his health fails completely and we need to get a deposition from him in the presence of a magistrate."

"I agree. But Searc tells me we can't trust any of the

other magistrates to come to Dalmigavie, never mind keep Wemys a secret. And if I were the chief magistrate, I'd find a dozen reasons to disqualify the testimony."

Finding the old man had been an unexpected gift, but Aidan knew he was in danger of losing the defector before he showed his usefulness.

"In the letters Wemys sent you, he claimed to know the person who set up and entrapped the Chattans. Perhaps if we get the name, I can go after him."

"I've been thinking the same thing," Aidan said. "But he's either sleeping or too sick to talk to me when I visit him."

"Convenient," Sebastian muttered. "I'll go see him. I'm far more persuasive."

"We need to keep him alive."

"I know, but the man is a viper whose every breath is a plague on humanity. I still can't believe he convinced you to—"

"Before you get too riled up, you should know that I'm going to Inverness next week. I need you to promise not to kill him while I'm gone."

"Why are you going?"

"I need to speak with the Chattans again. I want the names of their so-called friends. Everyone who was involved with their committee."

"When you saw them with their solicitor, they wouldn't give up any names."

"The lads were trying to be courageous and honorable, thinking they wouldn't get their friends in trouble."

"But one of those friends betrayed them."

"Exactly. I need the names."

"Wemys said they've already moved the scoundrel who was responsible for setting up the lads."

"And that gives us a fox to chase. If I come back and

put the list in front of him, maybe I can convince Wemys to tell me which one was responsible. And then you can go get him."

"Once you have your list, if you can't convince him, maybe *she* can."

Aidan realized they'd come to a halt by the weapons shed, and he followed Sebastian's gaze. Not twenty paces from where they were standing, two people were practicing with short, blunted daggers in the yard. Both were wearing stiff leather jerkins and thickly padded sleeves for protection. The taller man was Blair Mackintosh. It took a second glance to realize the lithe, young opponent with her back to him was Morrigan.

He recalled their encounter in the library. Every night since then, he'd gone up there, hoping that she'd come. At every meal he'd taken in the Great Hall, he searched the crowd, wanting to see her again. To his great disappointment, she'd kept her distance.

Today, she was dressed in men's clothing, a rough woolen shirt and trousers. Her hair was gathered in a thick braid that hung like a rope down her back. She moved with the grace of a panther—quick, agile, and competent.

Aidan found her as attractive in this outfit as the dress she wore the last time they met.

Morrigan fought Blair with both hands. Grabbing, punching, slashing, stabbing. She moved in and out. Lunge. Parry. Stab, stab. Retreat. Parry. Sidestep. Her hands were a blur of motion. Lunge. Stab. Retreat.

She changed her grip on the dagger effortlessly, attacking from down low or from above with equal force and ease. She was remarkably graceful, light on her feet. Her concentration was intense, and she lost none of it when she took hard blows, quickly learning and then avoiding the same mistake.

Morrigan was clearly fierce and skilled, and Aidan now realized exactly how fortunate he'd been in the alley. If he hadn't knocked the sgian dubh from her hand before she turned, she'd have probably gutted him like a salmon.

Aidan was raised with three brothers, and the women he'd come across in his youth fell into prescribed roles. Maidens looking for a husband. Wives and mothers. Workers for house or farm. When his world expanded to Edinburgh and beyond, he found women working in manufactories and in the trades: spinners, weavers, milliners, dyers, embroiderers, confectioners, bakers, brewers. And then, unfortunately, the less savory occupations.

In all his experience, however, he'd never met anyone like Morrigan and her family. One, a university educated doctor. The next, a political activist and writer. And then there was Morrigan. Smart and alert, she could assist in a surgery or cut down an opponent with the most lethal of skills. She needed no man to protect her.

He leaned against a post as Sebastian drew two blunt-edged dirks from a rack. Aidan had to admit, he liked the look of her long legs in trousers.

His brother walked across the yard to the two fighters. The three exchanged friendly words, and then Blair stepped back, continuing to instruct her how to use the longer dagger with Sebastian as Morrigan's training partner. The dirk appeared to be a weapon that was new to her, and she focused on what she was being taught.

Aidan watched them. Even with one arm, Sebastian was a formidable opponent for anyone. His skills had been formed as a lad and honed on the battlefield. It took a cannon ball to rob him of his left arm.

It wasn't long before she adjusted to the longer blade. He had no doubt she'd be as deadly with the dirk as the sgian dubh. As she became more obviously comfortable—

with the weapon and Sebastian—they began to talk between exchanges. He could only catch bits and pieces of what they said. He heard Morrigan ask how he'd lost his arm. Sebastian's response was as indifferent as if he were talking about the scar on his cheek.

The two of them were the same in their blunt manner.

Aidan was taken aback when his brother turned and motioned him over with a wave of the dirk. "Why don't you come and let this lass try these moves on you?"

Morrigan whirled toward Aidan. Her dark eyes rounded with surprise. She didn't know he was watching. The fight in the alleyway in Inverness was in the distant past. Their conversation in the library lingered in his thoughts. If he'd only known this was where he could find her, he'd have been down here every day.

"Are you planning to hide in the shed all morning?"

Morrigan's challenge was not to be ignored.

Aidan straightened. "Fools rush in where angels fear to tread . . . as the poets say."

"Well, you're no angel," his brother scoffed. "So have a go. You could use the exercise."

She gestured to the rack. "Grab a weapon."

"Here," Sebastian said, tossing him the dirk he'd been using. "She's tired me out, but I'd still like to cross swords with Blair, if he's willing."

"Aye, I'm always willing," the Mackintosh fighter said, going over to draw some weapons.

"Mark him up a bit more as you please, Miss Drummond," Sebastian told her. "But pray, don't kill him. He's the only brother I have left."

She cast a sidelong glance at Aidan. "I make no promises."

With a chuckle, Sebastian moved off with Blair, giving the two of them space.

They began in silence, testing each other with measured attacks. She was good, but he was better. She was fast, but he was stronger. If there was one weapon he could wield better than his brother, it was this one.

"I see you've been studying the books."

"My skills don't come from pages."

"Confident."

"I have to be when I spar with quick-witted barristers."

"Are you flattering me?"

"No, I'm trying to get you to let down your guard."

He would have preferred to stand around and talk. But she was the epitome of focus.

Morrigan had tremendous speed, but he also had the advantage of reach and height. When she attacked down low, he parried and knocked her backward with a jab to her shoulder.

She tried to get inside, and he deflected the move. She dropped her hand, and he had a chance to knock her on her ass, but he didn't.

His instincts were like the hammer on a cocked pistol. He knew what to do, and she recognized how good he was. She couldn't get to him.

In skirmish after skirmish, Aidan held his own but kept himself on the defensive. Like a gentleman, he held back.

Finally, she dropped her hands in frustration. "What was your brother going on about?"

"What did he say? I couldn't hear."

"He said you're an expert with the dirk."

"I am."

"Then attack me."

"I'd prefer to walk in the gardens or argue with you about your choice of reading."

She rolled her eyes. "We are in the training yard. Attack me."

"We've been doing well. Just because neither of us have been run through . . ."

She gestured to a straw-covered post. "I'd get more of a fight from that pell."

"A good lesson for me. I saw what you did to it."

"Are you going to fight or not?"

"I have been. You'll have to try harder."

Morrigan attacked again, but he managed to parry, striking her wrist sharply with his off-hand and knocking the dirk from her hand. He waited for her to pick it up.

"I understand now. You're being nice to me."

"I'm not."

"You have a bias against women being able to defend themselves."

"Not at all. The world being what it is, I'm in favor of it," Aidan told her. "Absolutely."

"How do you expect me to develop my skill with this weapon if you don't challenge me?"

"But I've seen your skill. I know you're already quite proficient."

She glared at him. "I love being patronized."

He waved her on.

"No, you come at me," she demanded.

Aidan lunged and retreated, fending off a flurry of blows as she pressed. Then, when he thought she was retreating, she darted in, tying up his weapon hand with her arm and stabbing him, head and neck, with lightning speed. She barely touched him with the dagger, but he knew if this were a real fight, she could have driven the dagger's point home in both places.

That thought was fleeting, though. Other sensations were running through him. The feel of her body pressed against him. She was strong and tough, beautiful and soft, and the heat from her flowed into him. Morrigan was completely unaware of the effect she had on him.

She disengaged herself and stepped back, glaring. "If you're not going to try . . ."

"Who is being patronizing now?" he muttered. "I would have been dead before I hit the ground. Let's go again."

Not about to be bested, Aidan stepped up his attack, using his long arms to shove her back and keep her off-balance. With a deft move, she sidestepped and lunged, but he caught hold of her jerkin and yanked her forward. As she spun to the ground, Morrigan punched upward, catching his barely healed eye with her fist and the butt of her dagger before tumbling off out of his reach.

"The deuce," he muttered as he went to help her up. She was on her feet before he got there. He could feel the blood running down his face and pressed a hand to his eyebrow.

"I'm sorry. I'm so sorry." She dropped her weapon. "I can't believe I hit you in the same eye."

"I'm fine." He headed toward a bucket of water by the shed.

"Let me see." Morrigan chased after him. "You're bleeding."

She scurried in front of him, blocking his way. She grabbed his wrist, forcing his hand down from the injury. She bit her lip, dismay registering in her eyes.

"It looks very bad. This time I cut you. What a brute I am! The blood is . . . Can you see?"

"Let me wash it, then I'll tell you."

She stepped out of his way but hovered like a mother hen, staying right at his side. When he put his hands into the water, her hands went in. When he splashed water on his face, she was using the cuff of her shirt to wipe it away.

He nearly laughed. The situation was comical. Never in his life had anyone fussed over an injury of his, certainly not one as minor as this. He did enjoy her attention, though, and considered pretending to pass out, just to see how she'd respond. He decided against it with Sebastian nearby. He'd never hear the end of it.

"I feel horrible, Mr. Grant. I can't believe I did that to you."

"I assure you, it's nothing."

"Now you're just being kind."

"Not at all. I can see perfectly out of my other eye," he told her.

Morrigan ordered him to sit on a nearby bench. He followed her directions. Luckily, Sebastian and Blair were still unaware of what happened. Aidan could only imagine the stories his brother would be inventing about this incident.

The numbness was quickly giving way to a stinging pain. Aidan tried to touch it, but she pushed his hand away and tilted his chin up.

Morrigan leaned closer to look at the wound. She produced a handkerchief from somewhere, and she used it to keep light pressure on his eye. Her soft breath teased his neck. Her free hand caressed his forehead as she brushed a lock of hair away.

Her skin was flawless, her dark eyes intense and unwavering. Aidan looked at her lips. The bruising was gone, and only a small cut remained, still healing.

His entire body became aware of her nearness. He'd thought her beautiful from the first moment he saw her in Inverness. But she had an aloofness that made her mysterious, an untamed fierceness that he found fascinating. Being near her was like standing by a loch at the onset of a summer storm. He wanted to be swept away.

She removed her handkerchief from his eye. "Blast. It's still bleeding. I should get Isabella. She might need to stitch it."

"I don't need stitches for something so insignificant."

"We can't let a scar ruin your good looks."

"Good looks? You think I'm handsome, Miss Drummond?"

"Passable." She dabbed the handkerchief against his eyebrow.

Aidan took her hand, forcing her to look into his eyes. "Only passable?"

She froze, and a deep crimson blush spread upward from her neck into her face. For a moment, time stood still. Her lashes were long and dark. A dusting of freckles kissed the tip of her nose. Aidan's gaze caressed her face, settled on her lips. He wondered what she would do if he tried to kiss her.

She wrenched her hand out of his grasp and leaped back. "I'll . . . I'll go and fetch Isabella."

"There's no need to trouble her."

"There is!" she exclaimed. "I'll fetch her."

Before he could utter another word, she was gone.

CHAPTER 11
MORRIGAN

Searc agreed to take Morrigan to Inverness for the day, but only conditionally. She needed to get Isabella's approval. So the night before the trip, she gathered up the collection of caricatures and went to the medical room and found her brewing a purplish decoction of roots and leaves. The brew looked and smelled foul, to say the least, but Isabella didn't seem to even notice.

"My intention is to speak to the women at Barn Hill. They might know the person responsible for these." She showed her the caricatures. "Based on what we see, the artist is a woman and is somehow connected to that estate. There can't be too many people who fit that description."

"What happens if the people at Barn Hill do know who drew these? Suppose they give you a name? What will you do, then?"

Find her. Hold her feet to hot coals. Break her fingers.

Honestly, Morrigan didn't know what she was going to do. After locating the artist, she fully intended to get some understanding of the woman's circumstances. And there was only so much she could accomplish in the time she had. They were leaving at dawn and returning very late in the day.

"I'll give the name to Searc," she said instead, hoping that was a satisfactory answer.

The incredulous look Isabella gave her spoke volumes. She didn't believe her. "I'm angry and I know you feel the same way. But I don't trust you. You like to take matters into your own hands."

"I admit I want to find her myself."

"For the purpose of stopping her?"

"Exactly." Morrigan had a feeling she knew where Isabella was going with this. "Once I locate her, I want to find out why she is doing it, who is paying her, and how we can make her stop."

"And you think you can do all that with a cool head?"

"I can be reasonable."

"You *can*, on occasion. But not always."

Morrigan had a temper. She'd be the first to admit it. During the years following their return to Scotland from Wurzburg, Isabella had witnessed more than a few tantrums. Those years had been difficult for her. Coming back to Scotland brought back the nightmares. Too many times, the corridors of their Infirmary Street house rang with her angry and frustrated outbursts. She knew even then that she was not an easy person to live with. Her father and other members of the household had borne the brunt of it. Isabella, however, had always been a pillar of self-control. She never allowed herself to be dragged into the arguments.

Morrigan felt she'd outgrown a great many things since then, and she also knew that much of her unhappiness at the time was caused by the forced silence about the past.

"Losing my temper with this artist, *if* I can find her, won't end their campaign against either Cinaed or the reform movement," Morrigan said. "They'll just go out and find someone else to create their falsehoods."

"You'll need to remind yourself of that when you find her."

"These days, I'm always in control. Well, mostly in control." Morrigan let out a sigh, looking at the unconvinced quirk of Isabella's lips. "Very well. I admit I still lose my temper occasionally."

"And hurt people, however inadvertently."

"I haven't hurt anyone." As soon as the words left her mouth, Morrigan realized her error. On Saturday, she'd fetched Isabella to inspect the cut above Aidan's eye. "I take it back. You're thinking of the accident in training yard."

"The man could have lost his sight."

She felt terrible enough without being reminded. She'd run all the way to Isabella's room. Everything about that morning kept coming back to her. Regardless of him holding back, despite her complaints, Morrigan enjoyed battling with Aidan. The competition wasn't only about skill, it was a battle of temperaments, of personalities. She felt a warm glow even now as she thought about it.

"We were sparring good-naturedly and—"

"Did your blow to his eye have anything to do with what happened between you two in Inverness?"

Numerous accounts of what had occurred continued to circulate within the castle walls, mostly as a result of Sebastian's enjoyment in deviling Aidan. She didn't think a supper passed when she wouldn't hear a new version of the story. She knew the younger brother was the source, for neither Aidan nor Morrigan spoke of it. And regardless of how they behaved toward each other, the teasing continued.

"Absolutely not," Morrigan assured her. "I was learning

how to fight with a dirk, and he was showing me a few defensive moves. I hit him very much by accident with the butt of the handle. Everyone gets hurt in the training yard at one time or another."

"That's exactly what he said. He took full blame for it, of course. Said it was entirely his own fault."

"It wasn't *entirely* his fault," Morrigan retorted. "I mean, I did actually strike him. But it was not to hurt him or blind him."

She didn't know why Aidan was continuing to do this to her. Being so blasted nice. Two days had passed, and she continued to think of him. They'd stood so close, his hand holding hers, and she'd seen the look in his grey eyes as he studied every flaw in her face. It was disconcerting.

She'd tried to avoid him since. He needed no stitches, but from what she'd heard from others, his eye looked quite bad.

"Well, you two will have plenty of time tomorrow to decide whose fault it was," Isabella told her.

"Is he coming too?" She didn't want to be happy at this news, but she couldn't help it.

"Aidan Grant is going to visit his clients in the Inverness jail. So I have a favor to ask of you."

"Of course. Anything."

"Don't hurt him, and come back in one piece yourself."

The sky in the east had barely begun to lighten from diamond-studded black when Morrigan stood in the courtyard, running her hand over the shoulder of her mount. As the others prepared to leave, she thought again of the conversation with Isabella. She was determined to honor her promise.

More Mackintosh fighters than the last time were accompanying the group going to the port city. She wondered if these trips were for the purpose of bringing back weapons. The rumors of an imminent attack by British forces from Fort George or Fort William were no worse than before. But with Cinaed gone, not every item of news reached her family's ears.

The excitement in the castle and the village was focused more on the upcoming celebration of Samhain, only a fortnight away. The festival, marking the end of the harvest season, was the time for taking stock of the clan's supplies of food, grain, and livestock before the winter cold set in. This was Morrigan's first autumn in the Highlands. She'd been hearing that the festivities at Dalmigavie were legendary. Eating and drinking, music and dancing. And of course, games of skill. Lachlan, Cinaed, and Niall were expected to return before then. Looking at the line of carts now, Morrigan thought it was quite possible they were simply conveying supplies for the holiday.

Morrigan spotted Aidan speaking with Searc near the castle gate. She led her horse to a safe place at the rear of the column. Carrying a torch, Blair strode along the line until he found her. As usual, he needed to check on her before their departure. He was still approaching when he launched into his well-rehearsed speech.

"Ye know how this goes, lassie. No riding off. No shortcuts. No lagging behind. No unexpected stops. Ye stay with the rest of us. Yer but a wee link in this great chain. Are ye listening?"

"I've sworn all of this to Isabella *and* to Searc."

"And now ye'll swear it to me."

"Again?"

"Aye. Again."

"I swear," she huffed.

"And when we reach Inverness, two of the men come with ye when ye go to Barn Hill. No abandoning them."

"No abandoning them," Morrigan repeated. She would, however, leave them outside. She wasn't about to have these brutes frightening a house full of old women.

"Searc sent a message. Said if ye run across any new barristers while we're in town, yer to leave them with their faces unmarked and with the use of both eyes, if ye please."

Smirking as he turned away, Blair moved past her to the men at the very end of the line. In the flickering torchlight, she saw him gesture toward her as he gave them instructions. No doubt the Highlander was putting every deuced eye on her.

She sighed. She'd have to prove herself and earn their trust all over again.

Morrigan knew they were only showing concern for her. What happened the last time she was in town could have turned out a great deal worse if Aidan hadn't been the one in that alley. When she thought back over that day, Morrigan knew that running into a couple of armed dragoons or a gang of drunken locals would have meant serious trouble. As angry as she'd been, next time she had to think first, act smarter, and be more aware of her surroundings.

The carts and riders wound their way through the narrow lanes of the village. Smoke from cooking fires already hung in the crisp dawn air. As they reached the end of the harvested fields where the lane disappeared into the forest, Morrigan became aware of a rider who'd left the caravan and sat waiting astride his mount.

Even from a distance in the greying dawn, it was not difficult distinguishing Aidan Grant from everyone else. In his tall hat and city attire, he was better dressed than any of the Mackintosh men, including Searc.

Morrigan had no choice. She had nowhere to go. There

was no avoiding him. As she drew closer, she noted his relaxed manner and the easy way he soothed the spirited beast he was riding. He exchanged jibes with the carters as they passed, and the sound of laughter reached her. Aidan made his life in the cities, but he was completely comfortable and at home here amongst these rugged men.

He tipped his hat when she reached him.

"Your eye," she murmured, forgoing polite greetings.

If she'd thought it had looked bad before, his eye was far worse today. Added to the lingering bruise along his cheekbone, the cut above it was red and badly swollen.

"I can't believe how much damage I've done to your face. I'm so very sorry."

"No apology necessary," he said good-naturedly, nudging his horse and falling in beside her. "It looks worse than it feels."

"Your brother must be enjoying this immensely. He does seem to take great pleasure in embellishing these mishaps you suffer at my hand."

No one actually saw her hit Aidan in the eye. That wasn't stopping Sebastian, however. From the stories he was circulating, one would think he was standing right beside them and watching every jab and parry.

"Indeed. He's the devil when he has an audience." The forest closed around them, and in the dim light, she could barely see his face. "But I don't really mind these wee bumps and scratches. In fact, I am grateful for them."

"Grateful? How?" Morrigan had thought he was simply being generous so she wouldn't feel bad. "I've heard some of your brother's stories."

"Sebastian sees these bruises as a lesson. He's always been concerned that I'm too reckless for my own good. That's why he's forever watching over me."

"Are you reckless?"

"I'm not, but I do believe I have luck on my side. I'm not tremendously worried about anything terrible happening to me."

"You're tempting fate, saying such things. Asking for trouble."

Aidan didn't respond, and they rode along in companionable silence. She peered ahead at the line of carts and riders. The sun had begun to filter through the foliage above. The road was descending steadily, and occasional glimpses of the gleaming river appeared alongside them.

Morrigan felt at ease riding along with him like this. If she could make herself forget the few moments in the training yard when he held on to her hand, or the night in the library when he'd teased her and stared at her like she was some ballroom beauty, then she was certain he'd join the ranks of men like Blair and Cinaed and Niall and Searc. Whenever she was in their company, she had no need to pretend to be something she was not.

At a bend in the road, he turned his attention back to her, serious and unsmiling. "Five Grants went off to fight in the war against Napoleon," he said, his voice low and somber. "At the Battle of Quatre Bras, our father died along with our eldest brother during a charge by French lancers. The second oldest, Noah, was dead as well before nightfall. Sebastian lost his arm when a cannonball ripped through our ranks. I walked away without a scratch that day and the final battle two days later at Waterloo."

Morrigan knew from the harsh tone, the hardened look on Aidan's face was hiding long-held feelings of mourning and guilt. She felt his sadness. They were living in Edinburgh when the news came of Napoleon's defeat. She recalled the days of celebration afterwards, before an understanding of the price of victory began to sink in for a wounded and hungry nation.

"Your brother told me he would not have lived if not for your heroism. You carried him to safety."

He shrugged as if it were nothing. "Sebastian lost an arm. I was unscathed."

Morrigan looked at him and considered all he'd been through, during the war and since then. Guilt was a sickness. It ate away at people, directing their lives. Morrigan had felt it in her own life. She saw it in her father. Archibald Drummond felt a deep-seated guilt that he tried to bury within himself. But it affected him. So many of the decisions he'd made in life were influenced by that guilt.

Morrigan brushed aside her own memories. "And thanks to me, you're no longer unmarked by battle."

He smiled, slowly shaking off his seriousness.

"And your brother owes me his gratitude as well," she continued, "for you now realize how valuable it is to have him at your side, keeping you safe."

"I enjoy Sebastian's company, but I need no bodyguard."

"Obviously you need more cuts and bruises. I'll be happy to oblige."

"Is that a promise, Miss Drummond?" He laughed, and the sound of it pleased her.

"You'll find me in the training yard most mornings."

"And I'll be working in the library most nights."

She knew and she was tempted to find an excuse and go there. But each time sanity prevailed. "Your mind is finely tuned, sir. It's your body's conditioning that needs work."

"There was nothing wrong with my health until I met you."

"Well, your brother serves a purpose and so do I. I'll promise to be a constant reminder that you're not invincible."

He shook his head and chuckled. "Your offer is very generous. And that reminds me, I have a gift for you."

"A gift?" Morrigan eyed him warily. She was unaccustomed to receiving gifts from strangers. While she was curious, she also didn't want him making any assumptions about their relationship.

He reached into his coat and pulled out something rolled in a piece of sacking. As soon as she saw the shape, Morrigan knew what it was.

She removed the weapon. "Returning my own sgian dubh to me isn't a gift."

"It is if I intended to keep it."

"You couldn't keep it. You knew it belonged to me."

"Any court would consider it to be 'spoils of war.'"

"Spoils of war?" she snorted. "We barely scuffled. You only took possession of it because I forgot to pick it up."

"You didn't forget to pick up your dagger. I wouldn't let you. Do you remember?"

"Oh, I remember," she replied. "And my offer stands about meeting in the training yard."

He laughed. Morrigan replaced the knife in her boot with her trusted one. She wrapped the other in the sacking and tucked it away. When she looked up, he was watching her.

"Tell me, how often do you draw that weapon?"

"Every time I train with Blair."

"Aside from our meeting, have you ever drawn it for your own protection?"

"Of course. Dozens of times."

"Dozens?" he scoffed. "How many times?"

"I have no real need for protection from the folk at Dalmigavie Castle."

"I was just wondering if you could actually use your sgian dubh to stab someone."

"You came quite close to becoming the most recent of

my many victims. You must have known I'd use it on you. Were you afraid?"

Their horses came close together, and her knee bumped again his.

The charming smile was back on his lips. "Afraid? Of you?"

Afraid. Her feelings for Aidan Grant were beginning to confuse her. She wanted some distance from him, but at the same time she enjoyed having him near. She was attracted and yet still afraid. Not afraid. Cautious.

"That would be wise, I think."

They rode along in silence for a while. Up ahead, one of the carters began to sing a Highland song, and others joined in on the chorus. These men had a shared past. They were together through troubles and celebrations. Clan folk were family. She'd never known such camaraderie before arriving at Dalmigavie.

"Do you know any Gaelic?" Aidan asked when the song finished.

"None. I know some German, but that's all."

"Have you any knowledge of French?"

She shook her head. "Why do you ask?"

"Searc told me you're visiting a Catholic house outside of Inverness. I heard a number of French nuns live there. A wee bit of their language might come in handy."

Morrigan wasn't surprised that Searc would tell him where she was going. "And I hear you're going to the jail to visit the Chattan brothers."

"You heard correctly." He paused a moment before continuing. "The jail is by the old bridge, not too far from your destination."

Apparently, he intended to keep her company right into Inverness.

"I'm going with you to Barn Hill."

She looked askance at him. "No. What for?"

"Our intrepid leader up there told me to accompany you."

Morrigan glared toward the head of the line, where she could see Searc's tall hat bobbing along.

"So, you're now in Searc's employ?"

"In a manner of speaking. He's the one who engaged me—through the Chattans' solicitor—to represent the brothers in court. Also, he's been using me and Sebastian as legal advisors, of sorts. So, I suppose I am."

There was no point in asking what kind of advice Searc might need. Morrigan knew he was involved in a multitude of ventures that straddled the legal line. "Thankfully, Mr. Grant, I have no need of your company or the skills of your profession."

"I have no doubt of it. However, our host told me to go to ensure that you continue to have no need of my services. I believe he considers it preventive."

Convincing Searc and Isabella to allow her to come today had gone more easily than she expected. Morrigan should have guessed the two of them would hatch a plan to keep an eye on her.

"I am speaking to a few nuns. A simple interview. I cannot see why I need your assistance. What kind of trouble could I possibly get into, going there alone?"

"I suspect you'll have no trouble at all. Unfortunately Searc thinks differently." He lowered his voice, speaking confidentially. "He also told me about the caricatures and about your quite astute observations. I believe he was impressed, and I don't think that is easily accomplished."

"I didn't come to any conclusions by myself. I had help."

"By the choice of the books you were selecting off the shelves, I should have guessed."

"It wasn't the books, but my family. The women who are like my sisters."

"Your humility is admirable."

"One of my many qualities," Morrigan said wryly. "But about coming with me. Blair has arranged for two Mackintosh men to come and stand guard over me like a pair of mastiffs. If you want to stand with them while I go in and speak with those women, you're welcome to do so."

"Searc might think you need physical protection, but no one knows the fallacy of that better than I. However, you might have some use for my social and diplomatic skills."

Morrigan doubted it. "And *your* humility is beyond admirable, Mr. Grant."

Aidan bowed, smiling at her barb. "Tell me, then. How do you plan to approach them?"

"I'll show them one of the etchings and ask them amiably if they know who the artist might be."

"*Amiably* sounds like the right approach, but the rest is wrong."

"What objection do you have?"

He frowned. "Why should they answer truthfully? They don't know you. Why should they answer at all? You have no connection with Barn Hill. You're not a Catholic. And you don't reside anywhere near them. Nor do you have a child or a family who might be interested in moving there. In short, they have no reason to trust you. I foresee failure in your quest."

Morrigan would have liked to disagree but she couldn't. He was right. Because of their faith, these women had surely been harassed for years. If she were in their position, she wouldn't trust a stranger either. She stole a glance at him and understood why Aidan had an excellent reputation as a barrister.

He wasn't finished. "What if the artist still resides there?

Approached by a stranger, they'll see it as their duty to protect her and themselves in the bargain." He shook his head doubtfully. "I think you'll have a difficult time even getting in the door. And if you do, you'll need to explain your visit in a manner that doesn't arouse their concern."

"I don't mean her or them any harm. I'll say curiosity brought me to their door."

"Curiosity over what?"

"The etchings."

"We've already established that doesn't work." His statement was final, like a judge addressing a jury. "You'll have only one chance at this. They might speak to you today, but if they have any suspicion of your motives, you'll be dismissed out of hand."

He was a man with two sides to him, Morrigan thought. Agreeable and good-natured. Then there was this other side. Strong-minded. Strong-willed. Unequivocal in his pronouncements. Dismissive of weak argument or approach. Very much the successful barrister.

"Very well. How would you go about it? How would *you* convince them to tell us what they know?"

"You'll see. You'll be with me." He tipped his hat to her and spurred his horse, trotting ahead past riders and carts, leaving her agape.

Morrigan couldn't believe it. The rogue had decided his company was essential for her today. And then she'd been dismissed.

She wasn't about to let Aidan get away so easily. Morrigan nudged her own mount and caught up with him halfway up the line of carts, reining in beside him.

"Yes, Miss Drummond?"

"I've decided that you may accompany me to Barn Hill."

"I thought that was already decided."

"And afterward, I'll go with you to the jail."

From the pained expression on his face, one might have thought she'd delivered another blow to his eye. "Absolutely not."

"You said the two destinations are not far from each other. And I've never been to a jail before."

"Surely, you're jesting."

"Absolutely not." Morrigan was indeed jesting, but he didn't know it. "You want to meddle with my business. It's only fair that I accompany you as you see to yours."

His features hardened and his eyes narrowed. With his bruises and cuts, he looked positively fierce. He leaned toward her and grabbed her hand. His grip was hard. All the good-natured affability in his demeanor had disappeared in an instant.

"You must *certainly* understand the folly in such an act. These people know who you are. They know your connection to the son of Scotland. Do not presume that you can stride into that jail and then walk out freely."

"Of course I can. Who is to stop me?"

"The Inverness jailer, for one."

"He is no match for me," she scoffed.

"And Sir Rupert Burney's henchmen?"

"I thrive on the ability to outwit and outrun such scoundrels."

"You cannot be serious."

"I am. And in addition, you've just armed me with my trusty weapon, Excalibur. Thanks to you, I'm now prepared to take on an entire company of dragoons from Fort George."

"Miss Drummond."

"Mr. Grant?"

He eyed her suspiciously. "What exactly are you doing?"

"I'd have thought a barrister of your skills and ability

would know when a witness was leading him on a merry chase." She slipped her hand from his grip. "Give me some credit. I have no intention of going anywhere near that jail. Once you get to know me, sir, you'll find I *do* have a lighter side."

CHAPTER 12
AIDAN

Aidan, Morrigan, and her two Mackintosh escorts left the caravan as the wagons followed the road past Castle Hill. He could see the steeples of Inverness when they turned off.

Long before his time and his father's time, an ancient castle once stood on that hill above the river, watching protectively over a village that would grow into a town and then into a bustling city. An arrow-shot from the stone walls, a seven-arched bridge was eventually built to span the Ness. From the castle's ramparts, knights and ladies watched ships from across the world bring their riches to the river's quays. Now, centuries later, the city and the port continued to thrive, but only a few stones remained of the once mighty fortress.

After the stops here and at the jail on Bridge Street, Aidan and Morrigan would continue on to Searc's house by Maggot Green and wait for the wagons to be loaded and ready to travel back to Dalmigavie. They'd have plenty of time for what they hoped to accomplish.

Leaving Searc and Blair and the others, they followed

an old road east, skirting the south side of Inverness. They immediately passed through the cattle market, crowded with buyers and sellers of traditional shaggy red beef as well as newer breeds of milk cow. The city ended here, and the neighborhoods gave way to fields and pastureland that surrounded estates which had stood since before the days of Oliver Cromwell. A few moments later, the four of them turned up a fairly long lane lined with ivy-covered walls. Several horses and ponies grazed on one side, and a garden rose in tiers on the other to a large, rambling house. Following the lane past a gate leading to the front door, they dismounted by Barn Hill's stables.

"I need to know your plan," Morrigan pressed as they left their horses with the Mackintosh fighters.

Nearly a fortnight had passed since the day he met Morrigan Drummond on the streets of this town. Seeing her now, Aidan realized his view of her had been changing. He still hadn't formed a firm judgment as to who she really was and what made her behave so differently from other women he encountered. At the same time, he'd made a few discoveries about her personality, the most obvious being her temper. It was dried kindling that took just a spark to set aflame.

He always did enjoy a good blaze.

"You're right. You should know my plan."

"What is it? What are you going to say?"

"I'll tell you when I know."

"I should have done this by myself," she huffed.

"We already determined that would not have worked out well."

"This is important. Your cavalier attitude is making me nervous."

He repressed his smile. "I can't imagine anything like

a casual visit making you nervous. Your charm is limitless."

Aidan nodded and tipped his hat politely to two middle-aged women supervising a half-dozen young girls in a group beyond a row of hedges. The students were huddled around a litter of puppies.

"Never mind the flattery, Mr. Grant."

When they reached the front door, he stopped. "Are we using our real names today?"

Her dark brown eyes rounded with alarm. "Why shouldn't we?"

"Well, you're a Drummond, and I'm a Grant."

"What does *that* mean?"

A serving lass opened the door, interrupting their discussion. She took Aidan's card as she led them through the entrance hallway into a drawing room. With a curtsy, she disappeared, leaving the door slightly ajar.

"You gave her your card." She seemed a bit flustered. "With your *name* on it."

He shook his head. "By mistake. I didn't intend to give her a card."

"So, we're using our real names?"

"We'll have to."

She let out a frustrated breath. "You argued that accompanying me here was a necessity. Now, please think. *Do* something. You *must* have a plan."

"I'm thinking of one now."

"Mr. Grant!" she scolded.

Aidan was enjoying the game he'd set out to play but knew he couldn't keep up this pretense of ineptness with her for long.

He put on his most thoughtful look and strode across the bright and well-furnished room. Bookcases lined one wall. A painting over the mantle depicted the estate in a bygone era. The tall windows looked out over the gardens, where an ancient gardener was digging up scarlet flowered plants and placing them in a wheelbarrow.

"I didn't realize geranium bloomed this late in the year."

"If you please, sir, either focus on the task at hand or wait by the stables."

Aidan looked over his shoulder at her. She remained by the door. A panther, ready to spring.

"You like to be in control, Miss Drummond. Don't you?"

"This is *important*," she said again, ignoring his question. "I'm no good at pointless social calls. So, if you please, tell me how you intend to proceed. No more idle chitchat about gardens or anything else."

"We'll have no idling about today, Miss Drummond."

"Thank you. But I warn you, unless you come up with a strategy immediately, I'll proceed the way I'd intended."

He walked back toward a cluster of chairs by the fireplace and motioned her to join him. She came farther into the room but did not sit.

"Our approach to our hosts is of paramount importance," he said, infusing a note of gravity into his tone. "You're visiting Barn Hill for the first time. What do you know about this beautiful estate?"

"I don't need to know anything about it. I'm not here for a tour of the grounds."

"If I may, allow me to offer you some advice from a man who spends far more time chasing down and interviewing people than he does standing before the court and arguing his client's case. Please, have a seat."

She did sit, but her tight-lipped expression said she was doing so under protest.

Aidan took a seat across from her. "If you're seeking

information from a mother, you mention how absolutely charming and well-behaved her children are. If you want answers from a weaver, you speak of unfair pay and long hours. If you—"

"I take your point," she cut in. "And what would a famous silver-tongued barrister use as an approach today, pray tell?"

"Do I detect a note of sarcasm, Miss Drummond?"

"You do, sir. But please proceed."

It was a good thing he had sound self-esteem. She could cut the faint of heart to ribbons with her tongue. "Based on my observations, I've determined the appropriate approach."

She was not trying to hide her growing skepticism. "What have you concluded from our few moments here?"

Aidan gestured toward the windows. "I'd say the house is set on approximately thirty acres, including the walled gardens, terraced lawns, and mature trees and rhododendrons we saw riding in. You must have noticed the old burial ground. I'm certain you'd find the fields covered with bluebells and daffodils every spring."

"Important observations," she scoffed, "if one were a botanist or considering leasing the estate."

"Very well." He let his gaze sweep slowly over the walls. "The books on the shelves indicate the political perspective of the residents. The furniture makes it clear that the women here are not suffering from any financial hardship. Note the new upholstery on these chairs. Indeed, they must have generous patrons. The painting over the fireplace tells us a great deal."

"The painting." She nodded skeptically. "What could you possibly learn from it?"

He took a deep breath. "I know that the house was built in 1754 by the Duncan family. A descendant donated the property to an order of nuns, I'd say about twenty years ago, with the stipulation that they offer a place of retirement for spinsters such as herself."

Morrigan moved to the fireplace, studying the painting. "How could you possibly know all that from . . . ?"

A tap on the door drew their attention, and Aidan stood. A round-faced woman with silver hair and a florid complexion glided in, all smiles.

"I am positively elated at seeing you, Mr. Grant. It's been far too long since we've had you here."

He bowed. "Thank you for receiving us, Mrs. Goddard."

She did not acknowledge Morrigan. She hadn't noticed her. From their many meetings in the past, he knew the good-hearted woman was severely nearsighted.

"How is your brother?" She didn't wait for an answer. "I've been following your legal successes through the newspapers mailed to me from Edinburgh. I do love seeing your name mentioned. This week, however, we were delighted to see an article about you in our *Inverness Journal*."

"You don't say?" He turned to introduce Morrigan, whose eyes were shooting daggers at him, sharper and more deadly than the sgian dubh she was so fond of.

"Aye, a lovely article. It was all about the upcoming trial of those poor men. The editor commented on how fortunate the Chattans were to have so excellent a barrister representing them."

"Mrs. Goddard, allow me to intro—"

"Your eye, Mr. Grant! Oh, dear!" A pair of spectacles appeared, and the mistress of Barn Hill gaped as she drew closer to study the damage done to his face.

"Who would do this to you?" Again, she didn't appear to expect an answer. "As soon as I read the article in the newspaper, I told Sister Martha that I feared for your life.

The local yeomanry has become a gang of undisciplined brutes, of late."

"They pose no threat to me."

"Then who did this to you?"

Morrigan stepped toward them, and Mrs. Goddard turned, shocked to find another person in the room.

"Mrs. Goddard, allow me to introduce Miss Drummond." He addressed Morrigan. "Mrs. Goddard is the mistress of Barn Hill."

The elderly woman quickly overcame her surprise, and the two exchanged greetings and a little casual conversation about the unexpectedly warm weather. Aidan noted that Morrigan could be very pleasant and charming when she chose to be.

"I must admit," she said to Mrs. Goddard, "I had no idea Mr. Grant was a friend of yours."

"Much more than friends, my dear. The Grants have been patrons of Barn Hill for years." She gestured toward the chairs. "Please make yourself comfortable. I'll tell you all about it over tea and sandwiches."

Without waiting for a response, Mrs. Goddard hurried out the door, calling to the servants.

Carrie House was only two days' ride from Inverness. Even though Scotland was predominately Protestant, pockets of folk who still practiced the old faith remained in the Highlands and the islands in the west. A number of Aidan's tenants were Catholic, and as Mrs. Goddard mentioned, the Grant family had maintained a relationship with Barn Hill for quite some time.

Today, when Searc mentioned the place, Aidan had been the one to suggest that he go along.

Morrigan came and stood beside him.

"If you reach for your boot," he said, "I'm going to dash for the door."

"You knew all about Barn Hill."

"I did."

"And you mentioned nothing of it before we arrived here," she said, her voice thin and icy.

"I didn't." He smiled at her. "There was no point of mentioning it and spoiling the surprise."

When she was angry, her cheeks bloomed with a bonny shade of red. He noted the rose color in them now.

"Are you entertained by seeing me riled, sir?"

He was, actually, but Aidan knew better than to say so. "Give me some credit, Miss Drummond. Once you get to know me, you'll find I *do* have a lighter side."

She opened her mouth to speak but closed it instantly. The hint of a smile touched the corners of her lips. The blush spread across her skin. Her eyes lifted to his, and the two of them were suddenly treading on an untried terrain. She was beautiful enough to take his breath away. And her toughness and independence pleased him beyond his wildest imagination.

Aidan cleared his throat and looked away at the windows. He was not a romantic by nature, but he always knew that he'd need to marry someday. With that idea came thoughts of how he could make an advantageous match, to help advance his career. Perhaps a politician's daughter, or a young woman with family connections to the courts. He didn't need his wife to have a large dowry, but it was greatly helpful to marry a person who could maneuver the rough waters of the social world.

Morrigan Drummond didn't meet that criteria at all. He was no cad, however. He wouldn't pursue her without honorable intentions. All this he knew, and yet he still couldn't quiet the eager kicks of his heart.

Mrs. Goddard's arrival was a relief. She bustled through the door with a servant carrying a tray.

"I want to thank you for your hospitality, Mrs. Goddard," Aidan told their host before tea was poured. "But I'm afraid I can't stay. I have clients I must speak with at the jail. I was hoping that I might leave Miss Drummond here with you. She has a question or two that you might be able to answer."

"I am disappointed you're going, but I certainly understand," Mrs. Goddard told him. She immediately reached over and took Morrigan's hand, giving her a conspiratorial smile. "We'll have a nice visit, and you can ask anything you want. I've known Aidan Grant from the time he was a wee lad in skirts, chasing after his two older brothers."

There was no point trying to clarify the purpose of this visit. Morrigan's smile at their hostess made it clear she had everything in hand.

CHAPTER 13
MORRIGAN

Morrigan realized that, almost in spite of herself, she was enjoying Mrs. Goddard's company.

In Edinburgh, she'd had no bosom friend. Invitations to dinner parties were nonexistent. She and Maisie were never asked to attend a ball or concert or soirée. Part of the reason for it stemmed from the fact that her father and Isabella led an existence that excluded them, for the most part, from social events. Morrigan always had a sense that suspicions about Archibald's support of radical reform kept them off invitation lists compiled by the more conservative members of the ton.

Though Morrigan was determined to learn what she could from Mrs. Goddard, she was surprised at the pleasure she was finding at this moment sitting and conversing with the old woman. The mistress of Barn Hill was interesting and well-read. Her opinions on matters were remarkably thoughtful. She also had a great many stories about Aidan's family.

"After the lads' mother died, Mr. Grant—the elder, I mean—had enough on his hands. An aunt of theirs came to help raise the four sons. She was an old friend of mine, so I visited Carrie House many times when they were young."

Morrigan thought back on her own life after her mother died. Archibald Drummond's life was consumed by his medical career and his covert politics. He had no idea how to bring up a daughter, and he was not alone in thinking that a girl needed more than servants to raise her. But he was wrong to think his daughter would be better off in Perth with his wife's family than with him in Edinburgh.

She shook off her dark thoughts and focused on Mrs. Goddard's words.

"I recall those days so well," the older woman continued. "The lads slashing away at one another mercilessly with their wooden swords. Arguing for no other reason than just being boys. Aidan was always the leader. It mattered naught that he was younger than Thomas and Noah and smaller in size than Sebastian; they always hearkened to him. He could settle any row, that Aidan. Where he is today is no surprise to anyone watching him through the years."

People did trust him. Morrigan knew Searc was not one to place his trust in someone lightly. Isabella said that Cinaed was eager to meet him. He did have a sharp mind and a quick wit. She thought of what he had done today. The devil had bested her. She had absolutely no idea he had a relationship with Barn Hill.

"The Grants of Carrie House are a very honorable family. And now Aidan is master there, with a fine career in the law ahead of him. Quite the eligible bachelor too, I'd say." Mrs. Goddard patted Morrigan on the knee and smiled. "So, do the two of you have an understanding?"

It took a moment for Morrigan to catch her breath. She'd somehow missed the direction their conversation was heading. But it was easy to see how a misunderstanding could come about. In his introductions, there'd been no mention of Dalmigavie or the Mackintosh clan. There was no word said about how the two of them knew each other. She was lucky the older woman didn't think worse of the nature of their connection.

"I apologize I didn't clarify things sooner. But I'm a family relation of the Mackintoshes, which is how Mr. Grant and I came to visit you here today."

"Kin to Searc Mackintosh? *You*, miss?" she asked, her eyes sparkling with amusement. "I must say I'm surprised."

Everyone in Inverness knew Searc, it seemed. Though he was an irascible sort, the man was also well liked.

"Well, I'm a family relation, of sorts, through marriage," she replied, hoping she wouldn't be pushed to further clarify the connection. "But it was on Searc's recommendation that I was first encouraged to come to Barn Hill. You're well known for your school's excellent reputation, Mrs. Goddard."

"Thank you, my dear. That's lovely of you to say. In fact, I am quite proud of what we do here. Our teachers are the most dedicated of women."

"Will you tell me a bit about them?"

"As you surely know, we have a number of nuns residing here, along with several widows and spinsters. So the lasses attending Barn Hill are fortunate in that they receive instruction from some very accomplished ladies."

Morrigan recalled Aidan's advice and smiled encouragingly at her host.

"We see the formation of character as our greatest goal. We teach each lass to develop a good and unselfish nature, and to remain cheerful in the face of adversity so that she can be a good wife and mother."

Morrigan would have failed miserably. "And you teach them other topics, I assume."

"Naturally! The domestic arts should be a basic part of

every woman's education. And then there is the instruction in both reading and writing in English and French, arithmetic, and we also provide music lessons—voice, the harp, and the pianoforte. Oh, I've left out drawing and painting, haven't I?"

Finally.

"I'm so happy to hear this. A friend of mine recently relocated to Inverness. She has two daughters, aged five and seven." Morrigan didn't think Fiona would mind that she was using Catriona and Briana to seek information. "Both children are especially fond of sketching. So I am here to seek your advice about hiring a tutor for them. Do you know of anyone?"

She waited, hoping she'd said enough. She wasn't disappointed. Mrs. Goddard's gaze flitted to the tall windows.

"Does the tutor need to reside with the family?"

"That can be arranged, if need be, but it's not essential."

"And the compensation?"

"I'm certain if the right person could be found, a mutually satisfactory amount will be agreed upon."

Morrigan watched as her hostess moved to the window. Putting on her spectacles, she peered out, looking for someone.

"I believe I have just the right person for your friend, Miss Drummond."

Morrigan joined Mrs. Goddard at the window. "One of the ladies living here at Barn Hill?"

"Indeed. But she's only here temporarily, until she can make other arrangements."

"Can you tell me a bit more about this lady?"

"Madame Laborde. Scottish by birth, thankfully, but she married a Frenchman. She's lived much of her life on the continent."

"Widowed?"

Mrs. Goddard nodded. "Unfortunately, she was left in a precarious state financially due to the untimely death of her husband."

"How long has she been with you?"

"She only arrived this past spring. Madame Laborde had been having quite a difficult time. She came to us after exhausting the hospitality of her husband's family and all of their friends. She had no other place to go."

"And she supports herself by teaching?"

"She does, but she's also been receiving commissions for additional work." Mrs. Goddard's expression turned serious. "Perhaps I'm speaking out of turn, but I know she's not happy here. Our quiet way of life is not what Madame Laborde has been accustomed to. She's told me herself that she's hoping for a chance or a means of earning enough money to return to France."

And what better way of earning money than to work for the British Home Office. Morrigan imagined they would pay very well.

"She must be quite good. What kind of commissions has she received?"

Mrs. Goddard hesitated before answering. "She is quite talented at creating caricatures of people."

"Caricatures, you say? How curious."

"Curious indeed. But I must tell you she's very good at it. The ladies here at Barn Hill are continually entertained by the likenesses she draws of each of us. Very amusing."

The headmistress was obviously *not* amused, however. The change in her tone made it clear she would be quite happy to see her guest moving on.

"Nonetheless, I believe Madame Laborde would be excellent with your friend's children."

"Would it be possible to have a word with her?"

"Of course." She looked out the window again. "This

time of the day, she generally walks in the garden. If the weather is mild, she likes to sketch or paint out there. I can introduce you, if you like."

"That would be lovely. Do you mind?"

"Not at all."

As they turned toward the door, a clock in the foyer chimed the hour.

"Oh my! The time. Would you give me a minute to speak to one of the sisters? I'll come back and take you out to the garden."

Morrigan had a name, and soon she'd have a face to the artist responsible for all the hateful images. She was certain this Madame Laborde was the person she was looking for.

"It's so lovely today. Would you mind if I waited for you in the gardens?"

"Not at all, my dear. I'll point out the way for you."

Isabella's warnings echoed in her mind as she followed Mrs. Goddard from the drawing room. A moment later, Morrigan was ushered onto a sunny terrace looking out into the garden. She needed to stay calm and keep her temper in check. It was already obvious, however, that what this woman was doing had nothing to do with politics or misguided feelings of patriotism. She was creating these caricatures solely for the money.

"Please feel free to stroll along the paths, Miss Drummond. I'll come back to you directly."

As the door to the house closed, Morrigan set off in search of the artist. She wanted to meet with the woman alone. She wanted to look into her face and decide if she had any understanding of the consequences of what she was doing.

She didn't see her right away, but the gardens were quite large, extending out from the side of the house and falling away in large broad terraces all the way to the road that led back to the center of Inverness. Walls of varying heights separated sections of the gardens. Near the house, a gate opened out onto the lane leading from the road to Barn Hill's stables.

They were quite close to High Street in Inverness—the church-like spire of the Tolbooth was visible just above the trees.

Morrigan passed by a group of youngsters engaged in what appeared to be a botany lesson in progress. She had no trouble finding Madame Laborde. At the edge of a green-sward on the lowest terrace, a slight woman in a blue dress and coat sat on a bench. She had a sketchbook on her lap.

Morrigan forced herself to take a breath and approached.

The artist's gaze lifted from the page when she heard the footsteps. The sketchbook closed swiftly, but not before Morrigan espied the caricature-style drawing she was working on.

"Madame Laborde?"

The woman hesitated but then rose to her feet, leaving the book on the bench. She was small and thinly built, but durable looking. The wide brim of her hat shaded her eyes, but from what Morrigan could see, she was still young and attractive enough to draw men's attention.

"I am she."

"I was speaking with Mrs. Goddard. She told me you were out here, and I hoped to have a word. I was . . . my friend is looking for a tutor for her daughters."

"Your name?"

She couldn't lie. Not with the headmistress coming out soon. "Morrigan Drummond."

"Any relation to *Dr.* Drummond?"

Morrigan felt her blood grow cold. "Do you know a Dr. Drummond?"

"Dr. Isabella Drummond. Or does she go by the name of Isabella Mackintosh now?"

Of course. She'd know a great deal about Cinaed's life, Morrigan thought. She was drawing him, making a mockery of his life. Unlike the other women who lived in the house at the top of the gardens, she was working for the British government.

Morrigan's sgian dubh sat at the ready in its sheath in her boot. She could force Madame Laborde to come with her. She could let Searc handle whatever needed to be done.

A dozen possible plans raced through her mind. She forced herself to be calm. Taking the woman would create chaos.

"You're her stepdaughter, aren't you?" the artist asked.

Morrigan's face caught fire. She hadn't been prepared for this, but there was no point in pretense. "I am."

"How did you know where to find me?"

"The nuns and children in your etchings."

"I see. You're quite clever."

"It seemed that you wanted to be identified."

She smiled. "Why are you here?"

"To speak to you. To offer you more than what they're paying you."

"The son of Scotland doesn't care for the way I present him?"

"He doesn't even know about your caricatures."

"Then why are you offering me anything?"

"Because I care about his cause." Mrs. Goddard said the woman needed money to leave Scotland. Searc could certainly arrange it. "I understand you want to go back to France. We can book passage for you to go immediately."

The artist frowned and crossed to a brass sundial on a pedestal at the center of the green space. She turned and looked intently at Morrigan.

"It's not just the money. Through my friends here, etchings of my artwork are now being posted in Tain, Nairn, Elgin, and Aberdeen." She motioned to her drawing pad on the bench. "I've been sketching and painting for all my life with no recognition."

"But no one knows who you are still."

"I've been promised that two separate printers in Edinburgh and Glasgow will be offering to produce my work, etched and hand-colored. I believe London will be next."

"But you're a Scot. How can you support the very government that is oppressing your own people?"

"I care nothing about politics."

"Innocent people are suffering. Dying."

Madame Laborde scoffed. "I understand your feelings. I learned a great deal about the son of Scotland and about your family. I know about you. I know about your late father."

She wanted to throw the words back in her face. If all this woman knew was what she learned from the authorities, then she had no idea of who Archibald Drummond was. And no idea of who *she* was.

"Your father supported and organized reformers in what is a losing cause. You think that's *your* calling too. But look at you. No home, no family of your own, no dowry, and no prospect of marriage. You have no future, Miss Drummond."

Those words meant nothing to her. This was a woman whose life had been dependent on the generosity of men. Morrigan wasn't here to argue the rewards of wealth and matrimony. What she had to do was to somehow convince Madame Laborde to change sides.

"You can continue to pursue your art. You can be recognized and paid generously for it too. All I ask is that you look about you. See what the British military and the wealthy absentee landlords are doing to Scotland and the Highlands."

"None of that means anything to me." She shook her head. "What I see around me are people who have more than I have."

"I tell you the Scottish people are suffering. Farm folk are being thrown from their homes. Tradesmen who assemble and protest are being trampled in the streets. My father was shot down in his own surgery."

"I'm sorry for your loss, Miss Drummond. But I see none of that here."

"You may not see it, but it's true nonetheless." Morrigan thought of Maisie's articles. "I can bring you newspaper accounts."

"And you think reading pathetic stories will change my mind?"

"I'm certain of it. I know when you see the truth, you'll have no difficulty deciding which side is more deserving of your talent."

Madame Laborde looked past her in the direction of the house. "Perhaps you'd have no objection to including this gentleman in our conversation?"

Morrigan turned and looked across the gardens. A wiry man with a pinched face and carrying a stout walking stick approached with a nimbleness that belied his middle age. Four bruisers trailed behind him.

"Have you met Sir Rupert Burney?" the artist asked, a note of amusement in her voice.

Morrigan couldn't breathe.

"I'm certain he'll be delighted to make your acquaintance and hear all you have to say."

CHAPTER 14
CINAED

A crowd gathered in greeting as the travelers rode through Dalmigavie's gate, and Cinaed had never been so glad to see their welcoming faces. It had been an eventful month on the road, to say the least.

He'd set out to see the leaders and the folk of the great Highland clans. With every stop and from every clan chief, he heard the same thing. The Highlanders were unhappy, fearful, angry. And everywhere, the same complaint rang out. Their lads had not come home.

To fight the French, armies needed to be raised. Now, every regiment composed of Scots and Highlanders was being moved to Ireland and to the farthest corners of the expanding empire. And militias from the south, as well as English regulars, were moving in to fill their places at Fort William and Fort George.

The rising was at hand, and the Crown didn't trust the Scottish soldiers' allegiance.

Whispers of coming war in the Highlands had been drifting northward. The Home Office was campaigning for it. English commanders in Edinburgh and the Borders were hoping for it. The rumored visit of the queen was being taken as an open threat in Westminster. Many believed it was far easier to crush out the sparks rather than wait and fight the inferno. But no consensus existed. There were other voices in Parliament who were against it. They feared the dire economic conditions of the country could turn a regional rebellion into a devastating civil war. A revolution like the one that toppled the monarchy in France just a few decades ago.

Before Queen Caroline returned to London, she'd told Cinaed what her own agents had reported. All opposition to war in the Highlands would be swept away if Whitehall were given a legitimate reason to attack. If the Scots organized and threatened England the way Bonnie Prince Charlie had done, the British military would leave a trail of blood that hadn't been seen since Culloden and the days that followed.

The Home Office needed a reason for war. One that would further divide the rich from the poor in Scotland, the aristocrat from the commoner, the Highlands from the Lowlands.

In his life Cinaed had done plenty to annoy the Crown. But there was an enormous difference between those nuisances and an action that would bring the entire British army down on the necks of unarmed people of the Highlands.

The English were trained and ready. The Peninsular War. Waterloo. The Gurkha War. The Pindari War. Those military campaigns had prepared the enemy. The navy would level every port from Stornoway in the Western Isles to Aberdeen. With the Caledonian Canal linking Oban to Inverness almost fully operational, the Highlands were cut in two. If all-out war were to come now, untold lives would be lost. Cinaed was determined not to give them the excuse they were looking for.

How to handle an unprovoked attack, however, was another matter entirely. No clan liked to see a laird wounded without retribution.

"Lachlan's leg is broken," Cinaed told Isabella as he dismounted.

As the men carried the laird to his chambers, Cinaed and Isabella followed. "A half-dozen dragoons appeared to be waiting for us by Loch Laggan. Niall thinks they were from Fort William. Lachlan's horse was shot from under him and rolled on his leg."

"Was anyone else hurt?" Isabella asked.

Cinaed shook his head. The attack had been little more than a glancing blow. The Mackintosh men had outnumbered the dragoons, who had fired on them and then dashed off as quickly as they'd come. Niall had been quick to say it was an old military tactic to lure them into a trap. These raiders were the bait.

After doing what they could for Lachlan, they'd brought him back here with the hope that his leg could be saved.

"When did this happen?" Isabella asked after sending Auld Jean to the medical room for what she'd need.

"Two days ago. We rode straight here. Lachlan is a tough old bird, but this nearly killed him. Where is Searc?"

"He and Blair went to Inverness early today. They're planning on returning tonight. Morrigan went with them."

Cinaed nodded, but as they passed a window on a landing, she stopped him.

"You have blood on your coat."

"From Lachlan's mount. I'm fine."

She wouldn't go another step until she'd inspected his chest and back, assuring herself he was unhurt. She caressed his face. "I've missed you."

He kissed her lips and held her tightly in his arms for

a moment. There was so much he needed to tell her, but it would have to wait.

The fracture in Lachlan's leg was below the knee, and Isabella set it with Cinaed's help.

Afterward, shifts were organized. The patient needed to be watched night and day. The laird was old and weak, and there was the worry of how easily his body would be able to recover after such an injury.

It was hours later when Cinaed and Isabella were finally able to get back to their rooms.

They held onto each other for the longest time. He told her about the journey through the Highlands. Isabella shared the news that Aidan Grant and his brother had arrived at Dalmigavie.

"I think you'll like him," she said. "He will be a good candidate to represent Inverness-shire in Parliament.

"Henry Brougham and my mother seem to think so."

"It's a relief for me, knowing you're pursuing a political solution instead of marching off to battle."

"It may not matter what I want." Cinaed explained to her everything he'd heard regarding Whitehall's desire for war. "Regardless of what I do, the Highlands are a powder keg ready to explode. And I don't want you in the middle of it."

She pulled out of his arms. "Where else would I go?"

"I've been speaking to Niall about it. He feels the same way. You and Maisie and Morrigan and Fiona and her family could go to continent. Perhaps Wurzburg. It'd be far safer for you there until some sort of—"

"Stop right there," she demanded hotly. "I'm your wife. I love you. And I'm staying beside you, wherever you are, whatever you do."

"You're not listening to me."

"And I am also a doctor. Do you really think I would leave you, leave the Mackintosh people, just to be *safer*?"

Cinaed shook his head. She could ignore it all she liked, but Isabella was still considered an enemy of the Crown. Like him, she had a bounty on her head. No one dared to come after her here, but their family continued to be a way for Sir Rupert Burney and the authorities to get at the two of them. If something were to happen to Maisie and Morrigan, Isabella would do anything to get them back, including handing herself in.

"If Niall can convince Maisie to go, will you consider joining her? To look after them?"

"Of course not," she snorted. "And Niall knows better than trying to suggest such a thing to her."

Cinaed didn't want to be apart from his wife, but he was worried and determined that she see the seriousness of the danger around them.

"And what about Morrigan?" he argued. "The lass is planning on leading troops into battle. She trains like she's in the king's guard. She's in Inverness only because Searc and Blair are watching her every minute. But she has a spirit that is hard to rein in. If the situation here becomes more perilous, she'll be impossible to protect. Do you trust her to keep herself safe?"

Isabella turned her face to the window as a breeze banged the shutter open.

"Morrigan is smart and resourceful," she said. "Of course, I trust her."

CHAPTER 15
MORRIGAN

To wait for Sir Rupert Burney would mean the end of two lives. His and hers.

The ruffians in suits he had with him trailed a few steps behind. They sensed no threat. Just two women in a garden. As he approached, she could see he was curious. His gaze was fixed on her. But she had no doubt the mention of her name would be catastrophic.

Morrigan thought of all the blood that had been shed because of this man. The arrests. The abuse of prisoners. All the people who'd suffered. The pain that Fiona and her children had endured.

At the Infirmary Street house in Edinburgh, she'd seen the carts bringing those who were injured after protests. She'd helped her father try to bring some relief to the people broken by torture at this man's command. The attack on the clinic last April had been ordered by the Home Office. Archibald Drummond was cut down in his own surgery. Dead at the hand of a hussar as he tried to save the lives of his wounded patients. An assassin most assuredly directed to their home by this man. Morrigan was there. She witnessed the tragedy, watched the blood pour from her father's body while Isabella tried desperately to save him.

Later, as Isabella forced her from the chaos, Morrigan was already planning her revenge. She would find and kill the person responsible for the horrors of that day.

She watched Sir Rupert as he drew closer.

Isabella, Maisie, and Morrigan had escaped through a back door with the aid of their housekeeper. In the alleyway behind the house, Morrigan killed a man to save Maisie's life. But there'd been no premeditation involved. It was a matter of kill or be killed.

Today was different. She'd been planning this moment for months.

A touch on her arm startled her.

"Why are you standing here?" Madame Laborde's face had grown pale, her eyes wide with concern. "Pay no attention to what I said before. You're young. You have a future that awaits you. Go!"

"You have nothing to fear. My business with Sir Rupert is personal."

"I don't fear for myself," she said with growing urgency. "Do not be fooled by the appearance of age. He is a fox, as keen and cunning as he is ruthless. He wears his age like a cloak. He is a true predator."

"And these are your friends?" Morrigan asked, her voice cutting.

"*Not* a friend," the artist admitted. "I have few choices in this world."

Burney slowed his steps and said something to one of his entourage.

"You see? He already senses danger. He won't kill you here. He'll take you to use for his own purposes. Think of your family. Is this what you want?"

Madame Laborde's words slapped her with the reality of her situation. Morrigan met the woman's eyes. She might be able to kill him, but what if she failed? She'd nearly been bested by Aidan in the alley near Maggot Green. He hadn't expected her to fight, however. She couldn't be sure about this man. Or the bruisers accompanying him.

She wasn't invincible. What if they did take her prisoner?

"Come with me," Morrigan said to the artist.

"Not now. I'm delivering new drawings to him today. He'll be on us in a moment if we both try to run. Neither of us will have a chance." She hesitated and then whispered, "I'll delay him. Come back for me later. Go now."

Twenty yards separated them.

"Please let me know, Madame, what you decide about the tutoring," Morrigan said loudly. With a quick curtsy, she turned and walked down the path to the gate at the bottom of the garden. Inverness and freedom lay beyond, if the artist could stall Sir Rupert.

She had no option about which direction to go. The Mackintosh men were waiting for her by the stables, but she had no way to get back to them. To reach the house, she'd have needed to pass the villain and his men.

She went through the gate and glanced back. Sir Rupert was standing with Madame Laborde. The woman was waving her hands as she talked. His eyes locked on Morrigan as he snapped an order at his men. Three of them immediately started down along the garden path after her.

Morrigan began to run.

This was exactly what Isabella had warned her about, keeping her wits about her. But she'd nearly committed an act that would have had disastrous repercussions. She'd nearly failed all of them. And she wasn't clear of the danger yet.

Morrigan lifted her skirts and ran hard. The cattle market lay directly ahead. As she reached the crowd, a shout
came from behind her to stop. She ignored it. The open
market was busier and noisier than when they passed
through it earlier. She thanked the stars. She crossed
through, mingling with the throng of buyers, sellers, and
drovers herding their animals into and out of pens. She cut
around a dozen men inspecting an enormous bull and darted
around the corner of a shed. A muddy lane wound down
a short hill and passed between a stone building and a tall
fence enclosing a livery yard. She hurried to the end of
the lane. A moment later, she reached the corner at the
head of Inverness's High Street and glanced back. One of
Sir Rupert's men appeared. He shouted over his shoulder
for the others, and then started to sprint after her.

The cobbled street was jammed with pedestrians,
carts, and carriages. As she threaded her way past vendors hawking their wares to small clusters of customers,
a gang of ragged children ran past her, two dogs barking
and nipping at their heels. A trio of British officers in
scarlet coats stood outside a milliner's shop, talking with
three well-dressed young women. Their attention turned
toward her as she pushed by them.

Moving in the direction of the river, Morrigan kept her
eye on the stone spire of the Tolbooth, which housed both
the courthouse and the jail. She prayed that Aidan was still
there. If she could elude the men behind her long enough,
perhaps she could get word to him, at the very least. Aidan
was far too public a figure for Sir Rupert or his men to
interfere with. He could go back to Barn Hill and warn
the Mackintosh men waiting there. Together, they could
bring Madame Laborde back.

The block directly across from the Tolbooth was lined
with shops. She stepped into the recessed doorway of a

stationer's store. Peering back up High Street, she saw them. The three bruisers were moving toward her, one on either side of the street and one in the middle. They were looking into the shop doors and studying the faces of women walking by.

The stationer's shop wasn't large enough to hide in. She could set out on foot and run for the river, but she doubted she could get clear of them. They were drawing closer by the minute.

"Blast," she murmured. She had no choice.

Keeping her head down, she walked across the street to a small doorway with a stout gate of wood and iron. The entrance to the jail. A smaller door was set into the gate and a guard leaned against it. He tipped his cap as she approached him.

"Help ye, mistress?"

"I was supposed to meet the barrister, Mr. Grant. Is he still here?"

"Aye, that he is."

"May I wait for him inside?" She glanced meaningfully at a couple of watermen sitting against the building, passing a flask back and forth.

"No better inside, mistress."

"I'd prefer it, if you don't mind."

With a shrug, the guard knocked on the door. A face appeared at a peep hole, and then a bolt slid on the other side. The door creaked open. The guard ushered her through and pointed to a bench just inside. Beyond the entrance, she saw a small dark courtyard surrounded by high walls. Windows of the courthouse and city offices looked down on the open area. A gallows sat ominously at one end. Just above the cobblestones on the far wall, a row of tiny, barred windows ran the entire length of the enclosed space. The sounds of the street were muted here.

The guard explained the situation to the gatekeeper, who bolted the door before disappearing into the building.

"You can sit here and wait, mistress," the guard said. He went into a small office space beside the gate, and the smell of tobacco immediately drifted into the courtyard.

She didn't have long to wait. A moment later, Aidan came out of the building with the gatekeeper. His expression upon seeing her inside the jail was murderous. He took her elbow and led her a few feet away. The guard went back out onto the street, and the gatekeeper bolted the door.

Aidan spoke in a hushed voice, but his anger was evident. "Have you lost your mind?"

"They're outside, looking for me on the street. They chased me down from Barn Hill."

"Who?" he asked, sending a cautious glance at the gatekeeper. "Who is looking for you?"

"Sir Rupert Burney's men."

His grey eyes met hers, and a hand wrapped protectively around her upper arm, leading her a few more feet away. She talked fast and told him everything—from finding out from Mrs. Goddard that the artist was living at Barn Hill to meeting the woman in the gardens.

"Sir Rupert arrived while I was speaking with her."

She left out her momentary impulse of putting a knife in the heart of the spymaster.

"I had to escape on foot. They came after me, searching in every shop along High Street. This was the only place where I thought they wouldn't look."

"No doubt, she told him who you were."

"She had no choice. She would have come with me if she could. I want to go back for her."

"You're going nowhere near Barn Hill," he ordered. He thought for a moment before leading her to the bench. "Stay here and wait for me. I'll be back in a few minutes."

She didn't argue. Morrigan watched Aidan approach the gatekeeper. A few words were exchanged before the man opened the door and let him out.

She sat on the bench, but she was too restless to stay there. She stood again. Twice, the guard's knock came on the door and the gate opened to admit visitors. Long minutes passed. The bells in the Tolbooth steeple above her ran the hour. Two in the afternoon.

While she waited, Morrigan studied the courtyard and the row of cell windows.

Perhaps there was once a time when she assumed only bad people were kept in jail cells. Murderers. Thieves. Brutes. Even those who were not violent. Frauds. Debtors. But assisting her father and Isabella in their clinic in Edinburgh had changed that assumption forever. She now knew citizens were being arrested and charged—or simply held indefinitely by the authorities—for their beliefs or opinions, for gathering in groups, for protesting against unjust laws. Those people now languishing behind barred windows all over Britain and Ireland were fathers and mothers, sisters and brothers, even children. They were people like Fiona. Like John Gordon.

Anyone could be robbed of their freedom, tortured and killed, even though they'd never stolen a ha'penny nor lifted a hand against anyone.

This was the new justice. Morrigan lost track of how long she sat there, deep in thought. She was startled at the sound of a knock at the gate. The door opened. Aidan appeared.

"Come with me."

He took hold of her hand, and the two of them walked out onto the street. As they passed the guard, Morrigan saw Aidan place some coins discreetly in his hand.

A hired post chaise was waiting, with Aidan's horse tied

to the back. The postilion sitting on the lead horse tipped his tall hat.

Morrigan barely had a chance to look up and down the street for the men who were following her. Aidan quickly ushered her in and climbed in after her. They set off without another word.

Instead of continuing down Bridge Street toward the river, the driver turned the carriage and went down Church Street. They were heading north toward the Maggot. They'd not gone two blocks before she spotted two of her pursuers looking onto a tea shop window. Morrigan pointed them out to Aidan as she sat back in the seat, hiding her face until Sir Rupert's men were behind them.

"When I hired the carriage," Aidan said, "I sent a messenger to Barn Hill to tell the Mackintosh men that you're with me."

Morrigan hoped the two hadn't gotten involved in any altercation. Her escorts had been waiting by the stables. She thought back to when she first saw Sir Rupert coming along the path in the gardens. Nothing had seemed amiss. They were not on their guard. Perhaps they hadn't seen the Mackintosh men waiting by the stables.

"What about Madame Laborde?" she asked.

"We'll need to act with caution. You said she's employed by Burney and seemed happy with the arrangement."

"At first, that was the impression she gave me. But that wasn't the case before I left. She was quite nervous. I think she would have come with me if the situation were different."

"Then we'll leave it to Searc to send someone back there. He can make whatever arrangements are necessary. Inverness is his town. He knows where he could put her that would be safe for everyone."

Morrigan understood that it was not up to her to offer

shelter at Dalmigavie Castle to someone like Madame Laborde. The artist could hardly be considered trustworthy at this point. Her mind immediately turned to Wemys. He was even less so, but the blackguard was dying.

The post chaise hit a hole in the road, and she was jostled into Aidan. She tried to slide away, but he reached over and took hold of her arm. He looked into her eyes.

"As angry as I was at the sight of you in the courtyard at the jail, I am glad about what you did. It was a smart decision. And it took courage, I'm sure, to go there. You acted responsibly getting away as you did."

Morrigan felt herself grow warm at his praise. Those moments in that garden when her desire for revenge nearly blotted out reason were still fresh in her mind. It was a weakness she needed to overcome. She'd done the same thing when she saw Wemys near Maggot Green.

She had to be smarter. Less hotheaded. She somehow had to make herself slow down and think before she acted.

"There is no bounty on my head. And even though I'm wanted for no crime, I know they would have taken me, anyway."

"And they would have kept you until they had Cinaed in chains," he agreed.

Morrigan frowned, thinking of Fiona. She was safe at Dalmigavie with her children now, but last spring she'd been taken by Sir Rupert's henchmen in Edinburgh. At the time of her arrest, she had damning letters and protest flyers in her possession. She told Aidan about that now. "I know it wouldn't have mattered that I had nothing but some of their own caricatures in my reticule."

"Lack of evidence means nothing to them. Lack of a crime means nothing. They'd hold you, and when the time came that they'd need to, they'd charge you with crimes that carry the maximum punishment. Knowing full well that you're innocent, they'd say you were conspiring against the government, abetting known traitors. They'd heap a dozen other charges on your head. It would be your word against theirs. But I can tell you one thing, if you were arrested today, Madam Laborde would never have testified on your behalf against Sir Rupert. She would have disappeared."

Morrigan shivered at the thought of the calamity she'd escaped. "You've seen these situations."

"Unfortunately, I have. I've been involved in a number of such cases."

Morrigan stared at their joined hands. His grip was firm, his actions back in the Tolbooth courtyard were confident. He didn't panic. He knew what to do. She watched the play of his thumb over her skin. A delicious twist gripped her belly. He was staring ahead, his thoughts on something else. She doubted he was aware of what he was doing.

"This is why Wemys is so important to me. His offer to testify against the Home Office is the first time one of their minions will provide evidence against them."

She pulled her hand away and slid across the seat, creating some distance between them.

"I don't think you should come back to Inverness anytime soon," he continued. "Burney now knows how close he came to getting his hands on you. He'll be on the lookout. You may not escape a second time."

"Would they be bold enough to come to the Maggot?"

"I doubt it. Searc has too many important connections for them to come after anyone in his house. Except perhaps Cinaed Mackintosh. And they'd need a battalion to take him."

Morrigan wasn't in Inverness the night the hussars set the Maggot on fire, but Isabella had told her about it. The end result had been disastrous for them.

After passing Maggot Green, the post chaise turned down the lane, stopping at the gate to Searc's house. The carts being loaded by Mackintosh men renewed her confidence. Blair appeared, coolly eying the carriage.

"You should go and tell Searc what happened," Aidan suggested. "I'll speak with Blair about keeping an eye out for Sir Rupert's men, just in case."

Morrigan agreed. As soon as the chaise came to a stop, she climbed out, not waiting for him to assist her.

Seen from the outside, Searc's rambling house looked as dilapidated as the rest of the area. The place was actually a number of buildings joined together. A warehouse was attached on the river side. Set back a little from the main road, the buildings were surrounded by high walls. The narrow lane where Morrigan left Aidan and Blair talking ran past a gated entrance and dropped off into the Ness. There were rumors about tunnels leading off from the house in a number of directions—to the river and to a livery stable some distance from the house. But she'd never seen them, and Isabella had been quite tight-lipped on the subject.

The area inside the walls included neglected gardens and a small stable. The Highlanders' horses were being tended there in preparation for the journey back. As she went in, Morrigan glanced up at a round, tower-like structure with a square block of a room perched on top. It was a curious place, and she'd never seen a house like it, even in Edinburgh.

Every time she came to Inverness, Morrigan spent some time inside the house. She was genuinely impressed at the way Searc used the run-down exterior to mask the shrewd and lucrative business dealings that he conducted inside.

The housekeeper told her that Searc was meeting with Captain Kenedy. Morrigan had met the man and his wife at Dalmigavie. The ship owner was an enthusiastic supporter of Cinaed.

She decided to wait in her favorite room in the house until the two finished conducting their business. Searc's Clan Mackintosh room. She liked to refer to it as the Armory.

Shedding her coat and tam, Morrigan walked along the dark, twisted corridors. Upon entering it, she closed the door behind her. Immediately, she felt better. All the lingering edginess of her escape from Burney and his men disappeared like a morning mist.

Weapons adorned every wall. Muskets and swords and pistols were displayed in a series of starlike designs. She ran her gaze over the shields and crossed swords and wheels of daggers. Lines of spears with wicked hooks and axe blades caught the light from large windows high on the walls. A great deal of damage could be done with the armaments in this chamber.

Above the fireplace, in a position of honor, hung the portrait of Bonnie Prince Charlie.

Morrigan heard a knock on the door and turned as it opened and Aidan came in.

"I knew I'd find you here."

"Did you guess how to get here, or did someone show you?"

"I knew about this room. I've been in here a number of times."

She shouldn't have been surprised that he'd been to Searc's house before today. Aidan Grant appeared to be quite familiar with Inverness. And Isabella had told her the Grants would be staying here during the trial.

"There are a few weapons on that wall that you still need to learn how to use." He walked around the room and stopped in front of one of the more impressive displays. "This battle axe, for example."

Morrigan came to stand beside him. "It would take me no time to use it successfully."

"I'll make sure I'm nowhere near when you pick it up."

"You'll suffer no bumps or bruising, sir. Your death will be quite quick."

He gave her a side look, a spark of amusement dancing in his grey eyes. "And this is what I get for saving your life."

"You didn't save my life. But I'll grant that you rescued me from a troublesome situation."

"I beg to differ. You simply enjoy disagreeing."

"I don't know what you mean."

"This morning, I gave you gift, a lovely sgian dubh, and you quibbled over its ownership."

"That was not a gift. The dagger was rightfully mine."

Aidan said nothing, but his hand reached toward her face. She froze, not immediately realizing what he was doing. He pulled a bit of leaf from her hair that she must had picked up running from Barn Hill. He offered it to her and she took it.

"I see that you're not going to give me any credit until I produce a proper gift."

"I want *no* gift from you, sir, except your continuing friendship."

His gaze was piercing, and Morrigan felt her body go warm.

"Our friendship, you can count on, Miss Drummond."

He'd left the door ajar, and she now heard footsteps coming down the hall. Morrigan stepped away from Aidan.

A moment later, one of her two Mackintosh escorts looked in at the door. "Relieved to see ye back here safe, mistress." The fighter, hat in hand, stepped just inside and told her how they'd seen the Englishman's carriage come up to the house at Barn Hill. They saw the five men enter a gate by the gardens.

"We thought ye were in the house. That's why we saw no need to follow 'em. We didn't know ye were missing until the lad Mr. Grant sent came to fetch us."

She was relieved how it had worked out. The consequences of what could have happened bothered her. They could have been hurt on her account.

"Did you see anything else?" she asked. "Did they leave finally?"

"Aye. Sometime later, we saw the old man come out of the gardens with just one of 'em louts. And he had a woman with him."

"What did she look like?"

"A wee thing, mistress. Thin as a stick. Wore a hat with a brim wide as a Quaker's. Wore a blue coat."

"They took Madam Laborde," Morrigan told Aidan. She should have convinced the artist to come with her when they had the chance.

"Was she struggling?" Aidan asked. "Did they force her to go?"

"Nay, Mr. Grant. The woman was willing. Thick as thieves, they were. Chatting all the way out of the garden. I heard her laugh as she climbed into the carriage."

CHAPTER 16
AIDAN

They arrived at Dalmigavie late and were immediately told that Cinaed and the others were back. Aidan knew the first order of business the following morning would be an introduction to the son of Scotland.

Aidan left his bedchamber early. On his way to the laird's study, he stopped to see Wemys. The cur's health had been continuously deteriorating, and the best time to converse with him was early in the day, before his medication was administered.

As Aidan had hoped, Wemys was sitting up in bed when he entered. The air in the room was close and smelled of sickness. He pushed open the window and a cool breeze wafted in.

"Are you trying to kill me with the chill?" the sick man snapped, pulling a blanket up to his chin. "You're not the face I've been looking to see."

"Too bad for you."

"Go on your way, why don't you? Send the doctor. She's the only one worth talking to."

Aidan sat in a chair near the bed and handed him the

list. "I saw the Chattan brothers yesterday. It took some persuasion, but they shared these names with me. Do you know any of them?"

Wemys stared at the paper.

The brothers thought they were among friends, sharing with fellow workers and members of their reform committee their frustration about what was happening in their town, in their country. As was the case all over Britain, however, their circle of trust had been infiltrated by a spy, a provocateur. They couldn't have been further from safe.

"Fourteen names," Aidan pressed. "I doubt the Home Office had every one of them in their pocket."

"You're right. And the man's name is here."

Aidan was relieved. Knowing the identity of the informant would be a tremendous help. He could send someone after him. He'd go after him himself. Perhaps the man would be cooperative if they offered money. If not that, maybe a threat would make him more agreeable. He and Sebastian were not above using the persuasive methods of the Home Office.

"Who was it?" he asked. "Which name?"

Wemys let the list lie on his lap.

"Tell me, by the devil, or so help me—"

"Today is the thirteenth day I've been here in this infernal castle. Nearly a fortnight. And my own niece hasn't seen fit to come see me."

Temper sharpened Aidan's tone. "I didn't bring you here to visit with your family. Our agreement was for you to help me with the trial. In return, I'd save your miserable life."

"Well, as we both know, you haven't done too well with that, now, have you? I'm dying."

"Not for lack of care."

"Dying, all the same."

"I could have just turned you over to the weavers in Inverness. They'd have known how to handle you."

Wemys gestured toward Kane Branson, looking on from the door. "I've asked your clerk. I get no satisfaction. I've begged the doctor to take my request to her. Nothing. All I wish for is to see my niece once more before I close my eyes. I have some things I should have said long ago."

"She doesn't care to see you."

Regardless of her denials, Aidan knew what Morrigan intended to do in that alley in Inverness. Her reaction to seeing her uncle in the cottage here later confirmed it.

Feuds between families were common in Scotland. Aidan's own family had suffered greatly from them. In the Jacobite rebellion of 1715, Grants fought on both sides. It was the same at Culloden.

"Forget about Miss Drummond," Aidan ordered. "Look again at that list and tell me the name."

"Put me out in the glen for the wild boars to feed upon. Drag me back to Inverness and let the weavers drown me in the Ness. Or let Sir Rupert's henchmen skin me alive. It makes no difference." He threw the list back at Aidan. "The doctor says I'm to die. Very well. Let's get it over with."

Aidan realized if, by some miracle, Wemys lived until the trial, his testifying would depend on whether Morrigan would see him or not.

The sick man turned his head away, but quickly looked back, pleading. "Ask her, Mr. Grant. Ask her yourself. Tell her that her uncle has a weight sitting on his chest that'll never be lifted until he's lowered into his grave. Tell her I'm begging her to let me say what I need to say."

A series of painful coughs overtook him. When he could speak, his breaths were ragged and labored.

"Afterward, I'll be yours. I swear to you. I'll give you

the name you want. I'll tell you where they sent him. God willing, I'll stay alive long enough to stand in that courtroom and testify for those lads."

Aidan left the room and descended to the keep's main floor. He didn't know how he was going to convince Morrigan to speak with Wemys. She was more passionate than reasonable, and she'd made her feelings perfectly clear. Perhaps if he told her more about Edmund and George Chattan. They were fine young men. Unfortunately, they were as hotheaded as they were naïve. It was their good heartedness and simplicity of spirit that made them the perfect gulls in this entrapment scheme.

Standing before the door to the laird's study, Aidan realized he couldn't think about it right now. Cinaed was waiting.

Once he entered and their introduction was complete, the two men sat in chairs by the hearth. A small wood fire crackled on the hearth, taking the edge off the chill morning. The son of Scotland had requested that they meet alone.

As they talked, Aidan was surprised at how at ease he was in the man's company, and he sensed that Cinaed felt the same way. He thought they were roughly the same age, and it was as if he'd known him his entire life.

"Right now, Sir Rupert is using every means at his disposal to make you look like a Highland Sawney Bean, living in a cave by the sea and eating children whenever you can take them." Aidan could tell this man was not one who smiled much, but that comment caused a momentary pull at the corner of his lips. "That serves several purposes. The folk of the Highlands will doubt you, and the city folk of the south will fear you. And he wants to anger you enough to draw you out."

"I recall a story about another cave, told by a minstrel

passing through here when I was just a lad. It was about the Black Douglas taking refuge in one during a tempest. He and Robert the Bruce had been taking a thrashing from the English. The Bruce was on the run as well. All their hopes for Scotland seemed to be lost. As he waited, he saw a wee spider was trying to weave a web, but the creature couldn't swing far enough to attach his silken thread to a wall. After trying six times, he made it. The Douglas took it as a sign. He and the Bruce eventually beat the English at Bannockburn."

"I recall that story. Do you plan to wage war for the next eight years?"

The son of Scotland shook his head.

"Our people in the Highlands were broken after Culloden," he said. "A new war would destroy everything that is left. All that will be left is empty moorland and English sheep."

Aidan agreed. "The Crown would love an excuse to crush the clans once and for all. The people in the cities in the Lowlands would see it, and any thought of protest or reform would shrivel and blow away like so many autumn leaves."

"Since we cannot destroy the empire, then my thinking is that we need to build our spider's web stronger. The more the Crown leans on the reformers, the more entrenched the desire for change becomes. We need to improve the laws. We need the right people in Parliament to increase the number of people who can vote. That's why I've been keen to meet you."

Since the end of the war against Napoleon, Aidan knew this was the direction he was going. Politics. He knew that many wanted the son of Scotland to wage war and fight for justice. They wanted him to finish what his grandfather had started. But Aidan knew that even more, people were tired of war and fighting. Times were changing. And as for him, Aidan had lost too many kin to support any kind of military campaign.

He was relieved to hear Cinaed's view. They had the same understanding of the political and economic nightmare the nation was facing. Although Cinaed was a warrior at heart and had spent many years sailing the seas, his vision of what needed to be done was the same as Aidan's.

"As you know, Charles Forbes holds the seat in Parliament for Inverness-shire," Cinaed continued. "But he has already indicated to Searc privately that he'll be stepping down next summer. Would you be interested in that seat?"

"Scotland's members in Parliament are still controlled by the large landowners and a powerful group of merchants and manufactory owners. I'm hardly popular amongst them."

"You can leave the campaigning to Searc and me, if you're interested."

Aidan thought of his father and the two brothers he'd lost on the fields of Belgium. They always believed that he'd someday rise to this position. He'd be good at it. He also thought of Sebastian. They could still work together if he stood for election.

Suddenly, Morrigan's face came into his mind's eye. Aidan wondered what she would think of Cinaed's offer. Would she even consider dividing her time between Inverness and Edinburgh and London? She would be so much safer from the machinations of people like Sir Rupert Burney if she were the wife of a member of Parliament.

He caught himself. The direction of his thoughts caught him off guard. He cleared his mind.

"I would," Aidan answered. "I'd be very much interested."

The next morning, after looking in at Wemys, Aidan was surprised to run into Morrigan on the landing of the tower stairwell. Both of them stopped and exchanged a brief greeting.

He'd looked for her the night before. The folk filling the Great Hall had been loud and boisterous as Lachlan was carried in a chair to the room to join the festivities. All were happy about the return of the travelers, and the added announcement by Searc and Cinaed that Aidan would have their support in standing for election to Parliament only added to the noise and celebration. Many approached to congratulate him. Countless words of encouragement were directed toward him, along with a few teasing remarks from Sebastian. He'd wanted to see Morrigan, to speak to her, to find out her opinion of this new change of plans. But she never approached, and the only time he saw her was as she left the hall.

Aidan noticed her gaze was drawn to the door of the room he'd just left. Perhaps it was the dim light of the hallway, but she looked pale.

"Would you care to go in?"

She frowned and shook her head. "I'm on the way up to the top of the tower." She stepped around him.

Aidan began to follow her. "May I join you?"

"I don't know why you ask, Mr. Grant. You always do what you want."

She nearly ran up the stone stairs, but Aidan kept pace with her.

"Dealing with you, Miss Drummond, I know it's better to ask first."

"I'm finished intentionally injuring you."

"So you admit that this last blow you delivered to my eye was intentional?"

"I admit to no such thing."

"You said 'intentionally,' proof that there was premeditated malice involved. You clearly had control over your actions."

She turned around to face him. She was standing on the step above him, and they were face-to-face. They had another flight of stairs to go to reach the top, but light poured down on her, bathing her in a beatific glow. She might have been an angel appearing from the heavens.

"I've apologized too many times already."

She peered closely at his eye. He stared at her lips. They were only inches away from his. He inhaled the scent of mountain pine in her hair. Thoughts raced through his mind of tasting her lips, gathering her in his arms, running his hands over the curve of her breasts.

Suddenly, he felt as awkward as a schoolboy.

She touched his bruised cheekbone with feathery softness, and Aidan felt his breeches tighten. Schoolboy or not, he wanted her.

"The swelling is almost gone. The black and purple are giving way to a greenish tinge. The colors improve your looks."

"Improve, did you say?"

"Of course. You look tougher. More battle-tested. A face like that says you're not afraid to go after what you want." She turned on her heel and ran up the rest of the steps to the tower.

Aidan remained where he was for a moment to give his body a chance to recover. How was it that this woman was so constantly in his thoughts? Wherever he was, he found himself looking for her. Wondering where she was, what she was doing, and when he'd see her again.

Over this past fortnight, beauty had been redefined for Aidan: she was tall with dark brown eyes and auburn hair, and she kept a sgian dubh in her boot.

He shook his head to clear it and continued up the stairs after her.

Stepping into the open air, he saw her immediately. Morrigan was standing in a gap in the crenellated parapet. She leaned over the edge to get a better view of the men in the training yard.

"Were you down there today?"

"Not this morning. Niall started everyone early."

Aidan knew Niall Campbell from their time in the military. Sebastian was a longtime friend of his. Campbell had been a career soldier and a good one. A lieutenant in the 42nd Royal Highlander Regiment, he had been recognized many times for his bravery and service. To have him now siding with Cinaed was a major coup for the son of Scotland.

"Does he mind you training with the men?"

"Of course not. Neither does Cinaed. Nor any of the Mackintoshes, for that matter," she told him. "Here in the Highlands, the men like their women tough and ready to do battle beside them."

"I know. I'm a Highlander too."

"My apologies." She gave him a side look. "It's easy to forget."

"And why is that?"

"Well . . . a barrister? A politician?" She paused, searching for the appropriate words. "Your chosen professions evoke certain qualities. A refined disposition. A certain genteelness of behavior, speech, attitude, dress, and bearing.

I believe all of those things are necessary for one to be successful as a member of Parliament. You, sir, possess all of them. I'm certain you'll be the toast of society in London. I can't imagine you driving a herd to market or sweating behind a plow."

"Genteelness of dress?" he scoffed. "Why do I feel like I've just been insulted?"

"You shouldn't. I meant it as a compliment." She turned her attention back to the men training in the yard.

Her comments and her conspicuously detached manner hinted at her true feelings. She now saw him as a politician, and she didn't care for it. He didn't know why. Someone needed to represent the people of the Highlands. Someone who knew the law and didn't have an agenda of personal advancement. This was the life he'd been preparing for.

"Well, before I schedule the requisite hours with my tailor, I have a few responsibilities as barrister that I need to see to."

"Good idea. Your clients will be grateful."

On their way back from Inverness two days ago, Aidan told her about the list of names he'd gotten from the Chattan brothers. He also explained briefly why Wemys's cooperation was critical in finding out which name belonged to the agent-provocateur in the government's entrapment scheme.

"Right now, my clients have nothing to pin their hopes on, unless your . . . unless Wemys agrees to cooperate and tell me who was helping the authorities."

Somehow, he needed to get through to her.

"Andrew Hardie and John Baird were sentenced to death and executed in Stirling on September 8. Hanged and beheaded." He spoke plainly, knowing she was not skittish about such bluntness. Perhaps that was what was needed to convince her to go downstairs and listen to what her uncle wanted to say. "Edmund and George Chattan are facing the same fate. They'll surely lose their lives if I can't secure Wemys's help."

Morrigan walked along the ramparts, and Aidan followed.

"He has the answers but refuses to help me unless you see him. If he lives to see next month, he'll renege on his promise to testify in court."

"He is of no use to you, then. I can help you, however, if you choose to throw him off this parapet."

She continued to walk along the perimeter of the tower. There was no hint of joking in her tone. Aidan had a strong suspicion she was dead earnest.

"I'd take you up on your offer, if the lives of two men weren't at stake."

She leaned to a dangerous degree out over the edge to stare at some people in the gardens below.

"Don't jump. I have no wish to lose you or your friendship. I promise, after this, never to ask you again." He touched her elbow, hoping she'd face him. "But for this one time, will you consider hearing what Wemys has to say? He promises they are the last words you'll hear from a dying man."

Morrigan turned and Aidan was stunned to see tears pooling in her dark eyes. "I can't, Mr. Grant. I'm sorry about your clients. Dreadfully sorry. But nothing you say, nothing he says, will ever convince me to go to that man."

Without uttering another word, she went around him and disappeared down the stairs.

Chapter 17
Morrigan

For the next three days, nightmares hung about Morrigan like spirits of the dead. Every dark corner of her bed-chamber seemed to be inhabited by shapes that shifted and changed and disappeared when she mustered her courage to approach them.

It was the coming observance of Samhain. It had to be. The ongoing preparations in the castle and the village were affecting her.

She had no desire to sleep. Closing her eyes would surely bring these spirits and fairies creeping across the wood floor, their fangs and claws out and gleaming in the moonlight.

She wouldn't give them the chance. With a blanket around her and a lit candle in her hand, she paced like a caged beast. Like a condemned prisoner waiting for the dawn. Waiting. Finally, she could walk no longer. She'd settle in her chair, fighting to stay conscious and alert. Then she'd doze, awaken with a start, and resume her nightlong watch into the dark places, praying for the rising of the sun. Praying for release from these night terrors.

As soon as the sky began to lighten, she'd descend to the kitchens, where the fires were lit and the smells of bread filled the air and bleary-eyed workers went about their daily tasks. She was safe here.

The Mackintoshes of Dalmigavie had a kirk in the center of the village, and a chapel in the castle. Both had seen changes in services performed within their walls. Several times. But the folk held to the auld ways for the most part, in their language, their traditions, and their beliefs. Christianity itself was still a newcomer in the Highlands, where the belief in fire and stone and oak and wind and rain and darkness was as old as the earth and the sky. There was the world that could be seen and the world that could not be seen.

Morrigan had come to learn that these Highlanders had a special reverence for the threshold places and threshold times. Borders, bridges, crossroads, doorways. Dawn and dusk. The spring and autumn equinoxes. Samhain marked the transition between summer, a time of growth and light and order—and winter, a time of death and darkness and chaos.

Morrigan had heard the Highland folk believed that time lost all meaning at Samhain. Past, present, and future became one. Now, living among these people, Morrigan knew it to be true.

She'd run from her past, ignored and hidden from it. But the past had caught up to her here, weighing on the present, and threatening all of her tomorrows.

For the three days since talking to Aidan on the tower roof, she'd walked past that door. Morning, midday, and evening. The words he'd spoken tormented her. If she rejected his plea and Edmund and George Chattan died because of her, Morrigan would not be able to live with herself.

Every time she approached, she broke out in a cold
sweat. Bile rose up in her throat. And each time, an inner
rage rose in response, fierce and hot. She couldn't trust
herself to go through that door. Morrigan didn't know if
she trusted herself to be alone with him. She didn't know
if she could see him, talk to him, and not put her dagger
in his shriveled heart.

By Sunday, guilt and exhaustion threatened to drive
her insane. Morrigan had heard that Aidan and his brother
were going to Inverness the following day. If she was going
to help him, if Wemys was going to give Aidan the name,
then now was the time. But she still couldn't bring herself
to face him.

Knowing that Isabella visited Wemys twice every day,
Morrigan went to her infirmary room around noon. She
was dressing the burned arm of a young boy who was stub-
bornly holding in tears while his worried mother looked
on.

When they were finally alone, Isabella turned to her.
"I see nothing bruised or swollen. But from your mood of
late, one would think you'd been kicked by a horse."

Morrigan had been rolling a strip of linen, but Isabella
took it out of her hand and put it on the table.

"What has he done? Or rather, what has he said to you?"

She knew who Isabella was talking about. Everyone
had gotten the wrongheaded notion that some sort of at-
traction existed between her and Aidan. From Sebastian,
most likely.

"Mr. Grant has done nothing wrong."

"You always say that."

"It's the truth." She heard the quaver in her own voice.

Isabella noticed, as well, and took hold of her hands.
"Morrigan, you can tell me what's wrong."

For years she'd hidden the truth from Isabella and

everyone else. Remembering her past was painful. In that moment, however, with Samhain nearly upon them, Morrigan realized she no longer wanted to carry the weight of that past in her heart.

"It's Wemys. He has information for Mr. Grant that will aid in the defense of the Chattan brothers. But he refuses to help unless I agree to see him."

"He's said nothing to me about the trial, but he has asked me repeatedly to use my influence with you. He desperately wants to speak with you."

Morrigan turned her face toward the window and forced down the lump rising into her throat.

"I've never been much of a mother to you, never mind a good one."

If there was one person who carried no blame, it was Isabella.

"I was always pressed for time because of my patients, and you were a capable and mature fifteen-year-old when your father and I married. I let Archibald keep his past, your past, and your family's past as private."

Perhaps this was where everything had gone wrong. Morrigan was suffocated while her father pretended all was well.

"But I knew something was wrong because of the way he treated you. He was worried about you when I could see no cause. He watched you constantly. He wanted to shield you from the dangers of the outside world, it seemed."

Too late. Far too late.

"So he kept you close at hand. He had his students, of course, but he always wanted you at his side, in the clinic and when he went to visit a patient. He needed to know where you were at every hour of the day."

Morrigan thought back over those years. Maisie came

and went as she pleased. Unbeknownst to the rest of the family, she was living the life of a radical reform activist, but no one ever noticed. Morrigan, on the other hand, was always under the watchful eye of her father.

"At first, I assumed it was because of your interest in becoming a doctor. That pleased me, to be honest. But that wasn't the reason, was it?"

She shook her head. Isabella took hold of her hands. Morrigan welcomed the connection.

"As the years passed, I came to realize that Archibald was watching you in the same way that a doctor looks for symptoms. At night, he often had nightmares, calling out your name. In his dreams, you were always lost, and he was searching for you."

Morrigan tried to steady her breath, but there was no hope. She tried to hold back the tears, but her eyes burned. When they began to fall, the droplets scorched her cheek. The last image that she had of her father was on the day the soldiers attacked the house. His eyes were fixed on her. He tried to speak, to get the words out, but it was too late. And then he was gone.

"Robert Wemys." Isabella said the name slowly. She tilted Morrigan's chin up and looked into her eyes. Her thumb gently wiped away fallen tears. "I saw the way you reacted to him. You're not the person you were before they brought him to Dalmigavie. Would you like to tell me what he's done to you?"

She knew. Morrigan felt a sob rise into her chest and expand, filling her with sharp pain. This time she let it go. Her anguished cry had been held in too long. It was a cry silenced for nearly a decade. The tears that followed could not be stopped. She didn't try to hold them in.

Isabella's arms encircled her protectively. Her body shook as she wept, but this loving woman didn't tell her to hush. She didn't ask any questions or demand the story. She simply held her tight and allowed her to empty out the agony.

When Morrigan tried to speak, to share the horror of her past, it was her decision. She *wanted* to speak. Isabella was her mother and sister, protector and friend. Morrigan trusted her. She felt safe with her knowing. In Isabella's eyes, she'd never be less of a person once the ugly truth was spoken.

"I was twelve years of age," she began. "My mother had passed, and my father was at a loss as to what to do with me, I think. He took me to Perth and left me with my maternal grandparents. We'd been to their house many times when my mother was alive. He assumed I'd be better off away from the city. I'd grow up near uncles and aunts and cousins. I'd have family around me. He thought I'd be safe."

Morrigan pulled out of Isabella's arms and stabbed at the tears on her face.

"Wemys is my mother's younger brother. I knew him from the time I was very little. I was happy to see him when he came back to Perth to visit his parents."

She'd been so innocent and trusting. She'd listened to his stories and been entertained by him. Impressed by him. He seemed to have traveled everywhere. He knew important people. He was clever and drew pictures with his words so easily. She never imagined someone could hurt a member of their own family. She never thought he would. She let her memories pour out. There had been no sign, no warning of what was to come.

She tried to continue, but she couldn't. Her throat had squeezed shut, robbing her of the ability to breathe. Isabella's eyes shimmered with tears, but she waited.

"I woke up one night and he was there . . . in my

bedroom . . . on top of me." Her voice broke, but she forced herself to continue. "Even now I remember the smell of whisky and smoke. I couldn't move. He held me down. He forced me. I tried to scream for help, but he had his filthy hand over my mouth. And when he was done, he told me I was to say nothing. If I was so stupid as to go crying, he'd deny it."

Morrigan didn't know if she was the one who reached for Isabella or if it was the other way around. But she was once again enclosed in her protective embrace.

"His family would never believe me, he told me, if I accused him. They'd throw me out on the street."

Even now, nine years later, she still lay awake in bed at night, listening. She should have heard him coming. She should have been prepared to do something. How could she have been so naïve? So trusting? So weak?

"I'm so sorry this happened to you, my love."

The rush of words could not be staunched now. She had to say them all. "I ran away that same night. I took my bag and my coat and left my grandparents' house with only a few coins in my purse."

Morrigan knew where she was going. She had to get back to her father. He was the only parent she had left. The only person in the world she could trust. She walked all night and most of the next day. She caught the mail coach at an inn in some village. She sat eyeing every person she saw, fearful they meant her harm. That they knew her secret, and that shame . . . that guilt . . . terrified her. She was alone and vulnerable. Before she reached Edinburgh, she swore she'd never be defenseless again.

The two women sat on a bench side by side. Morrigan spoke of her worries and vulnerability, of a child who was lost.

"I was exhausted when I finally arrived at our house in

the city. By then, my father had received a message from my grandfather that I'd gone missing. But he had no idea why."

"Did you tell him?"

The words hitched in her chest. "I had to. I felt so . . . so broken. I needed help."

Isabella leaned her forehead against Morrigan's. Their tears mingled and landed on their joined hands.

"What did he say? What did he do?"

"He said he was going to fix it. He was going to take away my pain." As if he *could*, she thought bitterly. "He took me to a husband and wife, close friends of his in Edinburgh. People he said he trusted like no one else. I was to stay there until he returned."

"He went to Perth?"

She nodded. "I never saw him with such rage. When he packed his pistol, I knew what he would do. He intended to go and kill Wemys. Part of me was happy. But I was also afraid. He was so angry. I worried that he'd never come back."

By the time Archibald Drummond arrived at Perth, Wemys was gone. No one knew where he'd disappeared to or when he'd return. Morrigan never knew if her father told her grandparents what was done to her. Or what had caused their twelve-year-old granddaughter to run away in the middle of night. Or why was it that he was angry enough never to speak to them, or go back there, or say their names ever again.

"He never *fixed* it. He couldn't. How could he take away my pain? My fear? After he came back, his solution was for us to forget it. To pretend it never happened. He thought I'd heal with time. We moved. And we moved again. That's how we ended up in Wurzburg."

Isabella caressed her back. She kissed her brow. "Six

years I was married to your father, and he never told me. But I'm here for you now."

They stood together, wrapped in silence and each other's arms, for a long time.

"What do you want to happen now?" Isabella asked finally.

Morrigan realized the heaviness was beginning to lift off her. The fist squeezing her heart was beginning to ease slightly. She knew Isabella understood that no one could make the past go away. No one could *fix* it, as Archibald had intended to do. Morrigan needed help, but the decision of what to do had to be hers.

"I want Wemys to suffer."

"He is."

"I want him to die slowly and painfully."

"He will. There is no escape for him."

"I think I know why he wants to speak to me."

"Knowing that death is imminent triggers regrets in many people," Isabella said, wiping the tears from under Morrigan's eyes. "They want to be forgiven for the sins and the crimes they've committed."

"I won't forgive him," she said passionately. "Never. And I don't care to hear *why* he did it. Or why he felt he had the right."

"Never think you need to see him or speak to him. Just say the words and I'll have him moved back to the village."

Morrigan shook her head. "He's dying. That's enough."

"There must be something I can do for you."

There was. Morrigan had already thought about it. "I'd like you to make a deal for me."

"What kind of deal? With whom?"

"With Wemys," Morrigan told her. "I want you to tell him that I am not playing his game. Whatever is left to his miserable life, he can spend it alone, stewing in his fears of what lies ahead for him. I'll not spend it at his bedside, listening to him drone on and on. He gets only one visit from me. One."

"Are you sure?" Isabella's brow was furrowed with concern. "You don't need to do this."

"But I do. I can't let the Chattan brothers hang because that horrible man isn't willing to reveal information he has," Morrigan told her. "The deal I am asking you to make is that he give Mr. Grant the information he needs *first*. Those are my terms. I'll not speak to him unless he helps."

"And if he agrees?" Isabella asked, still sounding unsure. "You're willing to see him?"

"I will," Morrigan decided. "I'll meet with him. But, devil take me, I'll never forgive him."

On Hallow-Mass Eve . . .

The Lady she sat in St. Swithin's Chair,
The dew of the night has damped her hair:
Her cheek was pale—but resolved and high
Was the word of her lip and the glance of her eye.
She muttered the spell of Swithin bold,
When his naked foot traced the midnight world,
When he stopped the Hag as she rode the night,
And bade her descend, and her promise plight.
He that dare sit on St. Swithin's Chair,
When the Night-Hag wings the troubled air,
Questions three, when he speaks the spell,
He may ask, and she must tell.

Sir Walter Scott
from "St. Swithin's Chair"

CHAPTER 18
AIDAN

Aidan thought about Morrigan every day that he was gone. Over and over, he recalled their conversation, skirmishes, arguments, her rejections. No, not rejections . . . evasions. Memories lingered of the night in the library, the day she looked after the bruise on his eye in the stairwell, the moment when he nearly kissed her. He also could not forget how upset she'd been the last time they met at the top of the old tower . . . when he asked her to speak to Wemys.

She told him she couldn't. But at least she'd asked Isabella to speak to the scoundrel on her behalf. Some kind of agreement had been reached. He didn't know the details. Still, the morning he and Sebastian left Dalmagavie, Aidan had the name he needed. He owed her and was grateful for what she'd done.

Even as he continually mulled over all of that, Aidan tried to imagine what their relationship would be once he returned. Were they only friends? Had Morrigan thought about him at all while he was gone?

For him, the nine days away felt like nine weeks. Nine

months. But the weariness of travel lifted off Aidan's shoulders the moment he laid eyes on her. No tam, no coat, she wore a dark green dress and a ribbon of the same color binding her hair in the back. The eve of Samhain was upon them, and the weather was unusually warm for the end of October.

She was standing in front of the kirk. A crowd of young people, most of them children, were gathered there, listening to storytellers. Near the market cross, a huge bonfire crackled and blazed, sending sparks high into the black night sky.

Samhain was the fire festival, celebrated here for as long as people lived in these Highlands. The long nights of winter had a connection with the world of the dead, and the power and light of the fires were needed to drive back the darkness. Two young lasses walked by him carrying their tumpshie lanterns—hollowed-out turnips with skull faces carved into them, illuminated from the inside with candles. On the hilltops and the craggy ridges of the mountains around Dalmigavie, a string of huge bonfires burned, visible for miles.

To celebrate the end of the growing season, the village market cross was the center for crafting displays and games of skill and courting rituals for the young and unmarried.

But Aidan had no time or interest in any of this. He had eyes only for Morrigan.

He approached but said nothing to draw her attention. Two women by the fire were attempting to best each other in their storytelling performance. Morrigan's hands were resting on the shoulders of Niall Campbell's nieces. Aidan had met the children before.

One of the women was spinning slowly, crying out in a singsong voice. "Samhain is the night of the Great Sabbat for the witches. But tell no one, do ye hear?"

Nervous giggles could be heard from their audience, and Aidan moved closer to them. He halted a step or two away, where he could see and hear her and yet not intrude.

"On this night, the witches of the wood gather to celebrate their auld ways and cast their spells."

A smile stretched across Morrigan's face as the girls pushed closer against her skirts, trying to get away from the women weaving through the audience and pretending to reach for them.

"Look to the sky."

All eyes turned upward to where the storyteller was pointing.

"They're flying through the air."

"Cover yer head, bairnies!"

"Look to the fields. Did ye see her?"

"There she goes! Quick as the wind, riding a black cat."

The women went back and forth, calling out with cries and whispers. The children gasped every time something else was evoked.

"A witch on a raven. There, by the kirk tower. Did ye see her?"

Heads bobbed.

Another woman strode in from the shadows, and the storytellers backed away with a cowering bow to her. Her hair was grey, and she wore a simple black robe. Her eyes flashed in the light of the torches and the fire.

"I am a MacDonald of Glen Coe, we of the tragic folk. Have ye heard? We have a witch who abides in the cave by the twisted oak on the banks of our woeful river."

Murmurs of awe rippled through the children.

"What's her name?" Catriona wanted to know, feeling brave and inching away from the safety of Morrigan's arm.

"Sidiethe." She pointed a long, bony finger at the five-year-old. "Ye see her only when the sun has dipped behind the wooded hill or just 'afore the break of day. A water witch, she is, with skin so fair and locks of flaming red."

Briana tugged on her sister's red hair and giggled.

"Sidiethe wears a dress so white, it seems to glow and a cape the color of midnight."

The child turned to Morrigan. "I want a white dress and a cape like that."

She laughed and whispered something in her ear that made Catriona clap her hands.

The woman glided along the edge of the audience, her voice rising in pitch. "Our witch sits on the banks of our tumbling river, her long hair trailing in the passing waters, singing her mournful songs."

"I like to sing," Catriona shouted boldly.

The storyteller turned and cut through the crowd to her. Suddenly, she didn't seem like an old storyteller, but the witch herself.

"Do ye ever hear weeping out yer window in the night?"

The child backed up and hid her face in Morrigan's skirt.

"Sidiethe weeps by the waters 'afore someone dies. The night 'afore the great death at Glen Coe, the MacDonald clan chief heard her. He made his way to the icy river. There Sidiethe crouched, washing a bloody scarf, moaning and crying her heart out."

The storyteller's gaze was fixed on a far-off hill where a fire blazed. She wrapped her arms tightly around her body.

"When the MacDonald blinked his eye, she was gone. But her weeping echoed off the hills and down the glen."

"Did someone die?" a child asked, her voice trembling.

"Aye," the storyteller replied. "I'll tell you all. It started with a letter and a far-off king . . ."

Aidan was familiar with the actual history. South of Fort William, the Massacre of Glencoe took place about hundred thirty years ago. After the end of a three-year

Jacobite uprising, more than thirty people were killed by forces of the earl of Argyll, who was angry that the Mac-Donalds of Glen Coe had not been prompt in pledging allegiance with him to the new British monarch.

Morrigan took the girls' hands and turned to lead them away. The story had suddenly become too serious for their young ears. Aidan decided that Morrigan probably knew the history too. The threesome nearly bumped into him.

"Mr. Grant." Morrigan stopped short, startled.

"Miss Drummond."

The smile on her face was the welcome Aidan had hoped for. She seemed happy and carefree and radiant. They exchanged a bow and curtsy.

"When did you get back?"

"This afternoon."

"Was your trip successful?"

He didn't want to talk about the chase that had taken him to Aberdeen, where it ended in futility. Not now. He and Sebastian followed the trail of government agent Wemys had identified all the way to the port town, only to find out that he'd boarded a vessel for the Cape colony a fortnight earlier. So Aidan was back to where he started.

Right now, he only wanted the smile to remain on Morrigan's face. He definitely didn't want her to think that her attempt to help him had come to nothing.

"It was as expected," he answered finally.

"How is your brother?"

"I tried to get rid of him on our travels. Unfortunately, the man couldn't be cast off, no matter how hard I tried. He's . . ." Aidan glanced around at the boisterous groups of people moving hither and yon. "Here somewhere. We may find him telling stories about us to his own audience of rapt listeners."

"That would certainly be too frightening for small ears." She bit her bottom lip and nodded toward the two girls, who were listening to every word he said.

"Miss Briana. Miss Catriona." He bowed with a flourish to the children. "How lovely to see you. Is this your first Samhain celebration in the Highlands?"

The girls curtsied and nodded, beaming up at him.

"What have you seen so far?"

"The storytellers. But I didn't really like that one." Catriona pointed to the woman from Glen Coe.

"I heard some of what she was saying. I'll need to bolt my door and shutter my window tonight." He made a face, and the little girl nodded soberly.

"Morrigan is watching us while our mother walks with Mr. Gordon to get her fortune from a woman teller," the older child announced.

This was news to the little one.

"Fort . . . teller?" Catriona asked. "What fort?"

"Not fort," Briana responded, swinging around the front of Morrigan and looking at her sister as if she were a total embarrassment. She motioned with her arm. "Fortune. Teller. There is a fortune teller over by the kirk."

"What does he do?" she persisted, craning her neck toward the church.

"He gives her money." Hand on hip, the seven-year-old leaned into the face of her sister and drawled the word. "*Fortune?*"

Morrigan cocked an eyebrow at Aidan. These two took what they heard quite literally. The girls tugged on her hand, and the group started walking.

"May I join you?"

Morrigan's nod was seconded by "Yes!" from each of the girls. Delighted, he fell in beside them. Aidan's gaze lingered on Morrigan's face as she laughed at something one of them whispered to her. She was happy, serene, obviously at home with these two. All her reserve was gone. She was quite different from the woman he usually saw—tense, alert, constantly on her guard.

Aidan realized this was the first time he was witnessing a maternal side to her.

Images immediately formed in his mind, adding to recent thoughts of what his life might be like with Morrigan beside him. While he was traveling, he'd found himself pondering that topic over and over. One thing he was sure of, whatever he'd imagined before as an ideal wife and partner had changed.

The raised voices of the children snapped his attention back to the present. They were discussing where they should go next. Each of them appeared to be passionate and determined to have their way.

"Bonfire!"

"Apples!"

"*Bonfire!*" Catriona tugged to the right.

"*Apples!*" Briana wished to go left.

"We have a man of the law with us," Morrigan interjected. "Perhaps Mr. Grant can settle this."

Two bright-eyed lasses were looking up at him expectantly. Equally strong-willed, one of them was bound to be disappointed if she didn't get her way.

"Very well," he said sternly. "Present your cases."

They stared at him as if he were speaking in a foreign tongue.

"You might consider keeping their ages in mind," Morrigan reminded him gently.

He got down on one knee and addressed Briana first. "Would you like to tell me *why* we should go to apple . . . apple . . ."

"Apple dooking," Morrigan clarified for him.

"Of course. How could I forget? Why should we go there first, rather than second?" he asked.

"Because I'm hungry for an apple *now*."

How could he refuse a child this adorable? The sad, serious face. The deep sigh. Quite dramatic. One would think her life depended on her having an apple at this very moment.

"A very reasonable request. Though we must consider whether dunking our heads into a barrel of water for an apple is a good *first* choice of activities." Still on his knee, he turned to Catriona. "And why do you think we should go to the bonfire first and not second?"

"Because it's warm now. It'll be cold later."

"So we should go the bonfire while it's warm?" He knew a troublesome witness when he saw one.

Catriona put her hand to her mouth and whispered, "We need to go *now*, or we won't *see* them."

He suddenly realized where this might be going, but he had to ask. "See whom?"

Catriona lifted her head and spoke to Morrigan. "*You* don't get naked when it gets cold, do you?"

"I . . . what?" Morrigan sputtered, seemingly lost for words.

Aidan looked up as well, interested in her answer. He was quite happy he'd followed this line of questioning.

"Auld Jean says this is the night when women take off their clothes and dance naked around the bonfire." She lowered her voice and whispered to Aidan, "*You* can't dance with her, though."

"No?" He put on his most disheartened look.

Catriona shook her head. "But if we go now, you can watch from the trees. Like Tam o Shambler."

God bless Robbie Burns, Aidan thought, slowly pushing to his feet. He was definitely in favor of going to the bonfire first. "Clearly, I'm bound for that line of trees. What do you say, Miss Grant?"

Morrigan had nothing to say, but the glare he was receiving said plenty.

No final decision by him needed to be made, however, for at that moment, the children shrieked with pleasure.

"Look, Old Napoleon is here." Catriona broke free.

"Fetch your weapon," the older girl shouted, running after her sister.

He glanced at Morrigan and saw her glare had softened into a smile.

Old Napoleon, the object of the girls' excitement, turned out to be their Uncle Niall, who was coming across the market square with Maisie. Campbell caught and lifted them, one in each arm, and their giggles rang out.

"It's an old game. They play Waterloo," Morrigan explained, coming to stand beside him. "Niall is Old Napoleon, and the girls get to kill him. Of course he comes back to life in time for the next battle."

"Leave it to the former lieutenant to play war games with children."

"And what kind of game will you play with your children?" she teased, her eyes dancing mischievously.

"I'll read to them."

"I agree books are excellent, but that won't fill all their free time."

"Said by the woman who pulls off *The Kinkvervankotsdarsprakengotchderns Anecdote* off the shelf."

Her eyes rounded. "I can't believe you remember that name."

"Or was it the *Kinkerpachydermsprackens*?"

"That's more like it. You're fallible after all. You don't remember everything." She patted him on the arm. "Something else. Parents need alternative battle plans."

"I'll teach them to develop an effective argument."

"You'll be sorry for that. They'll soon strip you of your authority." She motioned toward Niall. He was on one knee, and the girls were trying to climb him like a castle wall. "Children also need physical exercise."

"I'll leave that decision to their mother to decide. That is, unless she confuses the nursery with the armory. Of course, what's the harm of a weapon or two?"

Morrigan's gaze flew to his face but then darted away quickly.

Aidan cursed inwardly. What was he doing, saying such things? His life was completely at sixes and sevens right now. He had a pressing trial ahead of him. As much as thoughts about Morrigan never left him, he couldn't allow himself to be distracted by romance. Still, despite what his brain told him, his tongue seemed to have an agenda of its own.

The sound of fiddle and pipe, the voices, and the general noise of celebrating filled the air, but neither of them could find the right word to resume their conversation. Maisie approached them and they exchanged greetings.

"Niall and I can take the girls with us." She turned to Aidan. "Would you be kind enough to escort Morrigan to the bonfire? She's talked about nothing else all day."

Before either could say a word, Maisie ran off after her husband and nieces.

He and Morrigan both started talking at once.

"Do I have to stand by the trees?"

"I didn't mention any bonfire today. Not once!"

They both laughed. Aidan felt a weight had been lifted.

"Auld Jean is the best storyteller of all," Morrigan told him. "This morning, she was trying to convince us all to wear animal heads and skins and run through the village."

"That would have been quite a sight."

"Well, I'm sorry to disappoint you, but there won't be any naked women dancing around the fire at Dalmigavie tonight."

"Then we might as well go and bob for apples." He offered his arm and she took it. "But perhaps we should stop at the fortune teller first."

"I need no *fortune*."

"I see you've been spending far too much time with those children."

"Just the perfect amount, I'd say."

She was happy again. Curious about some of the activities, she asked many questions. The crowds were growing more concentrated as the two of them walked along. Aidan drew her closer to his side.

"Your very first Samhain in the Highlands," he said, stopping by a fire surrounded by a group of young villagers who were cheering loudly. "Did you mark your name on a hazel nut?"

"What for?"

He nodded toward the fire. "Two groups of hazel nuts are placed close to the fire. One group is marked with the names of the village's maidens, and the other with the eligible bachelors. As the nuts pop, the names of the pairs are linked."

"None of that silliness for me." She shook her head and tugged on his arm to continue their walk.

"It's all quite scientific."

She laughed. Near the kirk, they found the apple dooking, the busiest activity they'd come upon thus far.

"Among the Highland people, the apple has strong ties with the other world and even immortality," he told her.

"Then I'll take one. But you should take two."

They moved closer, standing where she could watch as men and women waited for their turns to plunge their faces into the barrels of water and catch the fruit with their teeth. Very few appeared to be succeeding.

"It seems easy. But it's not."

They joined in with the cheering and the groans when a young man almost had one but immediately lost it back into the barrel. "You have to catch the apple with your teeth. Otherwise it's gone."

"So you need a very big mouth."

She cheered on a young woman who went into the barrel up to her shoulders only to come out with her face and hair and clothes soaked, but no fruit.

"What's the prize if you get one?" she asked.

"Good fortune for the coming year."

"More fortune." She shook her head, smiling at all the excitement. "I like apples, but you won't catch me standing in a line to dunk my face in cold water."

"You might be very good at this."

"Ha! And have you and everyone else make sport of me? No, thank you."

Aidan tugged at her hand. "Come with me. There is a game here I know you'll enjoy playing."

"Will it involve an apple? Do I eat it afterwards?"

Aidan recalled Briana's grumbling about wanting an apple. Morrigan didn't sound much different. She wanted it *now*. "Of course."

Nearby, a group of young women were peeling apples. More people stood around them, urging them on. He put a hand in the small of Morrigan's back and guided her to the front of a crowd of onlookers.

"This doesn't look like a game."

"Ah, but it is." He nudged her closer. "You need to peel an apple all in one paring."

"That's all? That seems far too simple. Is it a race?"

"It's more difficult than it looks." He motioned to the person who was handing out the fruit. She offered one to Morrigan.

She eyed the apple. "Perhaps I'll just eat it."

This playfulness in her was something new. Her eyes sparkled with mischief. Aidan wanted to kiss the smile pulling at her lips.

"Peel it first."

The woman offered her a knife, but Morrigan shook her head and drew her sgian dubh.

"You don't need to kill it. Just peel it."

"You don't need to tell me how to use a knife. As you well know, I'm an expert."

He snorted and she stared into his face.

"You have no cuts or bruises at the moment, Mr. Grant. Some of these women might say you look handsome. So don't tempt me to use this on you."

He took her chin in his hand. Her eyes widened in surprise. They were deep black pools with glints of firelight reflected in them. Their faces were inches apart. "There are better ways to mark me than with the knife."

Morrigan's gaze drifted to his mouth. He wanted to kiss her. Right now. Aidan's hands itched to pull her hard against his body and tell her to do her worst.

She pulled away and fixed her attention on the fruit. A single line furrowed her brow, and her eyes focused on her task. She was all concentration as she peeled the fruit with precision and speed. Heads turned in their direction. Those around them cheered her as the entire skin came away unbroken.

"Fine work, lass," an onlooker called out. "Now throw the peel over yer shoulder."

Shouts came from all sides as Morrigan tossed the skin.

The women nearby all gathered around where the peel landed. Everyone had an opinion.

"What are we looking for?" Morrigan wanted to know, joining them.

"The letter. What letter do ye see?"

She took a bite of the apple and leaned down to study the pattern of the curled skin.

"It's an *A*," she announced.

Cheers went up all around her, and Morrigan stared at them in confusion.

Aidan always thought of himself as a man of reason. He used fact in his arguments. He largely ignored fantasy and old wives' tales. He liked to walk on solid ground and avoid slippery slopes. Still, he was a Highlander, and his heart beat a little faster as he stared at the shape of the apple peel on the ground.

"What does it mean?" Morrigan asked the women around her.

"The peel takes the shape of the first initial of the man ye'll marry."

She leaned over and stared at the pattern again for a long moment. When she straightened, her face was flushed, and she shook her head. "Rubbish."

Her denial prompted loud laughter, and she walked calmly toward him.

Aidan decided that she could say what she wanted, act as composed as she pleased, but even in the light of the torches, he could see the bright splotches on her cheeks.

"Who do you think it is?"

She didn't answer but held out the half-eaten apple toward him. "Would you care for a bite?"

"I believe I would."

He wrapped his fingers around her wrist and slowly

brought the fruit to his lips. Their eyes locked. Deliberately, he took his time—staring at her mouth, wet from the apple—before he took a bite.

He saw her lips part, and he released her. Everything around them disappeared. The crowds, the fires, the village, everything. Only he and Morrigan existed. They were two people drawn together by an invisible tie. Caught in this moment, this sublime instant, as time stood still.

"May I kiss you?"

She stared at his lips and nodded slightly.

Aidan took her hand, and the two of them moved quickly down a lane away from the light of the market square fires. Urgency seized them, and suddenly they were running. He didn't know where they were going until she pulled him to the gate of a dark cottage.

"You are so beautiful," he whispered, his gaze scouring every inch of her face. "So perfect and—"

Morrigan kissed him. Raising herself on her tiptoes, she crushed her lips against his.

There were no soft words. No coaxing. No wooing. Their kiss became the unleashing of repressed desire. Aidan's fingers delved into her hair, and his mouth devoured her lips, forcing her mouth open. His tongue surged inside. She gave a stifled gasp, and her body molded against him. Her hands encircled his waist, pulling him tighter.

Suddenly, she drew back. Her eyes were wide. She pushed him away, shaking her head. He backed up a step, his heart still racing.

"I can't," she whispered, alarm evident in her voice. "I can't do this. I'm sorry."

Morrigan turned and ran up the lane, and Aidan watched her go, confused and wondering what exactly he'd done to frighten her.

CHAPTER 19
MORRIGAN

Morrigan's lips tingled from the kiss. How alive she'd felt in Aidan's arms! As the castle walls loomed up in the darkness ahead, her heart raced. For the first time, she'd been overthrown by real passion. It struck like a summer storm, with lightning flashing and thunder shaking the ground beneath her feet.

Morrigan wanted to give and take. To sample and feel. To hold onto him and ask him never to let her go.

Aidan challenged her and—for all his teasing—respected her. He wasn't intimidated by who she was or what she was capable of doing. And her heart sang every time she was near him. Right now, her body burned, knowing he wanted her. And his words. The hints about matrimony and children.

Her steps faltered. She stopped.

What was she thinking?

Morrigan looked around her in the darkness. They said that tonight fairies, ghosts, and witches roamed unhindered. Spirits of mischief playing their tricks on humans. Making off with souls of the living. Tonight, she was being tricked into believing that she could have a life. Have a future filled with dreams.

But she wouldn't allow herself to be fooled. Aidan Grant was special. A man who cared about others. A barrister. Many hopes were pinned on his success in becoming a member of Parliament. The Highlanders needed him. And what did she have to offer? A father with radical views, shot dead by an English officer. A stepmother with a bounty on her head, married to the man who posed the greatest threat to the Crown in a hundred years. Her close connection to the rebels of the Highlands and her family presented a life fraught with scandal. And when the shame of her own past came out, Aidan would be ruined.

She needed to face the truth, she had no place in his future.

She stabbed at the futile tears on her cheeks, and her gaze drifted up to the castle. A light shone in a window of the ancient tower rising above Dalmigavie's keep. The room where Wemys lay dying. As she stared, anger filled her, building on her unhappiness. That lighted window was just one more reminder that she could never have a future where happiness existed.

Samhain. The night when time lost all meaning. Past, present, and future came together as one. Life and death too. A thin veil separated the world of the living from the world of the dead. At Samhain, the veil dropped away. The worlds merged.

Wemys was dead to her, but she had still a promise to fulfill. A door she had to close.

Morrigan had put it off for nine days. Nine days of fretting, of nightmares, of trying to decide if she should renege on her promise. Isabella wouldn't blame her. She'd already told her that much. Still, she knew she had to go through with it. She'd go to Wemys and allow him to

speak. He'd agreed to her terms. Done his part. Now it
was her turn. She had to do it, if for no other reason, for
Aidan. He might still need the blackguard's testimony for
his trial.

Only a few people remained in the castle tonight. A
watchman above the gate nodded as she raced through
the entrance. Most of the Mackintoshes were celebrating
in the village. Morrigan headed directly toward the old
tower.

Since they moved him here, she'd walked this way every
day going up to the parapets. She'd been testing herself.
Morrigan wanted to make sure she could do it and not fall
apart. She'd done fairly well. Grown stronger and harder
with each passing day. But tonight, each step was a stab
to her heart. Morrigan felt her head pound. Cold sweat
formed along her spine.

Damn him.

She was back in that small bedroom in Perth, trapped
beneath his body. His hand was covering her mouth. She
couldn't breathe.

Damn him.

Damn him.

Morrigan's knees wobbled as she reached the floor
where his room was located. She lunged into the dark corridor and stopped. She pressed her forehead against the
cold stone wall and tried to focus on her breathing, waiting for the weakness to pass.

"He can't hurt me."

She reached into her boot and retrieved her sgian dubh.
The feel of the weapon in her hand was reassuring.

"He can't hurt me."

A lamp hanging from the wall cast flickering shadows.
Tonight, the door between the living and dead was open.
Let the spirits pass back and forth. Isabella knew the truth,

but this was her battle. Her future depended on it. This was her chance to shove her own demons back into the darkness. She would not let them haunt her anymore.

She steeled herself for what she must do. Going to Wemys's door, she knocked.

Aidan's clerk, Kane Branson, was down in the village too. One of the serving women answered the door. Morrigan asked her if she could wait in the corridor.

The older woman quickly fetched her basket of mending and stepped out. Morrigan closed the door behind her. A candle flickered on a table next to the chair where she'd been sitting.

As the daughter of a doctor, she'd grown up knowing what death looked like. What it smelled like. The air in this room reeked of it. The form of the man lying in the bed, his face pointed at the ceiling, his skin waxy and transparent, could easily have been a corpse already. Only the irregular rise and fall of his sunken chest showed that Wemys still lived. And the sound of each wheezing breath.

Morrigan moved closer, until she could stare at his face. As she watched him, his cheek twisted and trembled as if he were being tortured in his sleep. She hoped he was being lashed or racked, tormented by devils in a horrible place where people like him burned and suffered for all eternity.

His face was blotchy and wrinkled. One would think he was ancient, though she knew his age could not be much past forty. Forty years of villainy. What a waste of life.

A cough erupted in his chest, thick and painful. He gasped for air and moaned, and suddenly his eyes opened. They filled with fear as he realized it was Morrigan standing over him. She stared back at him. A look of resignation settled over his features.

She felt no fear. He couldn't hurt her. No longer. She was not a defenseless, twelve-year-old child anymore.

"You're here. That's a blessing."

"One you don't deserve."

Wemys tried to push himself up in his bed, but he was too weak. He sank back on his pillow.

"You have no audience now. It's only you and me and your maker. Say what you have to say and be quick about it."

"Maker," he scoffed. He looked around the room as if to make certain she was telling the truth, that they were alone. His gaze lit on the weapon she held in her hand.

"Did you come to kill me?"

She lifted the dagger. The candlelight glinted along the polished blade. "I can give you no death as painful as the one that awaits you."

Another cough wracked his body, and Morrigan slid her sgian dubh back into its sheath.

Suddenly, a feeling of calm descended over her. Looking at this sorry excuse for a human being, wasted and too weak even to raise himself in his bed, she realized he was finished. There was nothing this man could do to hurt her again. There was nothing she could do to make him suffer more. The desire for revenge she'd harbored for so long lifted.

"I'm only here because we had an agreement. You revealed a name. And you *will* testify at court if Mr. Grant calls on you. I'm here now, as I promised, and you will get this chance only once. Now speak."

A fit, intense and painful, jolted him. He rolled weakly to the side, coughing up bloody phlegm. A cup of water sat on a table by his bed. He drank it down and waited for the attack to subside. He settled back, weak and exhausted.

"I'm dying," he said finally, pushing out the words between gasps for air. "They offered to bring me a priest. But the forgiveness I seek cannot come from any churchman."

"That's nothing to me," Morrigan replied, hearing the hardness in her own voice. She forced down the bile rising in her throat. This was what this man did to her. On that night, he robbed her of something soft, forgiving.

"I did you great wrong. I admit it. You were my sister's child. And you trusted me. But I was young. That night, when I came in from the tavern . . ." Emotion took hold of him again and he squeezed his eyes shut. "I was lost. My parents had refused to help me any longer. They took back their offer to allow me to continue studying art, saying I wasn't fit. They said I should enlist, fight the French, become a man. A lass I was courting heard about it. She shut the door in my face. I was drinking."

"Stop!" Morrigan's temper boiled over. She could take no more of his excuses. "Say what you did to me, to a girl not yet a woman. I want to hear you say it. What *you* did. *You.* Not your hard luck. Not your drinking. Not your failures. *You.*"

Her anger sparked in the air between them, hanging like a cloud of fire.

"Say what you did to me. The child of your dead sister. I want you to say it out loud. Admit what you did to *me.*"

He threw his arm over his eyes.

Morrigan waited. Tears of rage ran down her face, and she dashed them away. Finally, she could wait no more.

"Coward."

She turned to leave, but he called after her.

His words came, weak and rasping, slowly at first. Tears streamed down his face, staining his pillow. He broke down several times as he spoke, gasping and coughing. Morrigan waited and listened until he said out loud everything that he'd done to her that night.

To hear it from his lips as he sobbed with shame had a calming effect on her. A blade slid out of her heart, slowly but steadily withdrawing from a painful, ever-present wound that had festered and never healed, no matter how hard she tried to ignore it.

Once he was done talking, she turned toward the door.

"I did you grievous wrong. But please . . . please forgive me," he begged. "We're family. Look at me. I'm dying. Give me peace in my final days."

Morrigan shook her head. "You robbed me of my childhood, of my innocence. You stole my belief in goodness, in love of family. I did nothing to deserve what happened. You are the one responsible for this moment. When you held me down, when you hurt me, you felt no pity, no compassion. I was not your sister's child, your own kin. I was nothing. *You* took away my ability to feel pity or compassion for you."

Wemys gasped for air.

"What is forgivable is a sin one person commits toward another. But I was not a person to you that night. And I cannot forgive you because I may never be whole again. I'll never forgive you."

He started to say something, but a fit of coughing overtook him, and his wasted body shuddered. He reached a trembling hand for the cup by his bedside, but it was empty. He motioned toward a pitcher on the table across the room.

Morrigan ignored him and walked out. She couldn't bring herself to lessen his misery. Not for a single moment.

CHAPTER 20
AIDAN

"All rise for Lord Ruthven."

The justice made his way to his seat on the elevated dais, and the courtroom settled in. Aidan looked over at the Chattan brothers, standing together in the dock. Desperate men, and the strain showed in their faces. The stakes could not be higher, and they knew it.

Edmund Chattan was twenty-two years old. A weaver in Elgin, he was short and dark and wore a constant demeanor of unsmiling earnestness that, Aidan was certain, marked him even in the best of times. His brother George was fierce and hotheaded, quick to fight and quick to forgive. The two young men were not complicated fellows, and he knew they were more worried about their aging father than their own future.

Still, their long period of incarceration and the first day of trial had been hard on them.

The charges of treason were heavy. Conspiring to devise plans to subvert the Constitution. Conspiring to murder the Military Governor of the Highlands and the Lord Mayor of Elgin and a dozen other charges.

If they were found guilty of any one of them, the punishment would be swift and brutal. Aidan overheard that the plans were to erect a scaffold on Castle Hill for the execution. The Home Office wanted the spectacle to be as public as possible. The Chattan brothers were being portrayed as monsters, and their end would be seen as righteous, swift, and final.

Aidan knew who was directing these dramatics. Sir Rupert Burney was sitting in the front corner seat of the spectators. He and the judge, Lord Ruthven, exchanged a discreet nod of greeting. Known for his speed and lack of mercy, the judge was the scourge of the Outer Court of Session in Edinburgh. Loose in his interpretation of law, careless of justice, Ruthven rode roughshod over the rights of the innocent.

It was Lord Ruthven who was brought in to see that "justice" was done when young Hardie and Baird were duped into marching to the Carron Iron Works to seize weapons there. After a quick trial at Stirling, the two men were executed.

Aidan knew the judge well from skirmishes they'd had previously in Edinburgh. He was not just merciless; he was a fawning tool of the Crown. The man had been maneuvering for years for a position on the High Court of Judiciary. Hanging these men—after finishing the case with an eloquent final address to the jury—would serve him well. He had no more thought of fairness for a defendant than a butcher had for a side of old mutton.

As far as Aidan was concerned, there were only two monsters present in this courtroom, and one of them was presiding over this sham of a trial. The other, Sir Rupert Burney, sat wearing the alert look of a fox about to devour a hen he'd made off with. And he was not about to let this prize get away.

Lord Ruthven peered over his spectacles at his courtroom. Everyone was in place. Two journalists from government-supporting newspapers were in attendance, as they had been the first day of the trial.

Ruthven turned his attention to Aidan, gesturing for him to stand. "Before we begin today, Mr. Grant, I'm warning you that I'll not put up with your disruptions and the verbal gymnastics with which you clearly attempted to confuse the jury. Neither will this trial be used as a platform for your radical views. This is a court of law, sir. I insist that your addresses be pertinent to the grave matter your clients have been charged with. Do I make myself clear?"

Aidan scoffed, making certain his disdain was evident. "Since you appear to have brought your schoolmaster's rod to court with you this morning, Your Lordship, let me remind you that my duty here is not to sit by and allow my clients to be given short shrift by the prosecution nor anyone else . . . sir."

Yesterday, the groundwork for this mockery of justice had been established. After the jury was seated and the charges explained, the prosecution had made a daylong presentation of irrelevant argument, fabricated evidence, falsified documents and letters, and hearsay testimony sworn to by lying witnesses who'd obviously been coached and paid for their perjury. Aidan had spent most of the time on his feet, objecting and arguing with both the judge and the prosecutor. Once, when he'd caught his opponent directing the most condescending of smirks toward him, he'd been sorely tempted to drag the barrister over the table and thrash him. Instead, Aidan had to be satisfied with simply crushing him with a verbal assault that left the man ashen and humiliated.

"If you are suggesting, sir . . ." Ruthven sputtered angrily. "*If* you are suggesting that this court is interested in anything but the even-handed dispensation of justice, then your defense of these men shows a warped bias that will not be tolerated."

"My lord, I have not even begun my defense, so I question such an expressed judgment of 'warped bias' on the part of the court."

"Take care, Mr. Grant. Your attitude is veering dangerously close to contempt of this court. You are treading on exceptionally thin ice."

"Pray understand, my lord, that when it comes to *contempt*, I make a clear distinction between the *court* and the *individuals* present."

Aidan thought for a moment that, judging from the scarlet color of Lord Ruthven's face, his judicial wig might burst into flames. He *was* treading close to the line, but Aidan knew exactly where that line was located. If he nudged a bit over it, he was willing to take the risk. Arrogant bullies like Ruthven needed to be kept off-balance, even in their own court.

Especially in their own court.

While the judge was still searching for the correct words of admonishment, Aidan gestured toward the wide-eyed jury and the prosecutor, who was staring stony-faced at the table before him.

"If Your Lordship wishes," Aidan said calmly, "I am prepared to begin my defense."

Hardly happy with the exchange, Lord Ruthven glared at him for a full minute before nodding curtly. "Proceed."

Aidan looked casually at the notes he had spread on the table. At the back of the courtroom, the door opened, and two men entered, carrying satchels. He turned and gestured to the chairs reserved for the press.

"See here," the judge snapped. "Who are you?"

"Journalists, my lord," Aidan replied.

"I'm not addressing you," Ruthven stormed, turning his attention to the newcomers. "Whom do you represent?"

"*The Edinburgh Review*, Your Lordship," one replied.

"*The Scotsman*, my lord," said the other.

The judge scowled at them before glancing at Sir Rupert.

"Is there a problem, my lord?" Aidan asked innocently. He knew perfectly well the problem. They were independent publications, highly critical of Parliament and Crown policies in Scotland.

Before Ruthven could respond, the door opened again, and two more men appeared and made their way toward the press section.

The judge sat back in his chair, his gaze following them as if they were pheasants fluttering into range.

"And you two," he snapped. "Journalists?"

"Aye, my lord," they answered in unison.

"*The Manchester Observer.*"

"*The Times of London*, Your Lordship."

Ruthven swung his killing stare to Aidan. "Your work, I presume."

"I'm not sure what you mean, sir. But freedom of the press is one of bulwarks upon which our society exists. Even though certain branches of our current government see fit to manipulate and place restraints on our newspapers, the traditions of our noble land pertaining to such a valuable and venerable institution—"

"Enough! I need no lecture from you, Mr. Grant."

The judge adjusted his gown and, resting his elbows on the table, shot a look at Sir Rupert over his clasped hands. He was not difficult to read. Ruthven was trying to see how this could be turned to his own advantage.

When the judge spoke again, he suddenly sounded like a gracious host.

"This court welcomes the members of the press who

have come so far to bear witness to the justice of our system, and who will undoubtedly report the fair and impartial treatment that these defendants receive. And you may quote me, gentlemen."

"If I may proceed then, Your Lordship."

"The court is looking forward to hearing your defense, Mr. Grant."

Aidan gestured to the bailiff. "I'd like to call Robert Wemys to the stand."

At the back of the courtroom, the door opened, and the bailiff called for the witness.

A low rumble of murmur and whispered questions swept through the gallery. The pitch and volume rose, and Aidan didn't need to turn around to know that Sebastian had entered, supporting Wemys.

"I believe this witness will shed a great deal of light on this case, my lord, as well as a number of other cases."

Aidan looked up in time to see Sir Rupert Burney quietly whispering directions into the ear of a clerk, who immediately slipped out of the courtroom.

Lord Ruthven was staring at the spymaster, unsure of what threat this witness presented, but astute enough to realize that a problem had arisen.

Aidan watched as Sir Rupert's eyes slid expressively from the judge toward the press section.

Sebastian and Wemys reached the defense table. The journey to Inverness had taken its toll on the dying man. His face was grey, his breathing shallow and forced. His body seemed to have collapsed in on itself, and his clothing hung loosely from his bony shoulders. Sebastian leaned him against the defense table.

"Brace yourself, Wemys," Aidan whispered. "This is the moment in which you redeem your entire miserable life."

"If that were only so," he rasped.

Across the aisle, the prosecutor looked on blankly, unaware of who Wemys was but clearly unconcerned by the appearance of the surprise witness.

On the far side of the gallery, the motioning of Sir Rupert's hand toward the door of the judge's chambers was discreet but effective. Rising calmly, as if he'd just remembered another engagement, he sauntered out of the courtroom. But as he left, Sir Rupert directed a momentary and deadly glance at Aidan.

"The court will take a brief recess," the judge announced, standing and hurrying from the courtroom before anyone could move.

Aidan helped lower Wemys into a chair at the defense table. Minutes ticked by.

The audience in the gallery was growing louder, and the clearly bewildered members of the jury were glancing at the judge's door, wondering what was causing the delay. In the dock, the faces of the Chattan brothers showed their confusion.

Searc Mackintosh was sitting toward the back with the shipowner Captain Kenedy and another man that Aidan didn't know. Searc's bristly eyebrows were darting around the courtroom, taking in everything.

Finally, the door of the judge's chambers opened, and Lord Ruthven reappeared, looking like he'd been struck by lightning. He staggered to his chair and sat down heavily. Silence fell like a blanket over the room. Every eye was on him. He looked vaguely at the members of the press and pushed a stack of papers around on his table. Gathering himself, he was all business when he finally addressed the prosecutor.

"I must say that I am appalled, sir, by the shoddy preparation of this case. In fact, it has become abundantly clear that evidence of wrongdoing on the part of these two weavers has been tragically exaggerated." He straightened his judicial wig and then shook his head. "I'll not allow these proceedings to continue. Edmund Chattan. George Chattan. The charges against you are dismissed. You are free to go. Bailiff, release the jury. Court is adjourned. God save the King."

Everyone in the courtroom watched in silent disbelief as Lord Ruthven rose and scuttled off. No one moved for a long moment. Then, suddenly, the courtroom erupted in shocked cries.

Aidan turned to Sebastian. "Sir Rupert was willing to surrender the field, rather than have Wemys's testimony go into the record."

"That worked out well," Sebastian responded.

Friends surrounded the two weavers, whose faces showed that they still didn't believe they were free.

Aidan drew Sebastian aside. "Take care of our prize witness. Sir Rupert's men may take a run at him before you get ten paces from the Tolbooth. Get him to Searc's house. I'll send these distinguished members of the press after you. We don't want them to think they traveled all this way for nothing."

"I'll make sure they hear what Wemys has to say." Sebastian took hold of Aidan's arm. "Take care, big brother. You made a deadly enemy today."

Suddenly, the roar of a crowd outside could be heard.

"What's that?" Aidan asked.

"I believe your public has just learned the outcome of the trial," his brother said wryly. "You're a celebrity now, God help us."

CHAPTER 21
MORRIGAN

Morrigan had wanted to go to Inverness and watch the trial, but everyone had been adamantly against it. Isabella and Cinaed knew all about her brush with Sir Rupert.

Now, Aidan Grant was a hero across the Highlands, and soon his fame would spread throughout Scotland. He was the brilliant barrister who had cleverly bested Sir Rupert Burney and the most brutal judge in all of Britain in one trial. The Chattan brothers were free and had returned to Elgin to a hero's welcome.

Aidan's name would soon be in every newspaper from Inverness to London. The same journalists who'd interviewed Wemys were also going to print the court proceedings. They were planning to publish additional articles about the government's underhanded methods of coercion and entrapment. One of the reporters told Sebastian that a Glasgow printer was publishing a pamphlet about a spy there named Alexander Richmond. Now, to be sure, there would be more. And in every publication Aidan was to be proclaimed as a champion of the people.

Even though she admired Aidan's accomplishment, now that he'd returned, Morrigan kept her distance from him. Since the night of the Samhain celebrations, she'd avoided speaking to him. She was careful that they wouldn't be caught alone.

It hurt her that their lives had to be like this, but she knew it would be less painful in the long run. Aidan was leaving for Edinburgh, and Morrigan didn't know when he'd be back. She didn't know if they'd ever see each other again. And even if they did, she had her doubts that their friendship would survive what happened on the night of Samhain.

It was only a kiss, she kept telling herself. One that she'd ended in panic. But there was more to it, more going on between them. She couldn't quiet her emotions, didn't know how to stop thinking of him. The affection she carried for this man had no future, but Morrigan didn't know how to push him from her heart and close the door.

At dawn on the day he was to leave, she fled her room and went out to the training yard. The sky was steel grey and threatened rain. It didn't matter. She needed to let out her frustrations, and the battered pell took another beating from her. Every attack, however, every blow—right and left, slash and kick and stab—only managed to trigger another memory of him. No matter how hard she hit, no matter how breathless and light-headed she became from the exertion, she couldn't push Aidan's face from her thoughts.

Every look they exchanged was charged with meaning. She would never forget their fight in the alleyway. Or the way he came after her the first day he arrived at Dalmigavie. Or the morning when the two of them sparred with dirks and she again blackened his eye. His cleverness enchanted her. His wit at Barn Hill caught her off guard. He never forgot a conversation. Every word she said to him came back on her. Morrigan was never as well read as Maisie, or as accomplished as Isabella, but Aidan made her feel smart. Capable. He challenged her to think beyond the training yard.

She'd miss him when he was gone. She already did.

Frowning at the increasingly mangled post, Morrigan finally paused to catch her breath. A cold rain was now falling. She hadn't even noticed.

"You still rely too much on a two-handed grip. While I am gone, perhaps you could practice more using only one hand."

Morrigan's chest tightened. She looked over her shoulder at Aidan standing beneath the overhang of the weapons shed. His face was in the shadow, but she could see his long legs were sheathed in breeches and boots. He was ready for his travels.

"Anything else I should work on?"

He crossed the yard to her.

Morrigan stared into his handsome face. For the first time in her life, she understood what the poets and novelists meant when they described someone as "smitten." She was definitely smitten, unfortunately. Painfully, dangerously, irrevocably smitten. Blast.

"Practice your lunges and recoveries." He came to stand next to her. "Your footwork could be faster. You need to work on your agility."

"There is nothing wrong with my agility."

"You should also train with a sword in one hand and a dagger in the other."

Morrigan liked his idea, but she wasn't going to admit it. "When did you become an expert in training?"

"Also, practice with the sword held in your opposite hand. Attacking with your left hand always surprises an opponent." He took the weapon out of her hand and put it in the left.

Standing so close, feeling his touch on her hand and arm, thrilled her. She glanced up at his mouth, and the memory of their kiss returned.

He raised her left arm, but she let it drop. The point of the sword struck the dirt with a thud.

"You should definitely lift heavy things every day to build strength."

Morrigan spun the blade once in the air and drove the tip into the wet ground between them.

"Don't you have somewhere to go this morning, Mr. Grant?" she asked. "Some place really, really, really far away?"

He smiled and she caught herself staring. If she'd sighed out loud—as she nearly did—she would have had to throw herself off the top of the tower.

"I do have somewhere to go. But I couldn't leave without seeing you."

Morrigan wished he hadn't said that. She didn't need to feel worse than she already did.

"Well, you've given me a rigorous schedule of lessons that I'm already following." She tried to keep her tone flippant. "Have a safe journey, sir."

"You should also visit the library daily and make a list of interesting volumes you and I can discuss when I get back."

"You are an educated man, sir. You need no list from me."

"Oh, but I do. My education is severely limited. Besides, I have an ulterior motive."

"Which is?"

His hand brushed against hers. "Do you have to ask that question, Miss Drummond?"

She was relieved and disappointed when a number of

fighters entered the training yard at that moment, greeting Morrigan and Aidan as they passed. Two men stopped to talk to him. There wasn't a conversation at Dalmigavie that didn't involve the trial he'd won. He couldn't be more popular if he were a Mackintosh.

Morrigan decided this was the right time to disappear. She returned the sword to the rack and hurried out.

She didn't get far. Aidan caught up with her as she was passing through the garden on her way to the kitchens.

"Miss Drummond . . . Morrigan," he called out. "May I have a minute of your time before I leave?"

It would have been better for everyone to say no to him, to walk away. But she couldn't bring herself to say the words. The rain had eased to a mere mist, and they were alone in the garden. This was perhaps the last time they'd have a moment like this.

"I need to apologize for the way I behaved at Samhain. For taking advantage of you and the situation."

"You *didn't* take advantage of me. You asked if you could kiss me. How many men would do that? And I was the one who kissed you. But it was wrong. I shouldn't have." Morrigan felt heat rising through her chest and into her face. "And you would do me a great service if you could forget what happened between us and never mention it again."

"If you wish, I'll never mention that moment again. But forget?" He shook his head. "For me, that kiss we shared was too passionate to forget so easily. I'm afraid I'll never forget it."

Her fists clenched. How did it come to this? This is not what she wanted. Why couldn't she feel nothing for him? Confusion churned her stomach and scrambled her thoughts. She could no longer hold it in.

"Why? Why must you be who you are? If you were a

scandalous rake or if you were a dull and virtuous gentleman, I could cheerfully send you on your way. I could forget you. But you insist on being something in between. Why?"

"Not fish nor fowl. Not man nor beast. You're not happy that I'm going, and you can't forget me." He took her hand and placed a kiss on the backs of her fingers. "I have great hope for us."

Damn him. He was to be her ruin. Morrigan had no desire to wander around this castle for however long he was gone, drifty and misty-eyed, like Maisie before being reunited with Niall. She stole her hand back.

"Your fellow travelers must be waiting. Go."

"My fellow travelers are Sebastian and Kane Branson, and they can bloody well wait." His expression turned serious. "I wanted you to know that Searc has offered to move Wemys to Inverness. He can stay at his house in Maggot Green. He doesn't have much time left, but there is no need for you to put up with having him here."

"I've already spoken to Isabella. It'll be better if he remains here. She'll look after him until the end."

Wemys. Morrigan no longer felt anger at the mention of his name. She didn't feel any emotion whatsoever. As brief as their exchange had been, that conversation had closed a door for her. She no longer felt any need for revenge. And after what Wemys had done in dragging himself from his deathbed, going to Inverness for the trial, and telling the journalists of his involvement in Sir Rupert's schemes, she was content to let him be.

Isabella was a physician to her very core, and she had the ability to separate her personal feelings from the responsibilities of her profession. She knew Morrigan's history with Wemys, but she was still capable of performing her job. He could die as the maker had arranged.

"In that case . . ."

Morrigan noticed he was still reluctant to go. The longer he stayed, the harder it became for her to see him go. "You've given me unsolicited advice. You've brought up in conversation a dalliance that I wish to forget. You've made final arrangements for your informer. What else is left?"

"I have a gift for you."

"No gifts," she said. "Unless you've stolen my shoes and are returning them. Perhaps a handkerchief that I loaned to you?"

He reached into his coat and pulled out a few folded flyers.

Opening them, she realized they were two caricatures. "New work by Madame Laborde."

"I found them pasted on the walls near the courthouse and knew you'd want to see her latest."

Morrigan had thought a lot about the artist since the day she left her in the garden at Barn Hill. She hadn't been back to Inverness since, but even if she did go, she had no idea where to search for her. Looking at these etchings in her hand, Morrigan knew that she was alive at least, and still working for Sir Rupert.

She needed a dry flat space and Maisie and Fiona's astute minds to see what hidden messages, if any, had been conveyed in these drawings. Madame Laborde had to know Morrigan would be looking.

"Thank you. These are a gift."

He stretched out his hand. "Then I want them back."

She held them behind her back. "You can't take back a gift."

Morrigan was surprised when Aidan lifted her chin until she was looking into his eyes. "I knew you'd want to study these flyers to see what secrets they hold. I know that if they contain anything of value, you'll find it."

His touch lingered. She waited. That wasn't all what he had to say.

"But I worry that you'll do something unsafe to try to find this woman on your own."

"Me? Do something unsafe? Ha! Never."

"Morrigan, please listen to me." He searched for the words, and she feared what he would say. "I don't have near enough time now to make you understand how much I care for you . . . and how much I worry that something might happen to you while I'm gone."

She tried to say something flippant, but he placed his fingers gently against her lips.

"I'm asking you to take care of yourself and wait for me to return. We have more we need to say to each other. Much more."

His face was close to hers. Morrigan looked into Aidan's eyes, and she could not deny her feelings for him. What she felt was more than friendly affection. She never imagined she could love a man, but she loved Aidan Grant.

The hopelessness of the two of them ever being together was still there. But suddenly, it didn't matter.

His thumb traced her bottom lip. "May I kiss you before I go?"

Standing in the gardens with a hedge separating them from world, Morrigan kissed him first again. She pressed her lips against his, and Aidan's arms immediately encircled her.

She forgot to breathe, and the castle walls surrounding them disappeared. All she was conscious of was the consuming fire that was racing through her. The etchings fell to the ground, and Morrigan's hands moved of their own accord, slipping around him.

A noise emerged from the back of his throat, or maybe it was from hers. Powerful arms gathered her closer, pressing her to him until there was nothing left between their two hearts, pounding as one.

She'd never experienced passion before Aidan. She'd believed no one could ever conjure in her the need that gripped her now. She never thought any man would even tempt her. Not after what she'd been through. But this was different. Entirely different. Now, wrapped in Aidan's arms, she found herself burning. He drew her into a shadowy archway. When she pressed her back against the cool stones, his body followed. He tore his mouth from her lips and pressed it to her throat.

"Morrigan," he murmured. His hand glided down over her breast and stomach, and all she could do was clutch at his hair and drag his mouth back to hers for another searing kiss.

Sebastian's voice came from the garden entrance, calling out for his brother. The two of them leaped apart.

"Well, that settles two things," Aidan said, smiling.

"What is settled?" she asked, trying to catch her breath.

"You'll wait for me to get back."

"And the second thing?"

"I have to kill Sebastian."

With that, he brushed a final kiss across her lips and walked away.

CHAPTER 22
MORRIGAN

The three women examined the etchings closely. The artwork didn't differ greatly from the flyers Morrigan had brought back from Inverness. Making a mockery of the son of Scotland was the central theme. The nuns and students were depicted around the edges.

"Now that I've met her," Morrigan said, "it's easier knowing we were correct about how she uses the periphery of the artwork."

Maisie agreed. "It would have been impossible to locate her without the clues that placed her at Barn Hill."

Morrigan watched her and Fiona continue to study every detail. She had no idea where Madame Laborde was taken. Until Aidan gave her these, they had no way of knowing if the woman were still alive. Actually, they still didn't know for certain. These could have been made from the drawings the artist was delivering to Sir Rupert the day they met in the gardens of the estate in Inverness.

Morrigan had spoken to Searc about it when he returned to Dalmigavie after the trial. Now that they knew who she was, he had his people searching for her. But so far, nothing had come back. Even Mrs. Goddard was at a loss regarding where she'd gone, and she was quite concerned about it.

Maisie shook her head and stepped back from the table. "It's truly a shame that Madame Laborde should waste her talent supporting the wrong side."

"One would think she could have earned a decent income doing caricatures for your newspaper friends in Edinburgh and Glasgow," Fiona said.

"I doubt they would pay as well as Sir Rupert and the Home Office."

Morrigan agreed. "If money is her only motivation, then she's aiding the side with the deepest pockets." She thought back over her conversation with Mrs. Goddard and Madame Laborde. "She's a widow who has fallen on hard times. She has no family to go to. She's needed to rely on the charity of women who are strangers to her."

"Are you justifying her actions?" Maisie asked.

"Not at all. But it's important to understand her desperation." Morrigan owed her freedom to the artist. If she had not prodded her to go, reminding her of the consequences of what could happen, she might had been foolish enough to face Sir Rupert. "When it comes to survival, the fact that we're women stacks the cards against us. Take away marriage and inherited title and wealth, and we must rely on some talent that we're not averse to marketing. Marriage is not always an option or a preference."

The two women stared at her for a moment and then exchanged a look.

Maisie was the first to speak. "Has he asked you?"

"Who? Asked what?" Morrigan turned away and sat on the bed, smoothing her skirts. She had the answer to both of those questions, but she was unsettled. She didn't know what to make of how easily Aidan's attentions left her starry-eyed and hopeful, in spite of everything.

Still, they had no understanding as far as she was concerned, and she couldn't imagine how there ever could be. The obstacles were too many to count.

Maisie sat on the bed next to her. "Pray don't forget who you're talking to. I know you. What happened between you and Mr. Grant before he left?"

"Nothing." Morrigan was definitely not going to tell them that she'd kissed him. Twice.

"He's coming back," Fiona said.

"He has to come back. He's standing for the election when the time comes," Maisie affirmed. "Niall told me Searc and Cinaed already have a number of social events planned for him to attend around Hogmanay."

These would be social events where he'd be introduced to at least a dozen unmarried women who would no doubt make better wives for a politician. The pang of jealousy was sudden and sharp and left Morrigan disturbed. She stood and walked to the window.

The mountains heard that Samhain had come and gone, and a dusting of snow covered the peaks in the distance. The seasons were changing. Time was moving on.

Morrigan thought of the words Madame Laborde said to her in the garden. *Look at you. No home, no family of your own, no dowry, and no prospect of marriage. You have no future, Miss Drummond.*

"And no talent," she said aloud.

"Who has no talent?" Maisie asked.

Morrigan turned around and faced her friends. The artist had none of those things either. But the woman had her art. It was her only real means of survival. "I have no talent."

"That's not true. You're talented in so many ways."

"Don't exaggerate," she told Maisie. "Isabella is a fine physician. You, an accomplished writer. Fiona, you're a revolutionary."

"That's not a talent," Fiona said with a laugh. "It constitutes a lifetime of trouble."

They liked to tease, make less of what they did. But Morrigan knew the truth. She valued what they'd done and continued to do.

"You've accomplished things. You and Maisie established the Female Reform Society in Edinburgh. You have motivated women to break their chains and speak up. For representation. For just laws." Morrigan looked from one to the other. "But what have I done that has been worthwhile? And what can I do in the future that means *anything*?"

"I don't know a tougher woman than you."

"Or any woman braver," Maisie agreed with her friend.

"And what am I going to do with that? Disguise myself and join an army? Become a rebel leader and haunt these hills?"

She looked over her shoulder at the distant mountain peaks. Perhaps there had been a day not so long ago that such a life attracted her. But no longer. She'd always wished to be independent and proficient. She'd strived to protect herself so that no one would ever be able to abuse her again.

"My training with those weapons fulfills a need in me, like eating and drinking. It's a regimen. I don't consider it a talent. It certainly provides me with no way of supporting myself or contributing to society."

"For years, you worked at your father's side. Isabella swears that no medical student who ever assisted her matched your abilities," Maisie said. "Have you considered becoming more proficient in the area of medicine? You could study under her. She'd love to have you beside her."

"Isabella is university-trained. And she's brilliant. Beyond her academic training, she is also a born healer. And she has a way about her that makes people accept her. She doesn't let narrow-minded prejudices and fears get in the way of the care she provides for her patients. And she'd never turn her back on anyone who needed help." Morrigan thought of how Isabella continued to care for Wemys after learning the truth about him, regardless of how much she abhorred him. "She and my father both could separate their feelings and their duty. I don't have that ability."

Fiona motioned to the stack of books on the bedside table. "You're a reader."

"You could write," Maisie suggested.

"You have a wicked sense of humor," Fiona added.

"That's true," Maisie agreed. "Your tongue is as sharp as the dagger you carry in your boot. And I know. You've poked me with it enough times over the years."

"There you have it. You could write satire," Fiona concluded. "Prose versions of the kind of work Madame Laborde produces."

"I can't be someone else. I can only be myself. Even if I don't know exactly who that is. Even though I have no idea right now what the future holds or where I want to be a year from now, or ten years."

Morrigan turned to the window and pushed open the panels. A blast of cold air hit her in the face—exactly what she needed to stop the tears suddenly welling up in her eyes. She couldn't understand what made her bring up such a topic. In her mind, the fog swirling around the future was getting thicker. She doubted that anything said here would help her see what direction she was intended to go.

Maisie approached her from behind and wrapped her arms around her. Morrigan leaned her head back against the woman who had become a sister.

"I could suggest that this upheaval within you is due to the possibility that you're in love, but I fear you might throw me out this window."

"I think *that* is a suggestion right there."

"Am I wrong?"

Maybe she *was* in love, she thought. But that wasn't the reason for her unhappiness.

"Do you remember this past August? How you fussed and worried and had to talk to Niall before you two were married?"

Maisie sighed. "That was a difficult moment for me."

"I know it was. You knew who you were, and you wanted to make certain that he understood your dreams. That he respected your chosen path."

"Everyone finds their own path. But for some people it takes time," Maisie said softly. "This is just a morning mist that is obscuring the future right now. You need to keep moving forward, one step at a time. The path will show itself."

"I pray that you're right. But sometimes I feel like I hear a bell tolling, far off in the distance. I move toward it, thinking it's beckoning me toward the start of something new . . . but then I freeze. My fear is that my past will one day be exposed and become quicksand beneath my feet."

CHAPTER 23
AIDAN

Edinburgh

Aidan listened as the bells in the tower of the Tron Kirk pealed six. Sitting back in his chair at the Bull's Head Tavern, he wondered vaguely how many times he'd heard them ring the hour from this very spot.

Across the table from him, Captain Ian Bell took a long, satisfied drink from his tankard. It had been a good day for both of them. Bell was one of the directors of the Orphan Hospital in Bailie Fife's Close, not far from where they were having a celebratory supper. For several years, they'd worked together in situations where a father or mother had needed a barrister to represent them in court while the bairns needed a roof over their heads. Aidan provided the legal support, and Bell saw to it the children were cared for.

Today, Aidan had successfully defended a woman arrested at a protest last month. This evening, she'd been reunited with her children at the Orphan Hospital.

The captain had been relieved when his friend returned from Inverness in time for this trial. Aidan told him about the delays in the north, about the trial of the two brothers, and about meeting the son of Scotland. When he mentioned Isabella Drummond, Bell pushed his tankard away from him.

"The doctor . . . Isabella Drummond? The wife of the late physician, Archibald Drummond?"

Aidan nodded. Cinaed's name and rumors about his connection to the queen and Bonnie Prince Charlie had raced across Scotland like wildfire. He was a luminary who had suddenly appeared in the firmament, and everyone wanted to know more about him. The identity of his wife, however, was less well known. Aidan went on and explained their relationship.

Bell laid his hands flat on the table. "The entire Pennington family is indebted to that lady."

Aidan knew that his friend had married Lady Phoebe Pennington, but he was surprised they knew Isabella. A powerful and progressive family from the Borders to the Highlands, they had for generations been a force for change. Their politics had much in common with his own.

"Isabella Drummond operated on my wife's sister Millie," the captain continued. "Saved her life."

Before he arrived at Dalmigavie Castle, Aidan had heard about Isabella and her abilities as a doctor. Upon meeting her, however, he'd soon learned that her glowing reputation didn't come close to doing justice to the woman's prowess. She was a marvel.

As was Morrigan. He tried to be attentive of the conversation, rather than reminisce about the kiss in the garden before he left. He kicked himself for not going to her sooner. The day after Samhain. Those were precious moments that they'd lost. He missed her.

"Is there a chance you'll see her again?"

"Absolutely," Aidan said. "Why?"

"If you do, you can tell her that we think of her often

and fondly. Lady Millie just had a baby boy of her own this past summer. She's living up in Aberdeenshire."

He was a lost man, for even the mention of babies had him thinking of Morrigan. Maybe they'd be lucky enough to have a daughter first. A lass with Morrigan's eyes. Her strength. Her courage. He didn't realize he was running his finger over the mark on his eyebrow until the captain remarked on it.

"If you ask me, that wee scar over your eye gives you more of a soldier's look." Bell raised his cup to Aidan in a toast. "To my friend, who fought Napoleon to the end and still came home unscathed to do battle in the courtroom."

Aidan scoffed. Ian Bell had done his share of fighting on the continent, but he'd ended up languishing in a French prison in Lille after being badly injured and taken at Talavera. He and Sebastian both carried their own scars, though Bell's didn't show. All scars didn't come from the battlefield.

After returning from France, Ian had lost his sister to a murderer here in Edinburgh. In the course of his search for her killer, he'd found the love of his life. Though Aidan's knowledge of the full story was sketchy, he did know that it had taken the two of them to stop the predator.

"To my friend, who survived the French and the dangers of the Auld Reekie's Vaults. We'll see if you survive fatherhood." Aidan raised his own cup. "You must be anxious to get back to your family in Fife."

"I am, indeed. We have another bairn on the way, you know."

Aidan smiled. "Congratulations, my friend."

"Incidentally, I dined with Phoebe's brother yesterday. The viscount said the word around Advocate's Close is that while defending the two radicals from Elgin, you dragged that hanging judge Ruthven around the courtroom until he hoisted a white flag."

"Between you and me, the man is a heartless cur. Someday, I'd like him to feel the consequences of his actions."

"Well, my brother-in-law says the other judges in Edinburgh were quite happy to see Ruthven set back on his haunches. The man is a—"

The door opened and the captain stopped as Sebastian strode in. He spotted them and came over. Bell rose, and the two friends exchanged their customary greeting.

"Hullo, Cannonball."

"Good evening, Lille."

They sat down.

"Have you heard the news?" Sebastian asked.

Before he could continue, shouts and cheering were heard from outside. The noise of the crowds was growing.

"What is that?" Aidan asked, looking out the window as people poured out of taverns and coffeehouses. "From the looks of things, it can't be war. And it can't be a protest."

Just then, a red-faced fellow burst through the door, shouting, "The queen won! She beat them—king, lords, and all. And 'twas Brougham who done it! They say the crowds carried our lad on their shoulders through the streets o' London!"

A cheer went up in the tavern.

Queen Caroline had returned to London to stand trial before Parliament on charges of adultery. All based on falsehoods and accusations concocted by the jealous king demanding divorce that she was not willing to grant. Henry Brougham was defending her and had apparently carried the day. And as the cheering in the street affirmed, she continued to be the queen of the people.

"Well, there's my news," Sebastian said dryly. "But this came for you from the very man of the hour himself."

He pushed a letter across the table.

As the two men talked about the surprising turn of affairs in Westminster, Aidan opened the letter from Henry Brougham and perused the contents. The queen wished to see him immediately.

CHAPTER 24
MORRIGAN

The mail coach ran between Edinburgh and Inverness on a daily basis now, and for the past year, its route had been extended all the way to Thurso on Scotland's northern-most coast. The world was shrinking. From Inverness, a rider employed by Searc brought the mail every day to Dalmigavie, a convenience unheard of just a few years earlier.

Morrigan knew that since their arrival in the Highlands, Maisie regularly corresponded with the cities in the south. She exchanged letters with a woman named Ella who ran the meetings of the Female Reform Society in the absence of her and Fiona. There was also her ongoing communication with various newspapers about the publication of her articles. From midmorning on, Maisie always stationed herself by the laird's study and waited for the courier.

On a grey morning at the beginning of December, she delivered a letter that had arrived for Morrigan, much to her surprise.

"Who would write to me here?"

"Perhaps it's from Mr. Grant." Maisie's eyebrows went up and down suggestively. "I'll leave you to moon over every word."

The handwriting was unfamiliar, but she had no idea what Aidan's writing looked like. There was no initial or other mark on the wax seal. Surely, the Grant seal would be recognizable. Morrigan felt somewhat apprehensive as she walked to her window and broke open the letter.

It took only a moment to scan the brief contents, and she grew sicker with every successive line.

Miss Drummond,
I am in urgent need of a small supply of money, exactly one hundred pounds. I am a friend of your uncle Robert Wemys of Perth. More than a friend. I am like his brother. It was in the confidence of our relationship that he confided in me the details of a shocking and sordid event between you two.

Based on his own words, you conducted him with a boldness unbecoming of a young lady into your own bedchamber. Some conversation ensued, he informed me, from which it was quickly apparent to him that certain consolation was welcomed.

I had every intention of relaying this account to a number of newspapers that would pay handsomely for a report about certain women who not only entertain a familial connection with the son of Scotland, but who also have undertaken to have an understanding with a barrister, Mr. Aidan Grant of Carrie House. Acting out of a sense of profound honour and decency, I wish to offer my assurance to you that such scandalous information should never see the light of day.

I am anxious to receive the slight sum mentioned

above and would be honoured to meet with you personally. At that time, we can settle the matter of my financial needs in person at the auld hunting lodge off the road between Dalmigavie Castle and this city. If you find this suitable, we can meet on the eighth of December around the hour of ten in the morning.

> Until then, madam,
> I remain your humble servant,
> K. Baker

Her breaths were uneven, anger pushed a scream out of her chest. She had been a victim of villainy. And now this scoundrel intended to blackmail her. He would make public a secret that she'd lived with for all these years, an effort made for the sake of the peace of mind of others. She yanked open her door and charged out. This worm K. Baker was detestable enough, but it was impossible to fathom how a person could be so vile as to brag about a crime against a child? And lie about it? She read the letter again. There was no indication of a date when this occurred. Was he insinuating that she had been an adult?

Morrigan had heard that Wemys was declining rapidly by the day. But he couldn't die soon enough to suit her.

"Morrigan?"

She didn't realize where she'd been going until she came face-to-face with Isabella coming out of her medical room.

"What's wrong?"

She was too upset to speak, and the words died on her tongue.

Isabella immediately took her hand and pulled her inside, closing the door behind them. She glanced at the letter in her hand. "Did you hear from Aidan?"

"It's not from him. He has no cause to write to me." She waved the paper. "But why would a total stranger think there's something between us?"

Without asking, Isabella took the letter out of her hand and read it. As her fury grew, her face turned a deep shade of crimson.

"Who gave you this?"

"It arrived with the mail this morning."

"Who would do such a thing?"

"Wemys has to be behind this. He lied to some other scoundrel about what he'd done. The vile dog."

"You must get him to talk about this."

She was right. If Baker knew, then how many others had Wemys bragged to. He'd pretended he was remorseful and wanted forgiveness. But this proved there was no end to his evil. He'd trumpeted his sins about like a town crier. He was lower than scum.

"It occurs to me that the timing of this is very suspicious. Why now? If he's known about what happened for all these years, why wasn't he blackmailing Archibald? Your father would have paid any amount to protect you from public attention."

"Maybe he thought my father would murder him. There is nothing in here that says this didn't happen last month or last year."

"The same thing may happen to the cur now. I'm quite sure Cinaed and Niall and Blair—and Searc as well— would fight one another to be the one putting a bullet between the eyes of this man. You know how highly they all value you."

Blair would kill without asking why, but the others would need to know the reason. Hurrying toward the tower rooms with Isabella beside her, Morrigan's mind was on

Aidan. His future was being shaped in this moment. The hopes of so many rested on his shoulders. She didn't want to compromise him.

But how could this Baker know about her connection with Aidan? She supposed that anyone who'd seen them together at the Samhain celebration would suspect they had an attachment.

The letter burned her fingers. Nothing was simple. There'd be no quick end to this. If Baker's account was made public, there would be no mention of how young she'd been at the time. They'd print the lies and say she was an incestuous siren and seducer. She thought of the caricatures of Madam Laborde. They drew attention, regardless of the fact that they were lies and fabrications. Would there be caricatures of this? How low would they stoop in depicting such a vile event? Tears blurred her vision, and she brushed them away discreetly.

"Whatever it is, however this needs to be resolved, I'm beside you," Isabella said as they reached Wemys's room. "I'll help you, however you see fit."

Her heart ached. Morrigan thought she'd closed the door on what had been done to her. She wanted to let him die, put the mess behind her, and look to the future. But the door had been once again kicked open. She was exposed, vulnerable. There was no escape. His viciousness would outlive him.

They passed over the threshold, but she wouldn't venture in too far. Isabella spoke to the servant who'd been watching Wemys, and the woman quietly slipped out.

The emaciated skeleton of a body was all that remained under the blanket. He was far weaker than the last time she'd seen him. His breathing was labored and erratic, and his mouth moved as if to gulp at the air.

Morrigan watched Isabella go to the bedside. She closed her eyes as she tried to clear her thoughts and decide what she had to do.

Paying Baker wasn't the answer. Killing him was at best a temporary solution. Someone like him would no doubt have put in place the threat of others to step in with accusations of murder if he didn't return from the arranged meeting.

She didn't want to hurt the people she loved. Morrigan didn't want what little peace they had to be taken from them. She didn't want to put their lives at risk on her behalf. What if she went away? With her gone, there would be no connection that could harm Aidan at least. He had the most to lose. When Isabella and Maisie and Morrigan left Edinburgh, they'd been going to Halifax in Canada in order to disappear and start a new life. What if she did that on her own?

She hesitated. This was exactly what her father had done. He'd taken her and run away.

She watched Isabella check on Wemys.

"He's due to have more laudanum," she said as she came back to Morrigan. "But I'll not give him any until he awakens and you speak to him."

Morrigan had thought a weapon in her hand could protect her. What she needed more at this moment was a clear, strong mind. She needed a strategy to beat rogues like Baker and Wemys at their own twisted game. She sat on a bench by the window, and Isabella sat beside her.

Time ticked slowly by. Isabella refused to leave, even when Morrigan suggested it.

"I failed to be there for you for those first six years when you were in my life. But no more."

Morrigan felt herself once again able to breathe as the other woman's arm slipped around her. Mother, sister, friend—Isabella was all of those things to her and more. And right now, it was good to know she wasn't alone.

How long they waited, she wasn't sure. But eventually Wemys became more restless. Weak coughs bubbled up, and bloody froth formed at the corners of his mouth. Morrigan waited a while longer until the man's eyes opened. It took a few moments for him to focus on her. When he did, a tear ran down his face. His expression reflected fear and defeat and sadness.

"You're here to witness me crossing over."

"No." She handed him the letter. "This arrived today."

Perhaps it was the time she'd spent with Isabella. Maybe it was the knowledge that Wemys *was* dying. Or acknowledging to herself that she was a fighter. Whatever it was, a sense of calm possessed her that struck her as surprising, if not miraculous. For the first time in her life, Morrigan was above the chaos, observing events dispassionately. She was in control, capable of taking the time to think and make decisions. Aidan's strategy had been to use this man's testimony to counter the government's charges against the Chattan brothers. The thought occurred to her that perhaps she could get him to leave behind a letter, a document that stated what he'd done to her. There would be no secrets to expose then. Everyone would know the truth.

But did she have the strength to face this scandal here in Scotland? To fight this ongoing evil that haunted her? Or should she run? Even as the question crossed her mind, Isabella appeared at her side and took her hand.

Morrigan knew the answer before the complete thought formed. She would stay. She would fight. That was who she was.

The simple task of holding up the paper to his eyes took great effort. His hand shook. She watched his face as he read it. Finally, Wemys let the missive drop.

Morrigan picked it up. "How? How could Baker know? What are the lies you told him?"

He closed his eyes and tried to force air into his wasted lungs. Finally, he managed to get out a few hoarse words.

"That letter in your hand. It's not from Baker. He's just a tool. A messenger. Burney is behind this."

Morrigan felt the ground tilt under her. "How could Burney know what you did to me?"

He averted his gaze. He couldn't look at her. "Your father came looking for me. I was hiding in Baker's rooms. In Perth. He left a letter. He threatened to kill me for . . . for what I'd done to you."

Morrigan thought about her father leaving and going back to Perth. He'd packed his pistol. She was certain he would have killed Wemys if he'd found him.

"Baker had me confess what I'd done. He stole your father's letter and later gave it to Burney."

"Why?"

"We both went to work for him not long after. Burney collected information on everyone. He paid well for anything he could use against his enemies."

He coughed so violently that for a moment Morrigan thought he'd never take another breath. It took a few moments to recover.

"That is Burney's way. He ferrets out secrets, then twists them, creates scandal where there is none. That's how he gets people to work for him. And keep working." Wemys fought to take in air. "The old fox is using it now to get at you. He's created a story so shocking that it ruins you and everyone around you before you have a chance to explain. But all of it is a test. He's waiting to see how you react. If you pay, he knows he has you."

"And if I don't pay?"

"He still has you."

Morrigan thought of the caricatures. Could she live with herself if her likeness was at the center of one of those flyers pasted to so many walls?

"Beat him at his own game." Wemys groaned in pain. He was growing weaker. "He's thrown you a line. Grab hold of it. Yank the fox out of his hole. These Mackintoshes will know what to do with him."

She had so many questions now. She wanted to know as much about Burney as she could learn. Wemys talked to her. He told her what he could remember until he could go on no longer.

Isabella gave him another dose of laudanum to lessen his pain. The two women stayed at his bedside as he drifted in and out of consciousness.

Then, at sunset, he stopped breathing altogether.

CHAPTER 25
AIDAN

Brandenburgh House
Hammersmith, England

The drawing room of the queen's residence on the out-skirts of London was decorated appropriately with gold brocade curtains, Persian carpets, and Sheraton furniture of an earlier generation. Her defiant nature, however, was evident in a trio of Scottish Robert Adam chairs by the fireplace and the conspicuous display of Italian landscape paintings on the walls. In the eyes of the nation, she'd been absolved of her alleged love affair with Count Bergami, but she was not about to hide behind any pretense for her visitors. Aidan heard there was even a rumor circulating that she might publish a memoir.

Queen Caroline's trial in the House of Lords was behind her, but it was clear to Aidan that she knew her battles were not. As she stood by the window, she pointed out five places on the street beyond the wrought-iron fence.

"For a week, the good tradesmen of this village built celebratory bonfires out there, Mr. Grant." The queen turned her dark eyes in his direction and gestured to Henry Brougham, who stood by the fireplace. "My good friend here tells me the king was furious about the people's happiness over my vindication."

"It was very gratifying, Your Majesty, to see the country rejoice at your triumph," Brougham responded.

The queen waved him off. "Though it would have been even more gratifying to see Lord Liverpool's government fall and throw all of those scoundrels out, starting with that weasel, Lord Sidmouth."

"Indeed, ma'am. The Director of the Home Office has been entirely too independent, I'd say."

She turned to Aidan. "But I'm told Sidmouth and his pack of backbiting curs have been subject to your lash in Inverness, Mr. Grant. You outsmarted Sir Rupert Burney. Well done."

Aidan bowed slightly. "Thank you, Your Majesty. But it was a minor skirmish."

"Don't understate your victory. And don't underestimate the lengths they'll go to repay you for their humiliation." She looked at her lawyer. "We know that our enemies here will not rest until they've roasted us on bonfires of their own. Isn't that true, Mr. Brougham?"

"Quite true, ma'am."

The queen was a petite and energetic woman, and Aidan felt the same magnetic quality about her that one felt in the presence of Cinaed, her son. They both had a charisma that kept a person's attention on them. He couldn't help but think that Queen Caroline was a force that the king clearly felt he could not compete with. Rightfully so.

"Prinny's efforts to cast me off, however, have also brought out some unexpected friends." She gestured to the gilded, upholstered chairs by the fireplace, and the three of them sat. "That is the reason I asked Brougham to bring you to London. I've learned that even my own household cannot be trusted with secrets."

"I'm at your service, ma'am," Aidan told her.

"Thank you, Mr. Grant. And I know you can be trusted. I have a task of the greatest importance I'd like you to undertake." She drummed her fingers on the arm of the chair for a moment. "The king's younger brother William paid me a visit during the trial. Under cover of darkness, of course. Still, having the Duke of Clarence here in my drawing room was a kindness I'll not forget."

Her eyes wandered momentarily to the brightly colored painting of an Italian villa in summer. The scene was remarkable in itself, but even more so contrasted with the grey London winter outside the windows of Brandenburgh House. A reminder of sunnier days, Aidan thought.

"He and his wife, Adelaide, were the only ones in the family who sent condolences to me in Italy upon the passing of my daughter Charlotte."

Perhaps not altogether sunnier days. As Aidan considered her words, it occurred to him that in communicating with her, the Duke of Clarence was showing evidence of character that his older brothers lacked. The king had spent a life of dissipation and the Duke of York, the heir-apparent, was by all accounts eating and drinking himself into an early grave as well.

She was silent for a moment, but she rallied immediately. "William knows about my son Cinaed."

After her clandestine trip to the Highlands, rumors began to circulate widely, so knowledge of her connection with the son of Scotland was hardly surprising. Aidan sensed that the whole nation knew of it.

"Clarence was very interested to learn more about him—specifically, what his intentions are regarding the future of the Highlands."

Of course, he would be interested, Aidan thought. The

Duke of Clarence was a Hanover and third in line for the Crown. The son of Scotland was a threat to them all.

"I answered none of his questions. But when I asked if he would consider meeting with Cinaed, he was extremely eager."

Aidan couldn't help but glance at Brougham. The importance of such an event was not lost on him.

"Many believe that Clarence will be king. It's unlikely that either of his brothers will be producing legitimate offspring. The king will not, I promise you, unless he murders me. Which is quite possible, of course." She held Aidan's gaze. She was in deadly earnest. "But the point is that the duke knows it is in his and the Crown's interest to forge better connections with the north. He told me, confidentially, that he felt the government has failed miserably in its responsibilities toward Scotland."

The queen stood and the men did, as well.

"Clarence has agreed to meet with Cinaed. You, Mr. Grant, must make it happen."

CHAPTER 26
MORRIGAN

Two letters came from Aidan on the same day, and they couldn't have arrived at a better time. He'd written them more than a week apart, and Morrigan felt her spirits rising before she even broke the seals.

The first letter contained, for the most part, news of his travels. Writing from Edinburgh, Aidan told her about a court case he'd won and mentioned the mutual friends the two of them shared. The city was still seething with rebellious spirit and anger against the Crown. Without changing the seriousness of his tone, he went on to tell her that he'd visited the bookshops by St. Giles's. He'd purchased some volumes that he was having shipped to Dalmigavie. The title of one in particular was of great importance. It was "a philosophical tract on romance entitled *Love And Madness. A Story Too True. In A Series Of Letters Between Parties Whose Names Would Perhaps Be Mentioned Were They Less Well Known Or Less Lamented.*" He closed his letter with a postscript saying that his brother wanted to be remembered to her.

The second letter came from London. He'd been called there on business with Henry Brougham, who was the current focus of popular adulation following his victory in Parliament over the foes of the queen. Morrigan couldn't help but smile when he told her that a bookseller in Bond Street had sold him a political pamphlet of critical importance that he would be bringing back to the Highlands personally, since the mail service was far too unreliable. The title of the book was *Who Is The Bridegroom? Or, Nuptial Discoveries*. In his postscript he regretted to inform her that he'd been forced to murder his brother Sebastian after a period of intense provocation. Aidan was not at liberty to divulge the crux of the matter, however.

That same day, she had to head down to go meet with her would be blackmailer.

The moss-covered hunting lodge was ancient, but it was still an impressive building. Morrigan had stopped here once before, en route to Inverness when a cart horse had gone lame. Just a short ride from the road, the lodge was isolated enough for this meeting with Baker, but safe enough for her. This was still Mackintosh land, and she knew there were watchful eyes on her as she rode into the clearing that looked out toward the sparkling river in the distance and the glen.

By a tumbledown stable, a nervous little man in a thick woolen coat and tam stood beside his horse. Even as she approached, it was obvious he was shivering. She wondered if it was caused by the chill wind or fear.

Morrigan reined in her mare a dozen paces from him. She didn't dismount. "Baker?"

He removed his hat and held it into his chest and nodded. "Aye, mistress. Kenneth Baker."

"You sent me a letter."

For the first time, Morrigan had a clear look at him, noting the blotchy skin and red nose. Rather than looking steadily at her, his eyes darted nervously toward the path leading from the road. He appeared to be expecting a wild boar to rush out from the bushes at any moment and tear him apart, or a band of Mackintosh fighters. He pulled his tam back onto his head.

"I did, mistress."

"You asked for money."

"Aye. A hundred pounds. It said so in the letter."

"Do you get to keep the money, or do you have to give all of it to him?"

Baker stared at her, slow to comprehend what she was saying. "Give it all to who, mistress?"

"You know who. Sir Rupert Burney. Or do his henchmen take it from you? A bunch of rogues and thieves. Wouldn't you agree?"

He started saying something—his first impulse being denial—but he sputtered and backtracked and stuttered. Morrigan interrupted him. She couldn't take it anymore.

"I'll not be played for a fool, Baker, not by you or your master." She didn't wait for him to pile on more lies. "You will take a message for me. Tell him I wish to keep my past private."

Baker scrunched up his face, staring at the ground between them, and Morrigan knew this meeting was not going as he thought it would.

"Then pay the hundred pounds, miss," he said hopefully, though it sounded more like a question.

She frowned and shook her head. "I don't have access to that kind of money here in the Highlands. Sir Rupert should know this. And I'm not willing to ask anyone at Dalmigavie Castle for it, since your lies are the very thing I would not care for them to hear."

Baker straightened. He apparently felt he was moving onto more solid ground. "That sounds like a hard place you're finding yourself in."

"Not as hard a place you are in."

"What do you mean, mistress?"

"I want the letter you gave Sir Rupert. My father's letter."

The man stared, knocked off balance again.

"I know you got it from Wemys, and I want it back." Morrigan spat out the words. "This is not about a paltry hundred pounds. Your master needs to tell me exactly what he wants in return."

"I don't know, mistress. This ain't what he said . . . this is too . . ." He shifted his weight from one foot to the other. "Maybe you should talk to him yourself."

"I'll do that." She leaned forward in her saddle. "I'd have talked to him today if he had the bollocks to come himself. And you can tell him that too."

Baker's eyes widened at her words. "He'd never come." He glanced around him at the meadow and the surrounding forest. "It's not safe here."

"Exactly right. And yet he can send you. Look around you. You're on Mackintosh land. Do you know what the laird's men would do to a dog like you? Especially after I tell them Sir Rupert sent you?" She paused, letting her words sink in.

He edged closer to his horse.

"They'd string you up from the castle walls at Dalmigavie. You'd end up as food for their pigs. How does it feel to be expendable?"

"Not good." He was paler than when first she arrived. "But Sir Rupert won't be happy, miss. I had my instructions. I wrote the letter. You were to pay. And then he'd tell me what to do next. Maybe if you come back with me?"

"A helpless maiden like me?" she scoffed. "It'd hardly be safe for me, would it?"

He at least had the decency to shake his head. "Nay, miss."

"He's a villain. You know it. I know it. But we both know that neither you nor I can beat him."

"True, miss."

Morrigan watched him glance nervously at the road again. She guessed Burney wasn't the only one Baker was afraid of. He could already feel the Mackintosh rope around his neck.

"Very well, Baker. This is what I want you to do. Go back to Sir Rupert and give him my regards. Tell him I have no money. At the same time, I want no bad blood between us. And I want my father's letter."

Baker shook his head. "I'm telling you, miss, he won't be happy. Not happy at all. This won't come out well, not for you nor me. Sir Rupert likes to have his plans followed, just as he lays them out."

Morrigan wondered how many entrapment schemes Baker had been involved in over the years. According to Wemys, the man had successfully led a half-dozen unsuspecting reform groups into snares of Sir Rupert's design. He seemed too simple. Perhaps that was his charm, though. That and following Sir Rupert's instructions precisely.

"The world is not a happy place. Is it, Baker?" Morrigan reached in her pocket and took out a letter. She held it out to him. "This will make him feel much better."

His face clouded over with suspicion, and he squirmed. "Is this for me?"

"It's for Sir Rupert. For him only."

Morrigan waited until the lackey mustered enough courage to take the letter from her hand. He retreated quickly.

"What's inside will prove my value and worth. It

conveys to him my willingness to cooperate in exchange for my father's note. Trust me, he'll be satisfied."

Morrigan didn't wait for a response. She turned her horse and started back to Dalmigavie.

In her letter to Burney, she was providing him with valuable information—the location in Maggot Green of a warehouse containing a stockpile of weapons that disappeared from a British shipment about a year ago.

As Cinaed and Niall always reminded her, sometimes you had to lose a small battle to win the war.

CHAPTER 27
AIDAN

A letter from Morrigan had been waiting for him when he returned to Edinburgh from London. Her tone had been cordial. She'd found a well-read volume in the library that he needed to read, study, and commit to memory on his return to Dalmigavie. The title was *The Fault Was All His Own. In A Series Of Letters. By A Lady.* In her postscript she stated her absolute faith in Sebastian's recuperative abilities.

Winter had the Highlands firmly in its grip when Aidan and Sebastian returned to Dalmigavie. As the two men approached the castle the day before Hogmanay, a heavy snow blanketed the village. Regardless of the weather, Aidan's heart warmed at the thought that Morrigan was safe here within these walls.

Before coming to the mountains above Inverness, he and his brother had stopped at Carrie House for Christmas. For the first time since the war, Aidan had found himself looking out at his estate not as a reminder of the loved ones he'd lost. Instead, he'd conjured a future. A home where he and his wife could spend some time between his duties in the courtroom and possibly in Parliament.

Still, as he gazed across the snow-covered fields and moors, he couldn't wait to show Carrie House to Morrigan. Perhaps in the spring, when the fields were green with barley and the meadows were spattered with the purple of the thrift flower and the white blossoms of the whitlow grass. And everywhere, the air would be filled with the fragrance of the gorse.

Dismounting at the keep, he told himself he needed to meet with Cinaed before he saw Morrigan.

Cinaed and Niall and Searc and the laird gathered to greet him in the laird's study. Lachlan did not look well. He was growing frailer. Even with a cane, he could barely walk without assistance, and a profound weariness was evident in his drawn features. But regardless of his physical decline, his mind appeared to be as sharp as ever.

Aidan briefly explained the queen's request and the arrangements he'd made with the Duke of Clarence.

"He's the blasted nephew of Butcher Cumberland," the laird reminded everyone.

"But the least detestable one," Searc put in. "The man favors Scotland. And his mistress of twenty years was Irish. He sired ten children with the lass. He can't be all bad."

"He'll be king before he's done," Niall told them. "Everyone knows it. The War Department and the Admiralty respect him. More than a year ago, before the old king died, I heard that the Archbishop of Canterbury had declared openly that Clarence is the fittest to rule of them all."

Aidan concurred. "The king hasn't had his formal coronation yet, but Brougham says even his supporters in

Parliament are tired of his self-absorbed dramatics and his bullying."

The trial that Henry Brougham won on behalf of the queen was barely over before the king was demanding that his camp find another way to divorce her. But the latest word was that his advisors told him as clearly as possible that any further action would surely involve details about the king's own adulterous relationships becoming known to the public. The future of the monarchy itself would be jeopardized at a time when the nation had other, more pressing matters to attend to.

"But Clarence isn't next in line," the laird said. "There's that other one. The Duke of York."

"York's interests are limited to the enjoyment of London's high life," Aidan replied. "He can't see beyond food, drink, cards, and racehorses. And his health is failing. He was carried out of his box at Ascot last year. They said it was the heat, but the word is that the duke suffered a mild apoplectic stroke. At White's, there are wagers being placed right now that York won't live long enough to be king."

"So that leaves the Duke of Clarence," Lachlan said.

Aidan turned to Cinaed. His opinion was the only one that really mattered. "What do you think about meeting with the duke?"

"I heard he went to sea as a lad. We have that in common, anyway."

Although Aidan doubted Cinaed's experience was as pampered as the duke's, he kept his thoughts to himself.

"What do you think you can accomplish with this meeting?" the laird asked.

"If he's to be king, as my mother believes," Cinaed answered, "then we'll have the ear of someone who could support reform. Someone who could help Scotland gain a greater voice in the government."

Searc had been pacing the room throughout the discussion, and he stopped abruptly. "But what does he want in return?"

All eyes fixed on Aidan. "He wants to hear Cinaed say that he's not interested in sitting on Britain's throne." Those weren't exactly the duke's words, but the meaning was close enough. "I think he wants to judge for himself if the son of Scotland is a threat to his future."

Everyone here knew the answer. Cinaed had made it clear. He had no desire to be king.

"We need to show our faces to him. As Scots. As Highlanders," Cinaed said with conviction. "He needs to see more than the handful of landowners he might have raised a glass with in London. What could they tell him about the people going hungry in the Maggot?"

Everyone agreed.

"When was the last time an English king came to Scotland?" Lachlan asked.

"He's not king yet," Niall reminded them.

"He's close enough to the throne," Searc put in. "In two hundred years, none of them have come. And this one is coming to the Highlands. We're not sending you to him."

Aidan told them all the details of his meeting. He and Brougham had met the duke in the new west wing of Kew Palace.

"For obvious reasons, the king will never know about this meeting with you. The duke is supposedly coming to Inverness to look into the construction delays of the Caledonian Canal."

Everyone in the room began to speak at once. They all had an opinion on the disastrous project. It had initially been intended as an inland waterway to protect English shipping from the threat of French warships. Cutting at an angle from the western to the eastern seas, the canal ran through the Great Glen from Fort William to Inverness.

Aidan knew part of the push to build the canal had come from the Royal Navy, which gave the duke, as Admiral of the Fleet, a good reason for coming to Inverness.

"A seven-year project," Lachlan huffed.

"We're ten years past that already," Aidan added. "And close to eight hundred thousand pounds."

"In no small part due to a certain member of this clan," Cinaed said, gesturing toward Searc.

"It's true. I admit I might have had a hand in slowing things down a wee bit," he said, looking like he'd just swallowed the canary. "But I wasn't about to help the bloody English with their war effort, was I? And a man can't be faulted for making a few pounds where he can."

Aidan had heard the canal would be obsolete before it was finished. At fourteen feet deep, it was too shallow for many of the new ships being built.

"Who knows that the duke is coming?" Searc asked, obviously in favor of putting an end to the talk of the canal.

"I should think the military command at Fort George and Fort William will be notified," Niall suggested, drawing a nod from Cinaed.

"Then our friend Sir Rupert will know as well?"

Aidan turned to see a glint of mischief in Searc's eyes, and he wondered if there might be some other plot in the works that he hadn't yet been told about.

CHAPTER 28
MORRIGAN

With the severe cold, heavy snow, and ice limiting their time out of doors, Fiona's daughters needed to be kept busy, and Morrigan was glad to oblige. She, too, needed activity to distract her. Aidan was back, but she had yet to see him. The men had been sequestered in the laird's study all afternoon. She was excited and anxious, happy and nervous. She wanted to run with the children one moment, but considered locking herself in her room the next.

The large drawing room on the floor above the Great Hall provided a comfortable gathering place for the women, especially during inclement weather. An hour ago, snow had again begun to fall. Isabella was ensconced by the fire with a medical journal that Searc had brought her from Inverness. Auld Jean nodded in a chair opposite her, her mending on her lap. Maisie and Fiona had their heads together at a table in an alcove and appeared to be making plans to storm Westminster. The large fire in the hearth warmed the room nicely, and Morrigan and the children were at the far end, where they could play and carry on.

Three other youngsters from the household had joined Catriona and Briana. The current game they were playing was What's the Time, Mr. Wolf. In this case it was *Miss* Wolf, and Morrigan was playing the lead role.

She stood with her face to the wall while her playmates squabbled and tried to line up some safe distance behind her. All day, she kept thinking about the night of Samhain and Aidan's hints about choosing games and having a wife and children. Unfortunately, the warm glow of the memory was continually torn away and replaced by the chill, intrusive reality of her present situation.

After her meeting with Baker, Sir Rupert Burney had written her back. Of course, the letter came unsigned, but Morrigan knew the identity of the sender. He made no effort to disguise the contents. If the letter fell into the hands of the Mackintosh leaders, that was clearly Morrigan's issue to deal with. In the missive, he told her he was pleased with the information she'd provided. The warehouse had been raided, and the stolen weapons secured. No one had been at the location, and no proof established a tie with the Mackintoshes of Dalmigavie or with the son of Scotland. Sir Rupert warned that she needed to do better the next time, and she was to reply to K. Baker at the post office on Church Street. There was no mention of her father's letter or a face-to-face meeting.

"What's the time, Miss Wolf?"

The children's shout cut into her troubled thoughts, and Morrigan forced her attention on their game. "Two o'clock."

The youngsters counted their steps loudly and together, then the question came again.

"Five o'clock, my wee lambs," she called out.

There were some giggles. Five steps were counted out.

"What's the time, Miss Wolf?"

"Three o'clock, my sweet, fat piglets."

The laughter became louder. Morrigan heard women at the other end of the room chanting the steps too.

"What's the time, Miss Wolf?" all the players yelled out.

"It's dinnertime," she shouted.

The children shrieked and raced for the starting line.

Morrigan turned and lunged toward the players. She had to tag one person to make them the wolf, and she now knew why the adults were laughing. Aidan was standing right in front of her. He'd quietly come in and joined the game. His long legs had brought him closest, and he wasn't making any effort to escape her. She fell against him, and they both tumbled to the floor.

Aidan caught her by the waist, and she ended up sprawled on top of him. Her hair blanketed his face. Her breasts pressed against his chest. His arm remained around her, holding her. She longed for him.

Morrigan swept her hair back and tried to raise herself off him, but the devil held her tight. Their faces were so close. She stared into his grey eyes. It was far too easy to be lost in their magic. She wanted to press her lips against his. But they had an audience. The sound of laughter rang around them.

His hands fell away, and she was free to go.

"I apologize."

"I'm the one who needs to apologize."

"It was my fault."

"Hardly. The fault was mine completely."

Her knee pressed into his groin when she tried to raise her body, drawing a grunt. His hand grabbed her breast as he tried to help her. They kept trying to extricate themselves, but their hands were everywhere, the touches inadvertently inappropriate. By the time Morrigan and Aidan finally got to their feet, the children were jumping around them, and the adult onlookers were in hysterics.

Morrigan was mortified, but Aidan retained his good humor. He was already exchanging pleasantries with Isabella as if nothing out of the ordinary had occurred.

"We have a *Mr.* Wolf now," Catriona yelled excitedly, ready to play again.

Fiona took each of her children by the hand. "We promised Mr. Gordon a visit, didn't we?" She didn't wait for their answer and dragged them out of the room.

Isabella suddenly needed to see a patient who, oddly enough, was coming to the castle in the middle of the snowstorm. Maisie herded the other children toward the door, saying she could hear their parents calling. Auld Jean took one long, wistful look at the comfortable fire and shuffled toward them. She stared at Morrigan, then at Aidan, then back to Morrigan.

"That mutton's been simmering in the pot long enough. I'd say the meat's cooked." With a shake of her head, she made her way out of the drawing room, leaving the door slightly ajar.

Morrigan stared after her. Everyone was gone.

"I never realized I had this effect on people," Aidan said.

They were standing so close, their shoulders touched. A minute ago, she would have kissed him if they didn't have an audience. Now, she didn't trust herself being left alone with him.

"We should . . . I should go help Isabella."

She started to walk away, but he caught her arm and turned her around. This time, he didn't ask permission. He didn't wait for her to kiss him first. Aidan pulled her into his arms and lowered his lips to hers.

Morrigan couldn't remember why she'd wanted to run away. Her hands clutched at his back as the pressure of his mouth increased.

The give and take of their mouths continued. They were both starved for each other.

"I've missed you," he whispered. "Missed you every day."

She wanted to say the same thing back to him. She wanted to tell him how hard it had been. He was always with her, constantly in her thoughts.

His lips descended again, and their kiss deepened. His tongue explored her mouth, and Morrigan felt his hand slide down her back and encircle her waist. He pulled her even tighter against his solid body. She felt nothing but the incredible heat that seemed to possess them both. *Almost* nothing. His trousers did little to hide the hardening evidence of his arousal. But Morrigan wasn't afraid. She wanted him.

Suddenly, she was frantic to satisfy the hunger. Her hands moved inside his coat and felt the powerful muscles of his back. It was miraculous, the way her body felt, softening and molding itself to the hard contours of his.

The sound of footsteps and a dull clatter of metal could be heard approaching in the hallway. Clarity returned instantly and with it, sanity. The two of them jumped apart. She was breathless. He straightened his trousers and moved to the window, shoving it open to the chill wind and a flurry of snow.

A servant came in carrying a bucket with her tools. She was surprised to find anyone left in the room. "I'm so sorry, mistress. I was going to see to the fire."

"I'll take care of it," Morrigan said hurriedly, crossing over to the hearth. Not that she needed to feel any warmer.

The young woman curtsied and left, and Aidan closed the window before coming to her side. He took the pokers out of her hand.

"Allow me."

She stepped back and watched him. His hair was longer than the last time she'd seen him. Every time they were together, he grew more handsome, more confident in everything he did.

He put the tools away and stood up. The way his gaze moved over her, Morrigan wondered if he was going to take her into his arms and kiss her again.

She glanced meaningfully to the door that was now wide open.

"I had intended to get back here for Christmas, but Sebastian and I ended up spending it at Carrie House."

"Your brother is well?" she asked, recalling his letters.

"Resurrected like Lazarus from the cave. Unfortunately."

"The day was a quiet affair at Dalmigavie." She sat on a chair a safe distance away from him. "I understand the Highlanders make up for it on Hogmanay."

"Indeed. That promises to be a festive event."

He approached and moved a chair close to her. Too near and too tempting, she thought. If she leaned toward him even a little, their lips could touch.

"May I escort you during the promenade?"

She'd heard about the torchlit parade through the castle and the village on the eve of the new year. It was a coming together of the entire community, complete with pipers and fiddles, dancing and singing.

"You may. But I have to warn you, I'm a terrible singer."

"Not a singer? That surprises me." He cleared his voice. "Well, I'll try to make up for you."

She laughed. "You think yourself a fine singer?"

He nodded with fake humility and then smiled. "To be honest, what I lack in talent, I make up for with confidence."

A good reminder. The conversation she had with Fiona and Maisie came back to her. Talent. Did she have any at all? And what would a good dose of confidence add?

"Making a good show of it is half the battle in everything, is it not?" he continued. "Literature. The arts. Argument. Courtship."

Courtship? Is that what was happening? Morrigan watched him as he reached into his coat.

"I brought you a gift."

She touched the handle of her sgian dubh at her ankle, teasing him. "It's not my dagger or my shoes, so it must be that you brought me another flyer from Inverness. Or is it the book you promised?"

"The book can wait. This is a proper gift."

She stared at the small pouch made of green velvet in his hand. A red ribbon was tied neatly around it.

"Open it." He placed it in her hand.

Morrigan felt her cheeks catch fire. With unsteady fingers she untied the ribbon and emptied it into her hand. The most beautiful necklace lay in her palm. A gold chain with a pendant that was fashioned like a miniature sword. The hilt was decorated with a turquoise stone.

"Oh my! It's . . . it's stunning." She was too flustered to say anything more. No one had ever given her a gift so elegant and meaningful. "A dagger. So appropriate."

She started to put it around her neck.

"May I?"

Morrigan nodded, and he rose to his feet. He moved behind her and took the necklace. She held her hair to the side, and a thrill raced through her as his fingers brushed against her neck. He fastened the chain and sat in his chair again, eyeing her appreciatively.

"Beautiful."

She touched the treasure and looked into his eyes. She loved him. How she loved him. The words wanted to spill out into the open, but she couldn't allow it. Meeting Aidan Grant was the most wonderful thing that had ever happened to her, but she wouldn't ruin his future. She would not allow her feelings to take her to a place where hope led only to heartache.

Morrigan tried to think of something lighthearted to say. "If I knew we were exchanging gifts, I could have done some embroidery or drawn a portrait or written a poem in praise of your virtues. None of which I have any talent in, but I would have done them with *confidence*. And besides, it's the gesture that matters. True?"

He smiled. "I promise to give you the opportunity of doing all those things for me and more."

Morrigan watched him reach into his coat again, and this time he withdrew a small box. Her heart began to beat so fast that she feared it might burst out of her chest and fly away like a bird.

"Dear Miss Drummond, I thought only of you while I was gone." He moved to the edge of the chair and dropped to one knee. "I'm hoping that you would do me the honor of becoming my wife."

For a moment, Morrigan sat in stunned silence. She couldn't breathe. But the past snaked through the air like a whip and lashed at her. She tore her hand out of his grasp and jumped to her feet, edging away from him.

"I can't." Tears splashed down her cheeks. "I am sorry, Mr. Grant. I'm truly sorry, but I *can't* be your wife."

Morrigan turned and ran for the door.

"Wait. You can't? That's all?" he called after her. "Nothing more to say?"

Her steps faltered. She leaned a hand against the doorjamb for support. She couldn't look back.

"Don't I deserve to know why? Can't you at least tell me what I've done wrong? Is it someone else? Why would you acknowledge our affection, return the passion I feel for you, but deny us any future?"

She knew she should walk away, but he would come after her. Aidan was a man who was accustomed to getting answers. And what did it matter, anyway? Her past was no longer a secret when people as vile as Sir Rupert were weaving their own twisted tales about it. Wasn't it better if he heard the truth from her instead of the lies that would no doubt spread?

She took out a handkerchief and stabbed at her tears before slowly turning around.

Aidan stood watching her with the expression of a tormented man. She took a few steps into the room but held her hand up, motioning him to stop as he started to approach. She had to speak quickly, before she lost her courage.

"Wemys is dead."

His brow creased as he tried to understand what she was saying. "I know. I heard the news when I arrived. You are not upset about it, are you?"

"The first day we met in Inverness, you were correct. I intended to kill him."

"I suspected as much. But you never felt you could explain. And whatever your reason was for going after him, I have absolute faith that it was a good one. I trust you, Morrigan."

Her reason, she thought. She had reason. Shame. Guilt. Mortification. Morrigan had accepted that her father's approach was the only path. Walk away and forget. She'd never been able to do that. And when it came to Aidan, there was the fear that this man standing before her would think less of her. Her throat felt raw, constricted, but she pushed the words out while she still could.

"Wemys was my uncle. When I was twelve years of age, he . . . he raped me."

"Morrigan." The whisper of her name emerged as a painful sigh. He tried to come to her, but she held her hand up again, pleading with him to stay where he was. The line between the courage to speak and the cowardly urge to run away was thin. She had to say the words. The truth had to be laid bare between them.

She told Aidan everything—from her father's reaction to moving away to Wurzburg to that October day in Inverness when she saw Wemys again.

Aidan listened. When she was finished, he ran a hand through his hair.

"I'm sorry, my love. It breaks my heart to hear what happened to you. You . . . you had every right to go after him. To punish him for what he's done. Your courage . . . who you are, who you've become . . ."

He was pale, looking like a man who'd been run through with a sword. His voice shook and the words struggled to break free.

"And I am the greatest villain of all. I brought your worst nightmare back into your life. I delivered him here, where you were tormented day and night. I forced you to speak to him when he didn't deserve to be spat on."

"You didn't know."

Morrigan saw the anger building in the tension of his shoulders, the hard expression in his eyes.

"I wish he were still alive so I could strangle that blackguard with my own hands. I would have hung his worthless carcass—"

"Stop, Aidan. That would not have helped anything. No

one could take away my pain except me. No one could cool the rage I carried inside. No one could *fix* this for me. My father thought he could, but he was wrong. What We- mys did, he did to *me*. Only I could fix it. The battle was mine to fight." Morrigan spoke more calmly than before. "Isabella once told me that healing is a journey. Time is needed. And patience. And luck. The way it ended, watch- ing Wemys die, was part of my journey. I could not have healed any other way."

She started to leave, but he called after her again.

"I love you, Morrigan. The past means nothing to me."

One last time, she faced him.

"But it means everything to me." Her past controlled the present, and it controlled the future for both of them. No argument Aidan could devise would ever change that. "Sir Rupert knows."

Morrigan told him about the letters, about the lies that would be twisted to destroy her and Aidan both. He stood in stunned silence as she went out, shutting the door behind her. It was over. She could never marry him.

CHAPTER 29
AIDAN

Not everything a person did in life fell within their control.

Fighting in the war against the French wasn't Aidan's choice. It was his duty, particularly since his father and brothers were going. He'd pursued a career in law because of the encouragement and support of his family. The clients he chose to represent, however—those who were oppressed, who would never be able to pay for his services, who were targeted by the government—that was something he could control. It was a choice. His choice.

Somewhere along the way, Aidan had found a match between his ability and his passion. He knew what he could do, what he was good at. He could see a future for himself. He knew how he could be a valued member of society.

Politics, however, was a distraction that he'd gladly do without. To stand for election wasn't a need but more of an obligation. Serving as a member of Parliament was a position someone else could fill. There were a dozen persons more qualified than he was. He'd happily forego his place in Cinaed's plans if that was what kept Morrigan from accepting him. He'd give up everything and start anew, so long as she was beside him.

After she left him in the drawing room, he'd spent a great deal of time thinking about what she said. Guilt weighed heavily on him, for the truth had been looking him in the face all along. He'd never pursued the reason for Morrigan reacting in such a way to her uncle. At the same time, he accepted her belief that she had to deal with Wemys in her own way. It was her fight.

Aidan loved her because of who she was, inside and outside. Her will, her strength of character, saw her through this trial. Now he had to convince her that the strength of their combined will, their love for each other, would destroy any threat from the likes of Sir Rupert Burney. If they were divided, then they gave up that control over their lives. Then Burney would win. Aidan was not about to let the scoundrel dictate their future.

He loved her. He had no doubt that she cared for him as well. More than cared for him. He saw it in her face, heard it in the note of anguish in her words.

Tonight, he would find her and finish their discussion.

The celebration of Hogmanay was well underway. The Great Hall was brimming with the Mackintosh clan and their invited guests. The laird had been brought down, but he was pale and weak. Acting for him, Cinaed and Isabella hosted the festivities. Still, Lachlan had been keen to introduce Aidan to a number of landowners who came to dine with the laird and the son of Scotland.

Morrigan was nowhere to be found. He'd searched the hall, looking to see if she was sitting with Maisie and Niall. Nothing. And she wasn't with Fiona and her daughters, who were sharing a table with Auld Jean and John Gordon. Blair and Sebastian were carousing with a table of Mackintosh fighters, but Morrigan was not with them either. It pained him to think she wouldn't come down and enjoy the company of her family and friends on a night like this.

Aidan had looked for her in the training yard several times today, only to be told she hadn't been there. She wasn't in the drawing room, nor in the library. He'd checked everywhere except her bedchamber. If she was choosing to take refuge there, he wasn't going to intrude on her desire for solitude. Not yet, anyway.

People were settling down for dinner, and workers were carrying food out from the kitchens on great platters. Aidan was expected to join Cinaed and his wife at their table. He'd already been warned that an announcement would be made during the meal about the seat in Parliament, and Aidan was expected to say a few words.

"Has Miss Drummond fallen ill?" he asked Isabella privately.

"No, she's in perfect health."

"Why isn't she coming down to dinner?"

"She's already here."

Aidan was relieved to have a fellow conspirator in Isabella. He looked in the direction that the young physician nodded.

At the table closest to the kitchens, Morrigan sat with some people that he suspected were from the village. Her back was to him. She didn't see him approach.

"May I join you at this table for dinner?" he addressed everyone and not only her.

Good-natured greetings met him. The people of Dalmigavie had come to know him over these past months. He stood behind Morrigan, but he needn't have. Everyone knew where he wanted to sit. Men and woman cheerfully slid down to make room. A moment later, he climbed over the bench and sat beside her.

"Miss Drummond." He smiled at her surprised expression. The prettiest of blushes reddened her cheeks.

She looked over her shoulder. "Mr. Grant, I believe you're expected to dine with Cinaed and Isabella."

"I don't think they'll mind. They know where I am." He waved across the room at Isabella, and she waved back.

"I'm certain there are a number of guests here who were looking forward to spending time with you."

"That may be true, Miss Drummond, but I don't care to spend time with them. Excuse me for a moment." The couple seated beside him wanted to know the present whereabouts of the Chattan brothers. He answered them and turned his attention back to Morrigan.

"You're supposed to give a speech," she murmured. "You can't do it from here."

"I can and I shall, so long as you stand with me."

"I'll do no such thing."

"Then there will be no speech."

"You're being ridiculous, sir," she growled. "I believe I'll change tables. Move."

"Then I'll be forced to follow you. And if you move from there, I'll do it again. And if you decide to leave the hall, then everyone will wonder where we're going, because I'll not be quiet about leaving."

Her eyes sparkled, reflecting the candlelight from the chandeliers above. He was pleased to see that she was wearing the necklace he'd given her yesterday. The blue dress she wore accentuated the color of the gem on the hilt of the sword.

She leaned toward him. Their lips were close, and

Aidan was sorely tempted to kiss her, but he didn't want the entire Mackintosh clan giving him a beating tonight.

"Why are you doing this? Why are you being so difficult?"

"I'm not being difficult. I'm trying to get back to the proposal that you never allowed me to finish in the drawing room yesterday."

"Mr. Grant, we're done with that conversation."

"We're not. I'm certain."

"I explained."

"I didn't have the opportunity to present vital evidence."

"There's nothing more to be said."

"I'd like to repeat what I said to you yesterday. I love you, Miss Drummond. I love you." He said it loud enough that a few heads at their table turned to them.

She took his hand and squeezed it, trying to hush him. Aidan didn't think he'd seen this shade of red in her face before. Her dark eyes had become misty and shone like diamonds. He entwined their fingers under the table.

"I love you. I'm asking you to be my wife," he whispered in her ear. "We can't let him do this to us, Morrigan. We can't let Burney win."

Her chin sank to her chest. Behind them, the laird briefly welcomed everyone to this celebration. Cinaed stood to speak next.

Aidan's attention remained on Morrigan. He studied her profile, the tilt of her chin, her parted lips, the rise and fall of her chest as she steadied her breathing. Her grip on his hand was as strong as his. She wasn't letting him go.

Cheers rang out in the hall. Cinaed called out his name. This was the moment when he was supposed to stand and address the gathering.

He remained seated, calmly ignoring everyone, and Morrigan's gaze flew to his face.

"I don't want it if I can't have you in my life," he said quietly.

"But his threats?"

"I want you to trust me, as I trust you. He'll not defeat us."

Everyone around them was waiting for Aidan to stand. Silence had fallen across the hall.

"I need time to think it all through," she said finally. "Now please, speak to the people. All of us trust you. All of us believe in you."

Aidan didn't let go of her hand as he stood to the cheers of the Highlanders. The case was reopened.

CHAPTER 30
MORRIGAN

Sir Rupert had risen to the bait Morrigan cast last month.

The Mackintosh leaders were determined to beat him at his blackmail scheme. The warehouse of weapons had been the first lure. Next, she sent other information to keep him engaged. A prisoner transfer that needed to be deferred. A ship newly arrived from Hull that was carrying more cargo than had been reported to the exciseman. All the information came directly from Searc.

A weight had been lifted from Morrigan's shoulders, though she was not completely free of it. Still, her new attitude had come about because of Aidan. She hadn't agreed to marry him yet, but he wasn't giving up. Working together with him gave her a feeling she'd never experienced before. She had a true partner, and he was as determined as Morrigan to beat Burney.

During the second week of January, Searc brought back new flyers that had been posted from Inverness.

Maisie and Fiona had become obsessed with gleaning every bit of information they could from the caricatures. And they were quite good at it. Immediately, the three of them decided that the work was new, which was a relief. It meant Madame Laborde was still alive.

After some time spent examining the images, they found two more things of great interest.

Morrigan went in search of Aidan. Since returning to Dalmigavie, he'd again taken to using the small library upstairs from the Great Hall for his daily correspondence. As she passed the drawing room next door, she saw Fiona's children and a few others playing hide-and-seek. She knocked at the library door and entered.

He immediately rose from the writing desk. The way his gaze swept over her in greeting made Morrigan smile.

She waved the flyers at him. "I think we now know where Sir Rupert is hiding Madame Laborde."

She walked to the desk and spread the caricatures out for him to see. In both of them, the artist had included the Old Bridge that crossed the River Ness at the end of High Street. Directly above and behind the center of the bridge, she'd depicted Castle Hill. Just to the left of the bridge, the spire of the Tolbooth rose above the city. Morrigan was certain it was the view from her window.

"She knew we'd be looking closely at these, so she's telling us where she is. Her room is in a building across the river, north of the bridge."

"No doubt, you are correct." He ran a fingertip slowly down the side of her neck. "But you're not thinking of going there to rescue her."

Her stomach twisted deliciously. This was the way it had been between them since Hogmanay. When any chance presented itself, one of them pulled the other into a private space to steal a kiss, to caress, to tempt.

"I made a promise," she murmured. "And I shall go after her, but I'll not go there alone."

He leaned down and let his lips hover a whisper from her mouth. "Good. Because I insist on coming with you."

She glanced toward the door. She'd shut it, unintentionally, when she entered.

"I'm sorry, sir, but you'll have to convince me to take you along."

He took hold of her wrist and drew her closer. Morrigan's gaze slowly moved from his touch to his chest and lingered on his lips before looking into his eyes. He set her body on fire. She wanted him. He teased her but never took full advantage of what she offered. He'd told her straight out. His offer of marriage was part of the deal. There would be no making love until she married him.

"With the weather being what it is, we'll need to take Searc's carriage to Inverness. It'll be a very long ride with the two of us alone in a very confined space."

"It will be cold too."

"We'll need a blanket and each other for warmth."

Something melted deep in her belly, and the heat sank lower. Her breasts ached for his touch. Aidan wrapped an arm around her and brought her body hard against his.

"What do you say to that, Miss Drummond?"

He already knew her answer. Aidan kissed her, and Morrigan threaded her fingers into his hair. Their kiss became deeper, more carnal. His hands slid downward past the small of her back and over her bottom, pressing her tightly against his groin.

"I want you, Aidan."

With one sweep of his hand, he cleared the desk. Books and papers crashed and fluttered to the floor. He lifted her onto the edge.

"Let's go to my bedchamber," she suggested as his teeth raked against her throat.

"Marry me first."

"I am thinking about it. Someday, perhaps. But right now, I need you."

He pushed her knees apart and stepped between her thighs. His arousal pressed against her and she thrilled at the intimacy of it. He took hold of her ankle and raised it until it looped around his waist. He slid his hand upward along her calf and thigh . . . and higher. She bit onto his shoulder as anticipation rose as to what he would do next.

A faint knock at the door threw them both into a panic. She scrambled off the edge of the desk. Aidan picked up a book and strode toward the window, pretending to be reading. Morrigan straightened her skirts. There was no point to telling the intruder to enter; the door opened, and Catriona poked in her head.

"We're playing hide-and-seek. Can I use your curtains?"

Shouts ran out behind her. There was not enough time to hide. She was already discovered. She ran out, leaving the door to the library wide open.

Morrigan bit her lip and made quick work of gathering up everything that had been scattered across the floor.

Aidan joined her, helping. "Well, that was close."

Both of them tried unsuccessfully to hold back their smiles.

She found the etchings. They'd gone under the table during the avalanche. As she picked them up, she remembered the second thing Madame Laborde had hinted at in the drawing.

"Who knows that the Duke of Clarence is coming?" she asked.

"No one. No one outside of the government hierarchy, anyway. They don't want to bring any attention to this trip," he told her. "Once he arrives, I assume there will be some public announcement of it."

She showed him what they'd found in the caricature. Beneath one of the arches of the bridge, two fishermen were hauling in a net, filled with their fish. Mixed in with the catch, cleverly hidden, was a lion, a unicorn, and a crown.

"These wouldn't, by any chance, be on the duke's coat of arms, would they?"

Aidan peered at the image and a smile stole across his face. "I believe they are."

"What if I wrote back to Sir Rupert and told him I've heard here at the castle that the Duke of Clarence is coming to Inverness?"

"Better still, what if you wrote to the rogue and told him the duke is coming and that he's going to meet with the son of Scotland?"

"Why would we tell him so much?"

"Because no one knows it, except the duke and his closest advisors." Aidan paced the room a few times.

She could already tell he was plotting. "Tell me."

"Entrapment. That's the game Burney is famous for—tricking people into trusting someone they shouldn't, and then getting them to do the exact thing he can use against them."

"Are you planning to turn that ruse on the fox himself?" she asked.

Aidan nodded, closed the door, and told her what he was thinking.

Chapter 31
Morrigan

They now knew why no one had been able to locate Madame Laborde after Sir Rupert took her away in his carriage from Barn Hill. He didn't put the artist in a tavern or in some cramped room at an inn. He moved her into his own residence.

Once Morrigan discovered the approximate location, Searc's people were able to find the house Sir Rupert had taken on Huntly Street, a cobblestone lane that ran along the river. Searc knew the house. It had belonged to a successful old smuggler he'd done business with years ago.

Looking out the front windows of the grey stone building, one would see the exact alignment of the Old Bridge and Castle Hill, just as she'd drawn them in her sketches. Searc's people were also able to discern that no one went in or out of the house without Burney's approval. A burly footman turned away all callers whenever a passing vendor happened to go knocking. Only the occasional glimpse of Madame Laborde at an upstairs window confirmed she was there.

While they'd tried to find a way to meet with the artist,

Morrigan sent a letter to Burney containing the information they'd decided on.

*The duke is coming to Inverness. He plans to meet with
the son of Scotland.*

A letter had immediately come back to Dalmigavie addressed to Morrigan.

Where? When?

Morrigan responded with her own demand.

Give back my father's letter.

That left them at a standoff. Morrigan imagined that,
despite her handful of good deeds, she wasn't trusted. The
man had to know she would never betray Isabella and her
husband. All of this worked perfectly into their plans.

When Morrigan, Aidan, and Sebastian left Dalmigavie
with a contingent of men to accompany the carriage, a
white blanket of snow still covered the ground. Before
they even reached Inverness, however, she was surprised
to find the countryside was frozen but free of snow.

Their plan was simple. The back of Sir Rupert Burney's
residence opened out onto a lane that ran parallel with the
river. On the far side lay a large field that Searc referred to
as Fairfield Park. They'd discovered that Madame Laborde
left the house nearly every day in the midafternoon and
walked briskly around the park. They would approach
her there.

They waited for her at the edge of the park when she
emerged for her daily jaunt. As she passed the carriage,
Morrigan stepped out and approached her.

The artist was immediately alarmed. "I can't speak to
you. They watch me. One of his men always follows when
I go for my walks."

Morrigan already knew that. Sebastian was overseeing
a diversion that coincided with Madame Laborde going
out.

"We know." She motioned to the waiting carriage. "Come with me."

The artist looked back at the house. "I can't. My money, my jewels. It's all I have. I can't leave it behind."

"Just talk to us. Here. We can arrange for a time to free you when you have your belongings."

"We?"

"Mr. Grant and I."

"The barrister. I know of him." Whatever doubts Madam Laborde had, they seemed to disappear. With another glance back at the house, she followed Morrigan to the carriage.

Introductions were brief as they climbed in, and Aidan ordered the driver to walk on.

"I can't go far," Madame Laborde told him.

"I know this neighborhood." He called up to the driver, "Go as far as Wells Foundry and turn around. And take your time."

"I knew you'd find me." The artist turned to Morrigan. "I was certain you'd come."

"What happened that day at Barn Hill?" she asked.

"I told him everything, but I had to in order to save myself. Your name, why you were there, your offer to help me. What I left out was that it was at my urging that you ran." The gloved hand twisted the tassel of her reticule. "He ordered me to go with him immediately, that I was in danger. I had no choice but to go."

Morrigan had little doubt the relationship between Sir Rupert and Madame Laborde extended beyond her artwork. Aside from being closely guarded, she showed no signs of physical abuse. With the hat and gloves and heavy coat that she wore, of course, it was difficult to know for certain.

She had learned from Wemys that Sir Rupert Burney

was a widower. He didn't know what caused the death of his wife, but Burney was not averse to occasional acts of violence, despite his calm demeanor in public. Wemys said the man took a particular pleasure in interrogating the poor souls who found themselves in his clutches. In the surgery on Infirmary Street, Morrigan had tended to the wounds of his tortured victims.

Her mind flickered to Fiona. She'd been a prisoner of his. But Niall's sister still refused to speak of what happened to her during those long months. Morrigan hoped nothing evil had befallen her. Perhaps fear of the lieutenant had been enough to keep her safe.

"You have an arrangement with Sir Rupert that appears to suit you. Why do you want to leave?" Aidan's question was direct. The kind, amiable gentleman had disappeared, leaving the serious man of law in their company.

"I have no illusions. What I have now is not permanent. As I told you before, it is a matter of survival."

"Why not wait six months, a year? Certainly, what you're being paid for your artwork should allow you to return to France a rich woman."

"Ah, but what if I don't live so long?" She pulled at the collar of her coat, burrowing deeper into its warmth. "The day I met Miss Drummond, I had no choice but to go with him. Since I arrived at this house, however, I've been in his power. I am no better than a prisoner here. I'm told what to do, what to draw, who to entertain, when to smile . . . and . . ."

She stopped and stared out the window. No one had to guess at her other duties.

"We can help you get out," Morrigan told her. "The offer I made before still stands."

"But you don't understand. Sir Rupert is cunning. He

has his ways. He'll find me. I know so much more about him now than I did when I was at Barn Hill. I've heard things. He is dangerous. And he is driven by revenge." Her eyes moved from Morrigan to Aidan and back. "I want to leave, but I am also fearful he'll find me. And when he does, he'll kill me."

"Not if you destroy him first," Aidan suggested.

"That's impossible. He's too strong. Too shrewd. What can I do?"

"To some extent, at least, he trusts you. You can use that. As you say, you've heard things."

Morrigan took her hand. "You already know that the Duke of Clarence is coming to Inverness. You gave us the clues in your caricature."

Madame Laborde's look showed her approval. "I knew you'd discover the clue."

"What is Sir Rupert's reaction to this visit?"

"He is furious about it. He offered to provide for the duke's security, but he was flatly refused. He feels slighted, snubbed. This is the most important visit to Scotland by a member of the royal family in a hundred years, and the director of Home Office operations in the Highlands has been excluded entirely."

No doubt Morrigan had added fuel to the fire when she informed him the duke was meeting with the son of Scotland.

"What if you were to help us, without jeopardizing your situation as it is?" Aidan suggested. "What if we worked together to eliminate Sir Rupert?"

"Eliminate?"

"With your help, we shall expose him to the wrath of his own masters. We shall make him look like a traitor. He will suffer the consequences, and you will be amply rewarded."

"And free," Morrigan added.

Madame Laborde's gaze shifted from her to Aidan, where it lingered adoringly. She didn't blame the woman. She felt exactly the same way when he had explained his plans to her at Dalmagavie. She felt that way when they *weren't* making any plans.

"Is it possible?"

"Absolutely. He has already fallen out of favor with Lord Sidmouth. He failed to stop a meeting from taking place between Queen Caroline and the son of Scotland. Their confidence in him is nearly gone. He's teetering on the edge of an abyss. With your help, we can give him that final push."

Madame Laborde sat forward in her seat, her eyes flashing with excitement. "What can I do?"

"Two things, to start." Aidan glanced out the window. They were turning around. "You must pass on to him, in a very casual way, a rumor that you learned from one of the servants. The cook perhaps. Or your maid. Something they heard on market day."

"I decide on the menu. I speak to the cook every day. What shall I tell Sir Rupert?"

"Tell him there's a dinner and reception being given at the home of a Captain Kenedy," he told her. "The captain has a fine house down river, not far from here. Sir Rupert knows him. The dinner will be taking place next month, on the second Friday of February. Mention that the party is being touted as *the* event of the winter, so grand that one might think the king himself is attending."

"The second Friday." She thought about it. "But that coincides with the Duke of Clarence's visit."

Morrigan exchanged a look with Aidan. "Exactly."

"Is the duke to attend?"

"One would assume so."

"I know that Sir Rupert Burney has not been invited. And he won't be. He is never asked to attend such receptions."

"The Mackintoshes, however, will be attending."

"The son of Scotland, as well?" she asked.

"Perhaps," Aidan suggested.

"Oh, that will destroy him. He'll be so angry." She cringed. "He's so preoccupied with arresting and prosecuting Cinaed Mackintosh. If Sir Rupert thinks that deals are being made behind his back, he'll lose his mind."

"That is when we hoist him on his own petard."

Madame Laborde smiled with satisfaction at the thought. "That would be lovely, Mr. Grant."

"Tell me, madame, how good an actress are you?"

"Proficient." She gave a casual shrug and looked at Morrigan. "I was able to let you walk away unharmed, and I'm still alive. That says something."

"Do you have any influence with Sir Rupert?" Aidan asked.

She colored. "To some extent."

"Does he listen to suggestions you might make? Your ideas?"

"He thinks I am very clever. He enjoys my caricatures immensely."

Aidan leaned forward, his voice a soft caress. "Could a casual suggestion be made about how horrible, how unnatural it would be if the duke were attacked while he was visiting Inverness?"

He paused, letting his words sink in with their new ally.

"Perhaps while he was dining at an event like the one at Captain Kenedy's house," he continued.

She brought a hand to her chest in shock. "Highlanders attacking the brother of the king? It would mean war."

"Precisely."

Madame Laborde looked at them in silence as she pondered this. Finally, a smile pulled at her lips. "I understand. If Sir Rupert were to thwart such an audacious *plot*, he would emerge as the hero. He would *save* the duke and seize Cinaed Mackintosh in one fell swoop."

"Can you do it?" Morrigan asked.

"I can play this part." The artist pursed her lips. "But I have one condition. I must be taken from here the night of Captain Kenedy's reception."

CHAPTER 32
AIDAN

"*El amor y la guerra son una misma cosa,*" Aidan said to Morrigan as she stormed into the library. He rose from his chair by the desk as she came across the room.

"What did you just say to me?"

She was an open book to him. He knew all her moods now. He knew the difference between the blush in her face when she was angry and the blush when he kissed her or whispered all the things that he'd do to her once they were married.

Right now, she was definitely angry.

He read the passage from the book he held open in his hand. "'Love and war are all one. As in war it is lawful to use sleights and stratagems to overcome the enemy, so in amorous strifes and competencies, impostures and juggling tricks are held for good to attain the desired end.'"

"I just spoke with Isabella," she told him. "You can't do this."

"Thomas Shelton's translation of Cervantes's *Don Quixote.*" He closed the volume and offered it to her. "It is a wonderful tale. Life changing. You should read it."

"I've read it." Morrigan took the book from him and put it down on the desk. None too gently. "She told me that Charles Forbes has decided to give up his seat in Parliament earlier than planned. The election will take place in early spring."

"I heard the same thing." He picked up the book. "Did you know Cervantes is Sebastian's favorite author? I think it has to do with both of them losing an arm in battle, though I believe the author only lost the use of his left arm, 'for the greater glory of his right,' or something."

Morrigan was not to be deterred. "But you went to Cinaed this morning and withdrew your name as a candidate."

"It's true, *mi amor*. What else can a man do when the woman he loves refuses him?" He laid the book gently on the desk, touching the leather binding. "I've decided that my brother and I shall give up the law and travel the world. I shall be the noble knight-errant, Don Quixote, and he'll be my Sancho Panza, though I think he might be too tall."

She placed herself between him and the desk. "I never refused you. We talked about this."

"We never settled anything."

"I need to get my father's letter back first."

"We'll keep trying. But what happens if we can't retrieve it? And none of Sir Rupert's threats are about the letter. He is weaving his own tales."

Morrigan paled. "I know."

"Think of everything that is being circulated about Cinaed. Is any of it the truth? Is there any document that justifies all the lies? None. If their plan is to ruin me because I've been fortunate to make them look like fools in court, they'll come up with all kinds of falsehoods about me, anyway."

She hugged her arms around her middle. "I refuse to give them a scandal they can use to ruin you."

"Nothing they know about you can ruin me. And we're talking about Parliament. Public life," he reminded her. "To pursue that as a career, we have to be numb to the gossip. We can't run away and hide. Instead, we have to show them we're not afraid of whatever obstacles they hurl our way."

"So you *are* standing for the election," she said, sounding relieved.

"Not without you at my side."

"We'll talk about this later."

"I'll not be put off again. We are *not* talking about it later." He caught her elbow before she moved away from him. "I want an answer now."

"Aidan," she said softly, trying to pull away.

"My Dulcinea." He placed his hands on her shoulders and looked into her eyes. "Do you love me?"

"I love you. I love you. Of course I love you. I've told you that many times."

He kissed her and was once again taken by how passionately she responded. They stayed in each other's arms for too short a time, however. The door to the library was open and anyone could walk in on them.

"What really worries you, my love?"

She held his gaze. "I'm too passionate, too opinionated, too volatile. Aren't you afraid that I might put my dagger into the heart of anyone who doesn't show you the proper respect?"

"I'm counting on it." He kissed her nose and placed kisses on each of her cheeks. "What do you think Sebastian's calling has been?"

"I don't want to take his job."

"Have no fear about that. We could be going to London,

which is a far more dangerous place than Edinburgh or Inverness. I need you both in my life."

She was still uncertain. He could tell. "Talk to me. Tell me what I can do to put your mind at ease."

"It's not you," she exploded. "*I'm* the problem. Ever since you asked me to marry you, I have no difficulty imagining myself meeting you on the kirk steps. It's what comes afterward that fills me with doubts. I wasn't raised in a traditional household. We had no women coming to call; there were no return visits. No darning or embroidery or lacemaking. No arranging of dinner parties. What do I know about being a wife to a person of importance? What do I know about being a wife, at all?"

"What do I know about being a husband?"

"Exactly. All the more reason for us to wait."

He smiled. "I hand you an imaginary sword and there sits a pell." He gestured to a chair. "What do you do with it?"

"Right now?"

"Right now."

"I hammer it to pieces. Cut and slash it into kindling."

"Imagine this as a metaphor for our marriage."

Her eyes widened.

"When you're upset, when you need to release your frustration, you can use me like that chair. I'll be your trusted old pell."

She shook her head, a smile tugging at her lips. "A marriage based on the training yard. You've lost your mind."

"A marriage that says we will work hard on everything and solve our problems together. A marriage that begins and continues with the promise that we'll grow together and learn to complete each other." Aidan cupped her face and looked into her beautiful dark eyes. "I love you, and you love me. I respect you, and you respect me. I want to spend the rest of my days with you, and I know you want the same. It's foolish to let the lack of knowing a few parlor games get in the way of a lifetime of love. I would marry you today if you would say yes."

Her arms slipped around him. She pressed her face against his chest and held him. "I swear to you, if I could do it now, at this very moment, I would marry you. But I can make no guarantee about tomorrow. My cold feet could return by then."

He took her by the hand. "Come with me."

Aidan paid no attention to her questions or complaints. He took her out of the library and past the drawing room and down the stairs. They stopped by the laird's study.

She looked hopefully at him. "You're going to tell Cinaed that you've reconsidered your decision?"

"Marry me, Morrigan. Tell me now that you'll marry me."

"I just told you I would . . . if it were today. But I can't speak for tomorrow."

"Some decisions are irrevocable, my love." He drew her to the chapel door.

"What are you doing?"

"Will you marry me, Miss Drummond?" he asked, pulling the door open.

All of them were there. Morrigan's gaze took in the people who'd gathered in the chapel. Family, friends, everyone that Morrigan knew. Isabella and Maisie stood just inside. At the very front of the chapel, Sebastian was standing beside a priest.

Aidan knew her. He knew how she felt and what her fears were. If he waited, the time might never come that she conquered all of her doubts. Isabella had been indispensable in arranging this moment.

It was a chance he had to take. But Morrigan needed to say yes.

"What have you done?" she asked, her misty eyes meeting his.

"The rules of fair play do not apply in love and war."

"*Don Quixote*. I should have known." She took his hand. "I'll marry you, Aidan Grant. I thought you'd never ask."

CHAPTER 33

Aidan gazed across the Great Hall at his bride, who was speaking with Maisie and Isabella and a few other women by the fire. Food and drink continued to be carried in. There seemed to be no end to the Mackintosh hospitality.

The wedding service had been conducted efficiently and with appropriate seriousness. But this celebratory reception had already seen more toasts than a royal dinner. Indeed, sobriety for most of the folk gathered in the Great Hall was already a thing of the distant past.

And now Sebastian had cornered Aidan, with Cinaed, Searc, Blair, the priest, and a number of Mackintosh men forming a closed circle around them.

"As your younger brother and best man," he began, "In deference to our local man of the cloth, I've taken it upon myself to gather the wisdom of the ages regarding the conjugal aspect of your marital life."

Everyone boisterously raised a glass to the topic. By the devil, Aidan thought. This was going to be painful.

"To begin." Sebastian drew a sheet of paper from his coat. "After you've been married for three days—and there will be no intimacy before then, Highland traditions notwithstanding—there are a number of conditions that must be met every time before the act takes place."

"And you know all of this how?" Aidan challenged.

"I've been studying." Sebastian shook the page at his brother. "I've drawn up a list from theological tomes dealing with the subject."

"You've been studying marriage and sex. You."

"If you'd prefer, I have a wide range of damning tales about you, my dear brother. I'd be quite happy to have a nice long talk with Morrigan." He turned to the priest. "It's not too late for an annulment. Is it?"

"Go on. Continue with your inanity," Aidan suggested. "And keep your poisonous tales away from my bride's unsuspecting ears."

A toast to the bride's ears was followed by the pouring of another round of drinks.

Sebastian drew a deep breath and continued. "Under pain of the fiery pit, brother, you cannot have sex on any feast day. You cannot have sex on any fast day. You cannot have sex during Whitsun week. Nor during Advent. And I know that you certainly wouldn't dream of having sex at any time during Lent."

Sebastian paused to glance at his paper, and Aidan saw Morrigan eyeing them inquisitively. He made a gesture of wanting to strangle his brother. She smiled and shook her head. If she only knew.

"It is, of course, also a sin to have sex during Easter week. And you will not be having sex on Wednesdays, nor on Fridays, nor on Saturdays or Sundays. What day is today?"

"It's Wednesday," Searc barked.

"Very sorry, brother. Also, you cannot have sex at any time during daylight hours. You cannot have sex unless you're fully clothed. And, for heaven's sake, try to remember that you cannot have sex in church." Sebastian paused and bowed to the priest, who was staring wide-eyed. "And did I mention that the purpose of sex is to have a child?"

The men around Aidan all concurred heartily.

Sebastian placed the paper in Aidan's hand and addressed him again. "Once all these conditions are met, you may proceed, but the giants of theology are clear on the subject that no strange positions will be employed. The church is very clear on that. The natural order must be observed; males on top. And you may only perform the act once. But that may be the most she might expect, in any case."

Rowdy laughter ensued.

"And now, do I get a chance to present my argument?" Aidan asked.

"I don't really believe any rebuttal is possible, considering the high authority I have drawn from for my treatise. But as you please."

"Then have a seat and listen."

Sebastian pulled up a chair and began to sit. Before he succeeded, however, Aidan kicked the chair from under him, sending his brother sprawling. Laughter echoed to the rafters.

"There's you natural order and your high authority too!" Aidan scoffed. Striding across the hall, he took Morrigan's hand, and the two of them ran from the hall.

Morrigan and Aidan were married, truly and finally, and she felt almost giddy with excitement at what was ahead of them. Isabella had told them an apartment had been prepared for the newlyweds above the Great Hall.

As they started up the stairs, she asked if Sebastian had provided anything of value.

"I don't give a damn if it is a Wednesday," Aidan replied cryptically.

"What is significant about Wednesdays?"

"You don't want to know." He stopped in the corridor at the top of the stairs and pulled her against his body, kissing her lips. "I plan to make love to you seven days a week, day and night. Everywhere and anytime we get the opportunity. Does that suit you?"

Morrigan laughed. "Shall we start in our library down here?"

Maybe it was because the two of them had shared so many passionate moments in that room. Or maybe she simply wanted their first time together to be somewhere other than in a bed. She wanted no hint of her past casting a pall over their happiness.

"As my lady wishes."

Hand in hand, they hurried into the library and locked the door. It was dark, but a full moon bathed the room in a blue light.

"I wanted to kiss you and make love to you from the first moment I came in here and found you standing on that ladder."

He leaned toward her. All she could see were his lips as they brushed against hers.

"And I wanted you to make love to me every time you kissed me, touched me, and teased me, but held back, reminding me that we had to get married first."

Aidan's mouth took possession of hers. And as he pulled her tighter into his embrace, she felt herself melting, her lips parting, yielding to his, her body molding to him.

Morrigan rose up on her tiptoes as she returned his kiss. She felt, rather than heard, his groan of approval as her body pressed against him.

What they were doing and where they were doing it was

wild and sweet. Her senses were so alive, so ready for his next touch. She welcomed his kisses, thrillingly aware of her own exhilaration and the rising need within her.

His hands roamed over her body. He caressed her breasts, her back, the curve of her buttocks. When he pressed her back against the door, the feel of his erection elicited a gasp from her. She felt no fear, but a sense of wonder rippled through her.

"I want you so much, Morrigan," he murmured against her lips. "But you must stop me if I'm going too fast."

"And I want you."

Her body arched against him as he pushed a thigh between hers. She gasped at the sweet pressure. He pulled up her skirts, and she held her breath as his hand sought her beneath it. Morrigan gasped when his fingers found her sex. Her body tensed.

"I won't hurt you." His voice was a breath in her ear. "You can let go, my love."

Let go. Let go of fears. Let go of nightmares. Letting go of a lifetime of uncertainties. She focused on his touch. His palm was cupping her mound and his fingers slipped into her folds. A maddening pressure was building within her as he continued stroking her. This was unlike anything she'd ever known. She realized her breaths were becoming shorter.

She wanted more. Her mind screamed for more. Every part of her body cried out to be touched. An insatiable need was rising, pulsing through her. Her hands were around him, drawing him tightly against him. In the midst of this frenzy, she felt his hips press even more intimately against her. There was a shifting of her weight in his arms.

"Don't stop." She kissed his throat. "Give me more."

"There is no stopping," he laughed, his voice husky. "I'm too far gone for that."

He suddenly swept her up in his arms. She smiled as he carried her effortlessly to the desk.

With a sweep of his hand, everything went flying to the floor. But neither one of them cared as he lowered her onto it.

He paused. "I can still take you to our bed."

"Here. Now."

He pushed her skirts up, and she shuddered as he slid his hands along her thighs and over her hips. Stepping forward, he pressed himself between her knees.

She'd never imagined this would be the way. All the nightmarish memories of a night long ago were gone. As Aidan pressed his hard body ever closer, she welcomed the change in him, too. He was losing control.

"Wrap your legs around me."

She did what he told her as he opened the front of his breeches.

The moment was coming, and she held her breath. But when he touched her so gently with his fingertips, parting the folds and then probing and stroking her, she lost any lingering shred of hesitation. She rode his fingers, pressing herself against his palm, welcoming the pressure of his thumb. Her release was sudden and explosive, and she muffled her cries against his shoulder.

When he entered her, waves of pleasure continued to roll through her. She felt him deep within her. Slowly at first, and then with gathering speed, he began to move. Morrigan's brain began to take flight once again. To have him fit so perfectly inside her. To feel his breaths so warm on her neck, in her ear. To hear his heart drumming so solidly in his chest. He was driving them both to near madness.

Ever higher they rose, and she found herself matching the driving beat of his body with her own, until once again, as ecstasy obliterated all thought within her, she felt his straining body go rigid, and she knew, somehow, that they were soaring into the same sky.

Moments later, he placed his forehead against her cheek and softly kissed her. She felt wonderful. Amazing. Gathering her husband closer into her embrace, she also felt whole. New. Strong. And happy.

CHAPTER 34
MORRIGAN

Two weeks later

The duke's ship was expected to arrive in the harbor any time now, and the past few days had been a whirlwind of activity. Everything was in place, however. At least, Morrigan hoped so.

Inviting Sir Rupert Burney to dine with Niall Campbell, Maisie, and Aidan at Searc's house in the Maggot gave Morrigan the distinct feeling that they'd invited the fox into the henhouse. But because the dinner was being held with the added company of Colonel Wade from Fort George, the Lord Mayor of Inverness, Captain Kenedy, and the surgeon Mr. Carmichael, there was at least some sense of safety in numbers. Cinaed and Isabella had remained at Dalmigavie; they were both still wanted as enemies of the Crown by the Home Office.

As she looked around the table now, Morrigan was reminded that so many people in the room had suffered at the hands of Sir Rupert. Once he arrived, the tension in the room was barely restrained within the paper-thin veneer of civility.

For her part, Morrigan had promised Aidan that she

wouldn't cut the man's throat. She stayed true to her oath when she was introduced as Mrs. Grant, and the news of their recent nuptials was shared. Her foe stared at her with a look that insinuated he'd not given her the permission to be anyone's wife.

In recent weeks, the two of them had remained at loggerheads. She wanted her father's letter from him. Sir Rupert wanted to know the location of the meeting between Cinaed and the duke. After tonight, Morrigan guessed none of it would matter.

Searc had strategically arranged the seating so Niall would not sit anywhere near the Home Office official. The former lieutenant would certainly take Burney's head off with a butter knife at the slightest provocation. The bad blood between the two men was prodigious since, on one side, Niall's sister Fiona had been imprisoned for months by Sir Rupert and, on the other side, the Highlander had been a vital player in the reunion of Queen Caroline and Cinaed, an event that sent Burney's career spinning off course. In the process, Niall's efforts had cost Sir Rupert the service of an entire network of spies.

As course after course of food was served, Morrigan noticed Sir Rupert taking in his surroundings with an expression of understandable surprise. The dining room was grander than anyone would imagine, looking at the house from the outside. The finest crystal and silver gleamed in the light of hundreds of candles, and attentive servers circulated with the finesse one might expect only in the households of Britain's aristocratic elite. It was all part of the façade that the master of the house delighted in. A diamond had many sides, and so did Searc Mackintosh.

"Are you a first-time visitor to this wee oasis in the Maggot, sir?" Captain Kenedy asked of Sir Rupert, who was sitting beside him.

"I am, sir."

"Mackintosh is known for his hospitality and for spoil-ing his guests." The ship owner raised his voice, address-ing the host. "If you would only improve the outside of this place, then we could be entertaining His Grace, the good Duke of Clarence, here instead of at my humble abode across the river."

"Humble, you say." Searc snorted. He raised his glass in return.

"You're entertaining His Grace?" Sir Rupert asked. One would never have guessed from his expression that the fox knew anything about it.

"Aye, that I am. In three nights. A great honor, I don't mind saying. I'm only hoping that the weather holds, and his ship comes to port in time." Kenedy paused. "I'd have assumed that you would be accompanying His Grace?"

"Those arrangements will be determined once the duke arrives."

"This will be an historic meeting," Colonel Wade said from across the table.

"You know about the meeting, sir?" Rupert asked, un-able to keep a hint of accusation out of his tone.

"I learned of it here this evening," the officer replied. "But can you imagine, Sir Rupert, a prince of the Hanover monarchy and the scion of the Stuart dynasty breaking bread together? History in the making, indeed."

"More like treason in the making, sir," Sir Rupert re-sponded sharply. "A sworn enemy of the Crown meeting with the brother to the king? With no knowledge of the Prime Minister or the Home Office? The king will not be pleased. Or Lord Sidmouth either."

"Lord Sidmouth maintains his position by creating en-emies for the Crown," Aidan retorted. "Fear and hatred in the realm simply mean more influence and control for him, I'd say. *Any* meeting arranged to create lasting peace will not please him."

"What do you know about peace, Mr. Grant?" Sir Rupert huffed. "You who endanger lives by putting criminals like the Chattans back on the street."

"Have you forgotten, sir? You were too afraid for the case to reach its conclusion. Not I, but courts of law free men—like the Chattan brothers—who are unjustly accused. I only provide my services to protect the innocent against the plotting of men who clutch at power with both hands, men like you and your master Sidmouth."

"What plotting?" Burney scoffed.

"The Home Office lures innocent people into committing crime. You entrap them with your agents. You *create* the very crimes that you prosecute men for."

"Take care, Mr. Grant. We create nothing. We identify, we expose, we prosecute. We drag the vermin from their holes and show the public their twisted plots."

"How miraculous that you happen to discover these plots prior to any actual crime being committed. In case after case, you arrest reformers and political foes. You charge them with crimes that are nothing more than *thoughts.* Only you call it *conspiracy* and depict these men as dangerous extremists."

"And that's a credit to our organization. To our brilliance. We are everywhere. We hear everything. We are in people's homes. We know the crimes they are willing to commit before they take the first step."

"You pit friends against one another, Sir Rupert. You tear families apart."

"We do what we must to protect the Crown. *King and country.* Certainly you've heard the phrase, even if you don't know what it means."

"You are a stain on the honor of king and country.

You're a threat to free people whose lives you manipulate and destroy through your schemes."

"Save your speeches for the election, Mr. Grant. With radical opinions such as those, you'll never be elected to Parliament." He sent a sly look in Morrigan's direction. "Not that you're electable any longer anyway."

Morrigan put a hand on Aidan's knee to stop him rising to his feet. They'd been married such a short time, and already her temper had been passed on to her husband.

"Let me understand you, Sir Rupert," Searc said. "You're in favor of imprisoning men for crimes they may never have committed, but for your efforts to entrap them. For the sake of protecting king and country, as you say."

"Absolutely. We must stamp out threats before they come to fruition."

Before anyone could respond, the sound of pounding on a distant door was followed by raised voices. Searc was on his feet when the door of the dining room opened and a servant came in apologizing.

"They'll not go away, master. And they say they'll wait not another minute."

"Who are they?" Searc barked. "How dare they interrupt me and my guests?"

"The constable, sir. And four of his deputy constables. They've got a wagon and all in the lane."

"What do they want?"

"They're here to arrest someone."

"That's preposterous!" Searc pushed by him, shouting down the hall. "What is this nonsense about?"

A moment later, the constable entered, with his men close behind him. He was waving a document, and he bowed at the sight of the Lord Mayor.

"Explain yourself," Searc demanded curtly.

The constable's men spread out. They were armed with cudgels and looked ready to use them.

"We're here to take Sir Rupert Burney into custody."

Silence fell over the room.

"On what charge?" Burney burst out. "I am an official of the Crown. You have no right to take me anywhere."

The constable drew the warrant from his coat, pointing it at the accused.

"Sir Rupert Burney, you're charged with conspiracy to commit an act of violence against the person of a member of the royal family."

"Of all the . . . this is absurd," he sputtered. "Where did you get such a notion? I serve the royal family, and there is no member of—"

"Tonight, we arrested twelve individuals, hired by you, who were arming themselves for the purpose of breaking into a dinner at the home of Captain Kenedy three days hence. Their instructions from you were to murder His Grace, the Duke of Clarence and—"

"It's a lie." Burney jumped to his feet.

"We have confessions already from the men we took tonight."

Sir Rupert turned to the Lord Mayor. "These imbeciles work for you. If you don't take this in hand immediately, the Home Office will respond. This will not end well for you, that I swear."

Morrigan was impressed with how unperturbed the Lord Mayor appeared. He looked apologetically at his host before addressing Sir Rupert.

"I suggest that you go with these men so that any misunderstanding can be handled without any disturbance to our host or the ladies."

Burney swung around and pointed at Colonel Wade, who was already on his feet. "Do something. You represent the Crown."

"Such a charge is quite serious, Constable." The colonel crossed the room and took the paper from his hand. He read through the charges. "What you are saying is that Sir Rupert has committed acts of treason?"

"Aye, sir. You might call it that. And there's more to it."

Everyone waited while Colonel Wade thought for a moment before handing the warrant back. He gestured to the deputies.

"Arrest him."

CHAPTER 35
MORRIGAN

Entrapping Burney in a net of his own devising seemed too easy to Morrigan, and once they took him away, her worry only intensified. He was a cunning enemy, and his tentacles were far reaching. She wondered how many people he had still at his beck and call, agents like Baker. How many would follow their master's instructions, even though he was behind bars?

Sir Rupert's venomous gaze was directed toward only one person as he was being taken out of Searc's dining room earlier tonight. Aidan. He knew he'd been beaten at his own game, and he knew who was responsible for it.

Noises drifted into their bedchamber from the main road running from the quays through the Maggot. Voices of drunken sailors, the bark of a dog, the rattle and rumble of carts passing over the cobblestones. Morrigan had already heard stories from Sebastian about past attempts on Aidan's life. Having another foe as vicious as this one kept her awake and listening.

This was going to be her life. Tonight, tomorrow, for as long as they both lived. And as worrisome as the dangers were, she was proud of him for what he did, for the warrior that he was.

With a sigh, Morrigan nestled into her husband's arms and pressed her face against his naked chest. She loved him. She loved him. She could shout the words a hundred times and more, and it would still not be enough. She'd never known such happiness. Having Aidan trick her and convince her that it was time to cast aside her fears and marry him was stunning. And to love her, and make love to her, and teach her the thrill and beauty of their bodies as they joined was yet another miracle. Morrigan felt that for the first time she was whole, complete, healed.

And yet, she still feared. She feared losing him. She couldn't ignore that.

"You're digging your toes into my leg," he growled.

"My knees are bent. My toes are nowhere near your leg."

Morrigan drew back to look into his face, but he wouldn't let her get too far away. She could tell he was smiling.

"I was going to say the ruckus in your head is louder than what's going on in the street below this window, but that didn't seem very romantic. So I decided to complain about your toes."

Strange as his sense of humor could be at times, she loved the way he could put a smile on her face, regardless of the situation.

"I was thinking about Burney getting out of the jail and coming after you."

"He'll never get out."

"Sir Rupert has money and influence. When his trial happens, he could get a good lawyer."

"He'll never get out."

"His people could pay off those men who made state- ments against him. His friends at the Home Office could convince Madame Laborde to admit that she met with us. She could say we engineered the entire entrapment scheme, even though we only planted the seeds."

"He'll never get out," Aidan said again, tracing the frown creasing her forehead. The tip of his fingers ca- ressed her face, moved down to the side of her neck, inching lower to the curves of her breasts.

"They could move the trial back to London. Lord Sidmouth could assist him and—"

"He'll never get out." He rolled Morrigan until she lay on top of him.

Heat erupted within her as she felt his erection nestle against her. This was the way it was for them. Looking into each other's eyes led to lovemaking. Arguing about the color of the sky led to lovemaking. Lying in bed talking about nothing led to lovemaking. A touch, a brush, a kiss, a smile led to lovemaking. The man was insatiable and so was she. And now this talk of Sir Rupert getting out of jail or not was leading to lovemaking.

She raised herself to look into his face, and he took ad- vantage of the movement, nipping playfully at her breast. That was all it took. Her legs opened a little wider. Her body had a will of its own.

"Before we get distracted . . ." She took a quick breath, feeling him pressing into her.

"This is not distraction."

He took hold of her breast and brought it to his mouth again. Sparks exploded inside of her, and Morrigan could think of nothing but wanting him buried deep within her. She was ready for him. It seemed she was always ready for him. She moved her hips and he slid into her.

Later, when they were both spent and she lay sprawled across his body, Morrigan asked her question again.

"What makes you think that he'll never get out?"

He chuckled. "You're very difficult to distract."

"Tell me."

"For the same reason that Wemys was afraid and wanted me to hide him. Sir Rupert knows too much. And he can talk all he wants about 'king and country.' The only thing that matters to him right now is saving his own skin, and he'll do anything, make any deal to accomplish that. He would testify and bring down Lord Liverpool's government if he had to, without thinking twice about it. Burney would destroy the Home Office entirely to escape the gallows. For that reason, Lord Sidmouth cannot afford to let him live. I suspect one morning, quite soon, his jailor will find the prisoner hanging in his cell, and they'll swear it was done by his own hand."

CHAPTER 36
AIDAN

The reception and dinner at Captain Kenedy's house had all been a ruse to catch Sir Rupert in his own web. The actual meeting between Cinaed and the duke took place in the admiral's stateroom of His Majesty's ship *William & Mary,* docked at the north end of Merkinch Wharf, near the mouth of the unfinished canal.

Aidan boarded the vessel behind Cinaed, Niall Campbell, and a dozen Mackintosh fighters, who remained on deck trading glares with the ship's marines. Aidan believed that each side was operating in good faith, however, and that no danger would befall anyone. Happily, everything proceeded according to plan.

Cinaed and the duke were both men who possessed strong personalities. As a result, the discussion comprised as many disagreements as agreements. But in the end, the two of them reached a place of mutual respect and understanding. Promises of communication and support followed. They each walked away with the belief that when and if this son of George III were to become the monarch of the Great Britain and Ireland, both men would remember this meeting and abide by their promises.

It was with a sense of elation that they all went ashore hours later.

Cinaed and Niall and most of the men were returning immediately to Dalmigavie. Aidan was to wait at Searc's house until his wife returned from her visit with Madame Laborde.

The day after Sir Rupert's arrest, the artist had moved back to Barn Hill with Aidan's promise that financial arrangements would be made for her once Burney's trial was behind them. There could be no hint of impropriety between her and the Mackintosh clan. She would testify that she'd conveyed a number of rumors that she'd heard. She would admit that what she said may have induced Sir Rupert Burney to hire men to attempt an assassination on the duke. But she had no part in any such plan of his. And it would be clear to any jury that the spymaster would have benefited, regardless of the outcome.

They were standing on the pier, preparing to mount their horses when they saw Blair galloping toward them from Inverness.

"Burney has escaped," he told them as he reined in his steed. "They were taking the rogue to Fort George. The prison wagon was attacked before they even got out of the city. He's gone."

Aidan immediately thought of Morrigan. She'd taken a carriage to Barn Hill with two Mackintosh escorts, in addition to the driver. That should be the last place Sir Rupert would go, but he had to be certain.

Cinaed and Niall began to ask Blair what else he knew, but Aidan couldn't wait. Leaping onto his horse, he told them he was going after his wife.

Chapter 37
Morrigan

The enormous house on Huntly Street had been locked since the day after Sir Rupert's arrest. The servants were dismissed. His clerk and his henchmen had disappeared. Morrigan followed Madame Laborde out of the carriage. A frigid wind was whipping up the icy waters of the River Ness, and she promised the driver that they wouldn't be long.

The two Mackintosh fighters walked them to the door.

"The key is here somewhere." The artist searched the bottom of a large quilted bag she used for carrying her supplies around.

Morrigan had come along in hopes of finding her father's letter. Aidan said it didn't matter. She agreed. Still, the opportunity had presented itself when Madame Laborde mentioned that she wished to go back to the house and collect the rest of her things. Sir Rupert never returned to Huntly Street after the arrest. He'd had no chance to secure his papers or give them to someone else. That meant her father's letter could still be here.

"I found it." The key slid into the old lock, and the Mackintosh men went inside the house ahead of the women.

All was quiet inside. And cold. No fires had been lit inside these walls for three days. The windows rattled in their sills and a whistling moan came from the chimney in the drawing room.

"I'll go upstairs for my things." The artist pointed out a door to the right. "That is his study. I believe that would be the place to look."

One of the escorts walked into the study and looked around. She waited in the hall until he made sure no one was inside. He nodded to her that she could go in.

The study was furnished with a large table, a secretary's desk by a window, and chairs. Bookcases lined two walls. A cabinet with diamond-shaped openings for maps and scrolls stood empty. She pushed some papers around on the desk and opened drawers. Nothing caught her attention, and she began to wonder if his clerk had been here, after all. Or perhaps he had another office. Niall told her that in Glasgow, Burney had taken over offices in the City Chambers in the Saltmarket.

Morrigan recalled what Wemys told her. Burney kept secrets on everyone. All his spies and agents. All the people who worked for him. And anyone else he could use or manipulate. Looking around the room, she tried to think how he would keep this information close at hand. Perhaps there was a ledger that would lead her elsewhere.

As she stood thinking, she heard Madam Laborde call from upstairs that she needed help carrying a trunk downstairs. Footsteps moved away down the hall.

The volumes on the bookshelves were different sizes, and, from the coating of dust, many appeared to have been here for quite some time. She pulled out books that seemed to have been moved more recently. Working steadily, she went through them and looked behind the rows. Nothing.

As she was sliding items on the bookshelves of an inner wall, the wooden case moved slightly. She pulled at it, and the entire case began to swing toward her. A hidden closet. Of course. Searc said this house belonged to an old smuggler.

The bookcase groaned a little but swung open smoothly. Morrigan peered in. Shelves lined the opposite wall, and they were filled with books and ledgers and packets of papers tied with black ribbon and stacked neatly in rows. A metal cash box sat on a small desk and a large leather satchel filled with ledgers and papers was propped open beside it.

She stepped into the space and reached for the bag. She didn't get far. The keen edge of a knife pressed against her throat. She tried to twist to deliver a blow to the man standing behind her, but the jerk of his fist in her hair and bite of the blade stopped her.

"Mrs. Grant. How gratifying to find you here."

Sir Rupert Burney stood behind her. The bookcase swung shut.

CHAPTER 38

Mrs. Goddard's news that Morrigan had accompanied Madame Laborde to Huntly Street went through Aidan's chest like a hussar's blade.

As the hooves of his steed pounded along the lane and through the deserted cattle market toward Castle Hill and the bridge, he kept trying to convince himself that nothing was wrong. She wasn't alone. The women had two Mackintosh men with them. Nothing said that Burney would return to a house that was assuredly locked up by the authorities.

But all along the way, a feeling of doom clouded his brain.

Aidan only started to breathe when he espied the driver and carriage waiting outside the house as he reached Huntly Street. Reining his horse sharply in front of the house, he jumped down and rushed through the door. Male voices came from an upper floor.

"Morrigan!" he shouted.

One of the Mackintosh men appeared at the top of the stairs.

"Where is my wife?"

"In the study there."

He started to come down the stairs, but Aidan didn't wait. He didn't know the layout of the house. He called her name, looking in at the first door.

"The next one, Mr. Grant. In there. She was here but a minute ago."

They both went into the study. The window was shut, the curtains were drawn. No one was inside. There was nowhere for her to go.

"I know she didn't leave the house." The Mackintosh went out into the hall to look around.

The second man came down and joined the search. Immediately, Aidan was told the door going out to the back from the kitchen was still latched on the inside. The same was true of the windows and the other servants' entrance. The only way in or out was the way he'd come.

"Check the floors for a trap door." Aidan rushed back into the study and pointed at the bookcases. "Pull them down. Every one of them. There's got to be a door somewhere that leads out."

Leaving them, he raced out of the house.

Of course, there had to be a hidden passageway, Morrigan thought. And a tunnel. The house was on the river. She should have thought of it before stepping into the space behind the bookcase.

But how could she have known that Burney was free?

He'd ordered her to carry the heavy satchel. With his dagger prodding her in the back, they descended a steep set of stone stairs and started along a dank tunnel that smelled like a crypt. He replaced his knife with a small pistol that he carried with the muzzle pointed directly at her back. The passageway was narrow and slippery, and they passed under two small openings from which dim light and cold air filtered down. At a sharp turn, she looked ahead and saw the tunnel was brighter in the distance.

Morrigan could tell from the sound of his steps that he was close enough to shoot her, but far enough to be clear of any attempt she might make to try to kick at him or somehow defend herself.

She guessed from the weight of the satchel that he'd filled it with bags of coin along with whatever papers he thought would be most valuable to him. He was making his escape from Inverness, but he wasn't going empty-handed.

Morrigan thought back over their route. The passage led under the house toward the river. Since the turn, the tunnel must have been running parallel with the Ness. A smuggler's route, for sure.

"Where are we going?" she asked, slowing down a little.

"It's of no concern to you. Keep moving."

Screaming and hoping that someone would come to her rescue was no longer a possibility. Perhaps she should have done it when she'd first felt the edge of the knife.

"What are you going to do to me?"

"You'll soon find out."

The tunnel made a slight bend. In the distance, she could see a set of wooden stairs leading up through a trap door. She remembered seeing a dilapidated warehouse and dock not far downriver from the house. Someone had helped Burney escape. No doubt, he had henchmen waiting for him and a boat ready to take him beyond the reach of the law and the Mackintosh clan.

Whatever she had to do to put an end to this, Morrigan knew she needed to do it now.

"I cooperated with you. I helped you so you'd give me back my father's letter."

"Your father's letter," he scoffed. "That scrap of paper didn't matter a whit to him. Trust me, I tried to use it with him. Drummond wouldn't play my game. And don't try to play me for a fool. I know it means nothing to you either. If it did, you would have squirmed more."

"I thought we had a deal. I was doing my part."

"Your part? Liar. You manipulated me. You poisoned the mind of Roisin Laborde. You played her against me."

"I didn't do anything that you haven't done yourself."

"Don't give yourself so much credit. I know the two of you had a hand in this. You deserve each other. You and your lawyer. Too bad your marriage won't last."

The steps were just ahead. A freezing wind howled through the trap door.

"The joy I'll get from informing him of your pathetic end." His voice paused a moment before he continued. "Perhaps I'll keep you alive for a while. There might be some benefit in letting him think he can get you back."

She would never be a victim again. Never.

"Do not do anything foolish. Go up the steps slowly and stop at the top. I'll have my pistol trained on your back every moment."

Morrigan climbed as she was told, her mind racing. She'd run for it. Let him shoot. She'd jump in that river and drown in the freezing water if she must. Death was definitely preferable.

She climbed up and found herself in a small warehouse. The doors facing the water were open. She could see the dock. A boat bobbed in the icy river.

"Walk straight to the boat," he ordered.

As she moved ahead of him, she realized someone lay on the dock. Morrigan shifted the bag so she was holding it with both hands in front of her.

She stepped out of the warehouse. Not one, but two

people lay unmoving on the dock. She jumped to the side, planted her feet, and swung the weighted satchel with all her strength back toward the doorway.

She connected with Burney's shoulder as he rushed out, but his attention was not on her. Someone else was waiting on the other side of the opening.

Aidan.

The impact of the satchel's weight drove Burney into him. Aidan grabbed for the pistol, and she watched in shock as they tumbled over the edge of the dock together.

She rushed to the side and watched in horror as they fought in the icy river. Aidan went under first, but then Burney was pulled down.

She heard footsteps on the dock behind her. The carriage driver was here. The two Mackintosh men raced out of the warehouse onto the dock.

The driver drew a pistol from his coat but quickly realized who they were.

"Aidan went in the river. I can't see him." Morrigan leaned over the edge, ready to go in after him.

He'd come to her rescue. He knew she was in trouble. Aidan knew where to go and how to find her. He was the love of her life. Her future. He couldn't die. She wouldn't let him go.

"I'm going after him."

Morrigan was about to jump in when a pair of hands grabbed her from behind. She struggled to get free. Once again, she was back in the surgery in Edinburgh. Her father was dead, and she was being dragged out of the room. She was too late to do anything.

"Let me go," she screamed. "I won't let him die."

"There he is, Mrs. Grant. By the bank. He is coming out."

A few paces downriver she saw him. Aidan. There was no sign of Burney.

The men rushed down to help him out.

Suddenly, her knees wobbled. Everything had happened so fast. For a few insane moments, she'd nearly lost hope.

"Get blankets," she told the driver, gathering her strength.

Morrigan ran along the bank and threw her arms around him. A dry coat was thrown over him, and she pressed her face against his wet clothes.

"You're alive. Thank God. You're alive."

He held her and kissed her, then pulled away and ran his eyes over her face. "Did he hurt you?"

She shook her head. "I found a secret panel behind the bookcases and surprised him. He'd come to collect whatever valuables he'd left behind."

"When I couldn't find you inside the house, I knew."

"How did you know to come here?"

"Remember when Searc told us it was a smuggler's house?"

She nodded. Knowing but not paying enough attention.

"I've heard since I was a lad that many of the old houses along the river have tunnels that lead to the river. When I saw the boat tied up to the old shack and those two bruisers, I knew that was where you'd be coming out."

Morrigan motioned to the men still lying inert on the dock. "You did this?"

"The moves I saw you using on the pell in the training yard, I put them into action here."

He was soaked to the bone. His teeth were chattering and he was still in good humor. As they walked back toward the carriage, she spotted the bag she'd been carrying for Burney. She asked one of the Mackintosh men to bring it for them.

"What do you think is in there?" Aidan asked, holding her tight.

"A trail of frailty and fear." Morrigan looked up into the eyes of the man she loved. The man she would stand with and fight beside till the end of their days. "There is nothing that can touch us in there, but those papers might mean hope and freedom for scores of others."

Chapter 39
Cinaed

Brandenburg House, Hammersmith
Six Months Later

The satchel Sir Rupert Burney left behind when he drowned in the River Ness was filled with magic. Besides the letters and records that kept the innocent in the spymaster's grasp, they found a plethora of incriminating evidence of wrongdoing by many politicians from both parties. Some of that evidence even pointed to those working in the intelligence-gathering sections of the Home Office in London.

Sir Rupert valued information just as much as Searc did, but Cinaed preferred to believe the man who had watched over him from childhood was not as indiscriminate in ruining lives.

Aidan was elected to Parliament, representing Inverness-shire. He and Morrigan were already settled here in London. Sebastian joined them from time to time, having decided to keep open their law offices in Edinburgh. He wanted to be prepared for when they chased his brother out of Westminster with torches and pitchforks.

Thanks to Aidan's discreet negotiations—using Sir Rupert's records of some rather indelicate transgressions on the part of high-ranking government ministers—all charges against Isabella and Cinaed were dropped this past spring. The bounty on both their heads was rescinded. They were free. No one was more relieved than Lachlan Mackintosh, who had decided it was time to pass the title of Laird of Dalmigavie on to Cinaed.

It had taken Cinaed a long time to realize it, but he was more Mackintosh than Stuart. He and Isabella cared deeply about these people. They were at home at Dalmigavie. Neither wished to move on to Nova Scotia and leave those they loved behind. He'd humbly accepted the honor.

With their lives settled, Niall and Maisie had taken up a long-standing offer from James Watt. Long months ago, Niall had secured an investment in the steam engine manufacturer. Now he accepted the position of helping the company expand its operations into the industrial north. As a Highlander and a former military man, his success was almost guaranteed. They were to live in Aberdeen, and Fiona and her family were to join them. No formal announcements had been made yet, but Cinaed had a strong feeling that John Gordon and Fiona would be announcing their engagement very soon.

The only one complaining about the change was Auld Jean. She hated to have everyone so far away. After a great deal of cursing and grousing, however, she decided to stay with Isabella and Cinaed at Dalmigavie, for the two of them—"a simple, good-hearted flatlander and a sea dog"—needed her help more than the rest.

And they did need her, for Isabella was with child.

Cinaed took a deep breath, trying to hold the feeling of happiness intact, for he'd arrived in London at the request of his mother. She was dying.

The same night that the king's coronation had been

held—an event that Caroline had been banned from attending—she fell ill. Over the next three weeks, she'd suffered more and more pain as her condition deteriorated. His mother was only fifty-three years of age.

Although Cinaed and Isabella were both free of their troubles with the Crown, at the suggestion of Brougham and Aidan, they arrived under cover of darkness. This government wasn't to be trusted. Some of her physicians claimed the queen had an intestinal obstruction. Others attributed her condition to cancer. Since arriving, Isabella spent a great deal of time with Caroline, and she suspected that she'd been poisoned. But too much time had passed and too much damage had been done to save her life.

On the night of August 7, Cinaed and Isabella sat beside her bed and held onto Caroline's hands.

She knew about her grandchild that was to be born before the year was out.

She'd been told of the promises made by the Duke of Clarence about the future of Scotland.

She knew that the streets around Brandenburg House were surrounded by people who even now prayed for their beloved queen.

At twenty-five minutes past ten, Caroline died.

And on her coffin, per her instruction, Cinaed saw to it that an inscription read: "Here lies Caroline, the Injured Queen of England."

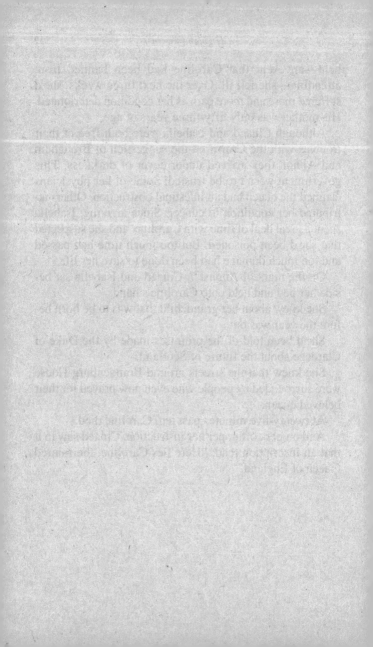

EPILOGUE

William Henry, Duke of Clarence, was crowned King of the United Kingdom of Great Britain and Ireland and King of Hanover on 26 June 1830. He reigned as William IV.

During his reign, the British Parliament enacted major reforms, including the Factory Act, preventing child labor abuse; the Slavery Abolition Act, emancipating slaves in the colonies; the Poor Law Amendment Act, standardizing provision for the destitute; and the Scottish Reform Act, extending the vote from 5,000 adult males to 65,000 voters. Still, nearly a hundred years had to pass before full voting rights were finally granted to all women over the age of twenty-one.

But that, perhaps, is another story.

followed us over the decades know that we hate to say goodbye to our characters. In fact, we never will. Side characters find their own stories. Main characters come back in critical roles. No story is ever done, for once we've created them, our characters are family to us. Some of you might have noticed, but we couldn't finish this book without making a mention of our beloved Penningtons. If you are interested, there are ten books that follow the family through two generations . . . and counting.

Before we sign off on this book, we'd like to thank Pamela Sutherland of Inverness Botanic Gardens for her expertise and help.

We're also grateful for Peter Mackenzie, Glasgow journalist, publisher and lawyer (1799–1875). Through his periodical *The Loyal Reformers' Gazette*, we learned so much about the political views of the time, particularly the campaign for parliamentary reform.

Many of you know that we've been busy creating a vast, interconnected world of stories spanning centuries, from the medieval Highlands to Georgian, Regency, and Victorian England and Scotland. If you're interested to learn more, our website is a great source of information.

As authors, we love feedback. We write our stories for you. We'd love to hear from you. We are constantly learning, so please help us write stories that you will cherish and recommend to your friends.

Please visit us on our website at www.MayMcGoldrick.com for our latest news and write to us at May@MayMcGoldrick.com.

Finally, if you enjoyed *Highland Sword*, please consider leaving us a review . . . and recommending it to your friends. We greatly appreciate your support!

Wishing you peace and health!

—Nikoo and Jim McGoldrick

AUTHOR'S NOTE

Hope you enjoyed *Highland Sword*.

As writers, we are in love with history and love to share it with you with a cast of interesting characters.

When we set out to write the Royal Highlander series (*Highland Crown, Highland Jewel, Highland Sword*), our goal was to weave the lives of three extraordinary women into the fabric of a revolutionary, but largely forgotten series of historical events called the Radical War of 1820.

From that mindset, the characters of Isabella, a university-trained physician; Maisie, an early activist for suffrage; and Morrigan, a militant revolutionary, formed in our imagination. Our research directed us to real historical figures of the Georgian and Regency Era who served as models for our heroines. Women like Dorothea Erxleben, physician; Mary Fildes, political activist and an early suffragette; 'William' Brown (birth name unknown), an African woman serving in the Royal Navy; and María Antonia Santos Plata, a rebel guerrilla leader in South America.

Those exceptional women led us to this moment, the end of *Highland Sword*. Many of our readers who have